Praise for *Me and Johnny Blue*

"*Me and Johnny Blue* is old-fashioned storytelling raised to the level of homegrown art, told in an American language that is almost gone."
— Loren D. Estleman, four-time Spur Award–winning author of *White Desert*

"Wildly comic and darkly compelling."
— Robert Olen Butler, Pulitzer Prize–winning author of *A Good Scent from a Strange Mountain*

"Real cowboys never lie . . . except sometimes, and usually only to make a good story better. This rollicking big windy has occasional grains of truth, but not enough to keep it from being very funny."
— Elmer Kelton, six-time Spur Award–winning author of *The Good Old Boys*

"*Me and Johnny Blue* is a tragicomedy with the humor transcendent. It is an original, imaginative work. A delight. Do not miss this one."
— Max Evans, Spur Award–winning author of *The Rounders*

"Take a pair of pugnacious cowboys who never saw trouble they didn't like, mix them with a fiendish villain and his diabolical filibusters, and the result is comic delight. Joseph West brings to this engaging novel an encyclopedic knowledge of the West. He keeps the body count sufficient to satisfy gluttons, frosts his cake with bawds, throws a few wolf... a boxer, and a patent medi...
rings in all the Wester...
seasons the stew with...
— Richard S.

DONOVAN'S DOVE

Joseph A. West

A SIGNET BOOK

SIGNET
Published by New American Library, a division of
Penguin Group (USA) Inc., 375 Hudson Street,
New York, New York 10014, U.S.A.
Penguin Books Ltd, 80 Strand,
London WC2R 0RL, England
Penguin Books Australia Ltd, 250 Camberwell Road,
Camberwell, Victoria 3124, Australia
Penguin Books Canada Ltd, 10 Alcorn Avenue,
Toronto, Ontario, Canada M4V 3B2
Penguin Books (NZ), cnr Airborne and Rosedale Roads,
Albany, Auckland 1310, New Zealand

Penguin Books Ltd, Registered Offices:
80 Strand, London WC2R 0RL, England

First published by Signet, an imprint of New American Library,
a division of Penguin Group (USA) Inc.

First Printing, July 2004
10 9 8 7 6 5 4 3 2 1

PUBLISHER'S NOTE
This is a work of fiction. Names, characters, places, and incidents either are
the product of the author's imagination or are used fictitiously, and any
resemblance to actual persons, living or dead, business establishments,
events, or locales is entirely coincidental.

For my editor
DAN SLATER
who showed me the trail

1

"I'll see your twenty-five and raise you fifty."

Zeke Donovan didn't know it then, but that simple statement was about to land him in a world of trouble and more long-term grief than any man should reasonably be expected to handle.

Before him on a rickety table covered by a worn cloth of green baize lay $250 and an expensive gold and enamel watch, a fine repeater made by the esteemed Berthoud of Paris.

The watch was the valued property of gambler and itinerant pimp Ike Vance, a man with an explosive temper and considerable gun skills, an unfortunate combination for those who incurred his displeasure. He had eight dead men to his credit, and it seemed to those watching that Donovan was rapidly shaping up to be number nine.

"Your call," Donovan suggested mildly.

From over the top of his cards, Vance's cold eyes met Donovan's.

"Don't rush me, boy," he said. "I'm studying on it."

Donovan, twenty-seven years old that fall, shrugged and said nothing. He'd been trying to out-run a year-long streak of bad luck that had begun back in Fort Worth, Texas, and tonight it looked like the cards were finally falling his way.

Three months before, his fellow gambler and some-time friend Luke Short had given him a road stake, as he'd done several times in the past. By nature, Luke was a generous, openhanded man, much given to helping orphans and poor widows and the like, but from him such a donation always came at a price.

And that price was a sermon—in Zeke's case usu-ally concerning the error of his ways and his propen-sity for low companions and persons of ill repute.

"And that," said Luke, his eyes accusing, "includes cattle drovers, dance hall loungers, razor grinders and soiled doves—and I won't even begin to read to you from the book about your love for bonded whiskey and Mumm's champagne."

The sermon went on for some time, but finally sum-ming it all up, the little gambler sighed and said, "Zeke, you can't run away from a losing streak. Luck, fate, destiny, whatever you want to call it, is a pretty weak apology for a man's own faults. Eventually you're going to have to stop running and play the cards where they fall."

Well, now Donovan had stopped running and he'd run a fair piece.

This dark, smoky saloon was a far cry from the glit-tering, chandeliered gambling palaces of Fort Worth and Denver with their elegant, frock-coated patrons and beautiful, sophisticated and willing women.

The saloon stood in a sod and green timber cow town north of Fort Laramie in the Wyoming territory. It was ten miles off the route served by the Cheyenne and Black Hills Stage Line and seventy hard miles from the Union Pacific's iron road.

No spur line would ever be laid to this town. In that year of 1879, the place was a bleak annex of limbo, a ramshackle settlement, stillborn but not yet buried, now teetering on the edge of oblivion with no stake in the booming Black Hills gold rush further to the east.

It was a sad, seedy, shabby, down-at-heel kind of town and Luke Short would have told you this description also perfectly fitted the young man who was now studying Ike Vance so intently.

Donovan, tired from days on the trail, let his hazel eyes stray to the railroad clock above the bar, if rough pine planks laid across three whiskey barrels could be called such. It was two in the morning and fatigue lay heavy on him, the energy draining out of him as the clock ticked away the slow minutes and hours.

To Donovan's right an old, bearded miner who had already thrown in his hand watched Vance with eager, red-rimmed eyes. A few idlers at the bar, lean punchers in from one of the local ranches in wide hats and high-heeled boots, regarded the action with growing interest.

It was said by those who knew that Ike Vance had never stepped away from any poker table a loser. But it seemed to those who watched that his jealously guarded reputation now hung precariously in the balance.

Vance himself was a huge, handsome man in a black frock coat and checkered vest. He stood four inches taller than Donovan's even six feet and outweighed him by sixty pounds. Clean-shaven but for the full dragoon mustache then in fashion, Vance carried a Colt .45 at his waist and a Smith and Wesson .32 hideaway in the leather-lined back pocket of his pants.

He could use either equally well.

"Your call, Ike," Donovan said wearily, his impatience apparent to everyone. "It's time to ante up or fold."

Donovan knew the watch on the table represented the last of the pimp's liquid assets and the man's eyes revealed increasing desperation as he turned and hurriedly glanced around the saloon.

Two of his whores, pale, undernourished and overworked, stood beside the bar.

The girls shared a flimsy wood-frame-and-tarpaper line shack out back, but tonight, not being a Friday when the punchers got paid, there had been no demand for their services.

Vance rose abruptly and pushed back from the table. "I'll meet your raise and be damned to ye," he said, his eyes malevolent and wild.

He stomped to the bar and roughly grabbed one of the girls by the arm. She was small, thin and dark-haired, wearing a faded red dress a couple of sizes too big for her and high-heeled shoes that had been bought for a woman with much larger feet.

Vance pushed the girl to the table and thrust her at Donovan. "This whore is worth fifty dollars American in anybody's money," he said, turning, arms spread wide to the grinning men lining the bar as though enlisting their agreement. "I raise the dove."

A cowboy laughed and said, "Well, don't that beat all. You're a real sporting gent, Ike, an' no mistake."

Donovan lifted a quizzical eyebrow. Fifty was a steep price for a lay, considering that the going price up until a few moments ago had been two dollars and even that, given the shabby, straight-up-and-down homeliness of Vance's whores, was anything but good value for money.

But tired as he was, Donovan just wanted this thing over. And the fact that his luck seemed to be changing for the better made him willing to be magnanimous. The young gambler reckoned Vance's $125 and gold watch wasn't a bad night's work and besides, he was eager to return to the hotel and seek his blankets.

"Okay, Ike," he said, smiling, even as he shook his head at Vance's desperation. "I accept. Now, let's see what you're holding."

To Donovan's surprise, Vance had just two pair, queen and nines, no match for his own kings over deuces full house.

For a few moments the big man stared at Donovan's cards in stunned disbelief. Then he jumped angrily to his feet.

"Damn ye for a cheap tinhorn!" he roared. "Believe me, boy, this night's work was ill done."

Vance turned and stomped to the bar where he stood and glared at Donovan through the curling blue pipe and cigar smoke and dank gloom that the saloon's sputtering oil lamps did little to banish.

The old miner leaned close and whispered in Donovan's ear, "Sonny, you just made yourself a mighty serious enemy. A gunfighting pimp like Ike Vance ain't a man to be trifled with."

Donovan shrugged, raking in his winnings. "Hell, if a man can't afford to lose, he shouldn't play poker."

Vance's voice, calling from across the saloon, stopped him in midmovement.

"You listen to me, boy," he said. "Don't you go wearing that watch around. I see you flaunting it and I'll kill you." Vance's right arm hung loose, his hand very close to his holstered Colt. "If I even hear you've been showing off my watch, I'll come after you. I won't call you out and I won't much care if your front or your back is to me. I'll just come a-shooting."

Somewhere back on the trail, Donovan had heard that Ike Vance had recently killed a man down on the Cherokee Strip over an Indian woman and before that a deputy sheriff in Wichita. Like all known and dangerous gunmen, Vance's restless wanderings were closely followed by even the smallest cow town newspapers and his shooting scrapes reported with relish and usually more exaggeration than fact.

But there was no exaggerating the man's ability with a gun and right now the big pimp was very much on the prod and hunting trouble.

In a shoulder holster under his left arm, hidden by the generous cut of his threadbare frock coat, Donovan carried a .44 Colt. He'd had the barrel cut down to two-and-a-half inches and the front sight removed by a gunsmith in Dodge.

Vance stood about twenty feet away and Donovan knew that even if he had the gun skills of Hickok or Hardin—which he hadn't—he couldn't hit him at that distance with a short-barreled revolver.

Besides, the concussions from the first shots fired would blow out the few oil lamps in that tight, sod-built room. Then he and Vance would be forced to step closer to each other, blasting away in the darkness, blinded by the flash of their own guns.

No fool, Zeke Donovan did not relish the prospect. Despite the apparent upturn of his fortunes, he doubted that he'd come out ahead in such a close up shooting scrape.

The young gambler made no reply to Vance, but his hands moving slow and careful, he took two silver dollars from his pile and laid them in front of the old miner by his side.

"What's that fer?" the old timer asked, puzzled.

"If I don't make it out of here alive, hang one of them on my watch chain before they bury me," Donovan said, his voice low and quiet. "When I get to the pearly gates, I want the Good Lord to know I was finally standing pat."

"What's the other one fer?"

"That's for you."

"An' suppose you don't get kilt?"

"Then spend 'em both and get drunk."

The old man beamed, flashing toothless gums. "Damn it all, I like you, boy, an' I sure hope ol' Ike don't kill you. You're true blue, an' stone me if that ain't a natural fact."

The miner quickly scooped up the coins as Donovan rose and shoved his winnings into his pockets. The watch he dangled from its chain, looking steadily across the saloon at Vance. For his part, Ike was closely studying how the young gambler handled the watch, but as yet he seemed unsure of its significance.

Finally, his voice cold and ugly, Vance said, "You heard what I said about that watch, boy. I know and now you know that I won't repeat myself."

Donovan was tired and irritated, and to his surprise he suddenly found his irritation overcoming his good sense. "You've been riding me mighty hard, Ike," he said. "I have friends here and I won't be buffaloed, so now it's time to back off."

Beside him, Donovan was aware that the whore's face was pale and frightened. She edged away from the table out of the line of fire, wide eyes following Donovan's every move.

"Maybe you should try and make me back off, boy," Vance said, his voice low and flat, alert and ready for what was to come.

A sudden tightness in his chest, Donovan knew he'd opened his mouth and said the wrong thing at the wrong time and now there was no escaping a gunfight. His hand moved toward the Colt under his coat and he saw Vance tense, ready for the draw.

But even as the moment seemed to stretch on forever, the saloon doors suddenly burst open, letting in a blast of cold fall air, the crash of wood against the sod wall an abrupt exclamation point of sound that brought a quick halt to the tension.

The local sheriff stepped inside, flanked by two tough and capable-looking vigilantes. The lawman was a typical small town sheriff, the front of his collarless shirt mostly hidden by a black beard, the ragged tin star pinned to his coat cut from the bottom of a peach can. But the man's hard blue eyes missed nothing and the sawed-off, American Arms 12-gauge scattergun in his hands was all business.

The lawman's eyes moved quickly from Donovan to Vance as he swiftly summed up the situation.

"Ike," he said to the tight-lipped Vance, rightly pegging him as the more dangerous of the two, "this is my town. If there's killing to be done, I'll do it."

Vance considered that statement for a few moments, then his shoulders slowly relaxed. "Suits me, Sheriff," he said. "There's killing to be done all right, but here or somewhere else, it doesn't really matter much to me. Just know that it will be very soon."

The lawman turned his head only very slightly in Donovan's direction, keeping his eyes on the fuming pimp. He knew you didn't take chances with a gunman like Ike Vance and it showed.

"You, boy," he said, "get on out of here and go on your way rejoicing that you didn't get the opportunity to try for your gun. Vance here would have killed you for sure."

Donovan smiled, pretending a bravado he didn't feel. "Maybe," he said. "Maybe not."

The sheriff shook his head. "Son, if you'd tried to shade Ike Vance I'd be burying you at first light and hanging him come noon. Now, do like I told you and get on out of here."

Donovan turned to leave but stopped beside the whore. Her brown eyes looked huge in her small, peaked face and she was bravely trying to smile, revealing little teeth that were close to the gum and surprisingly white.

"Sorry, darlin'." Donovan smiled. "Maybe some other time." He turned toward the scowling Vance and made a show of slipping the watch into his vest pocket, patting the gold chain with its silver wolf's head fob into place across his flat stomach.

"Some day very soon," Vance gritted, his face black with anger, "I'll kill you for that.

"Out!" the sheriff snapped at Donovan, and this time there was no give in him, his shotgun leaving no room for argument.

With a single backward glance at the huge and glaring Vance, Donovan stepped outside and walked through the cold and muddy darkness toward the hotel.

He patted the round bulk of the watch in his vest pocket and realized for the first time his hands were trembling.

His luck had sure changed, he thought.

Or had it?

2

The only hotel in town was a low sod building with a tin roof. A crudely lettered sign above the door said, THE REST AND BE THANKFUL, and under that in smaller letters, NATHANIEL P. WALTROP PROP.

The hotel boasted six rooms, arranged shotgun style, so that Donovan had to walk through three other rooms, each with its odorous and snoring occupant, before reaching his own.

Each room was partitioned by a piece of canvas hanging from a string and each was furnished with an iron cot spread with a couple of doubtful blankets. There was a two-by-four thrust into the wall for hanging clothes, an oil lamp hanging from a hook attached to the roof and nothing else.

Worn out as he was, Donovan was eagerly looking forward to sleep, though he was sure those stained, half-washed blankets would be the site of considerable nocturnal activity of the bug and flea kind.

He lit the lamp, then took Vance's watch from his pocket and thumbed open the cover, figuring it must be almost three o'clock. Immediately the watch softly chimed the Stephen Foster tune "Beautiful Dreamer," delicately picking out the melody with notes that rang like tiny silver bells.

Donovan shook his head and in the habit of men who ride much alone said aloud, "No wonder ol' Ike was such a sore loser. This is a watch any man would set store by."

"An' so he did, boy."

Donovan turned slowly and found himself looking down the twin barrels of the sheriff's scattergun. The lawman motioned toward the watch with the shotgun. "Turn that thing off, damn it. You'll wake the whole town."

Snapping the watch shut, ending the tune in mid-note, Donovan sought the man's eyes in the gloom.

"If you're here to warn me about the narrow escape I had, forget it, Sheriff," he said. "You've done told me that already."

The lawman shook his head and smiled, his lips thinning. "I'm not here to tell you anything, boy. I'm here to run you the hell out of town."

"It's three o'clock in the morning!" Donovan protested, his face flushing. "I need some sleep."

"Well, that's real unfortunate and I sincerely beg your pardon for it," the sheriff said evenly. "But you're leaving tonight. I don't want a killing in my town come morning."

A sudden rain spattered on the roof of the hotel and the oil lamp flickered, a small globe of orange light dancing on the gray tin.

"Hell, Sheriff," the young gambler sighed, "this isn't a killing matter. If Ike wants the timepiece so bad, he can have it back and pay me ten dollars. I guess the watch means something to him, but it means nothing to me."

Behind his beard the lawman's lips twisted into a humorless smile. "You just don't get it, do you, boy? Ike Vance took that fancy French repeater off the body of a riverboat gambler he killed down Natchez way a few years back. Like you said, he set store by the watch and just about everybody from here to Texas to the Dakota Territory knows it."

The sheriff reached out and touched the smooth gold of the watch case. "Ike was reckoned to be the best poker player west of the Mississippi, but when you took this from him so easily, him trying to buck a full house with two pair an' all, you dishonored him and he knows the word will get around.

"If you try to give the watch back in exchange for ten dollars, as an act of charity like, he'll lose face even more."

The lawman poked Donovan in the chest with a thick finger. "Don't get me wrong, Ike wants his watch back, but he plans to take it off'n your dead body. And like I already told you, that he probably will, and mighty soon. But not in my town. Now, you go get on your way an' get yourself killed someplace else."

The sheriff nodded toward Donovan's carpetbag. "Get whatever you own packed. I already woke up ol' man Fenton down to the general store and told him you'll need supplies and there's a man sleeps all night in the livery stable. He owns the place and he'll help you with your horse and pack animal."

Lightning flared in the window like a white sheet as the lawman continued. "Fenton now, he has plenty of coffee and flour and some right tasty smoked bacon brung all the way from Ireland by clipper ship. Any women's fixin's you might need, calico dresses an' bonnets an' sich, well, I reckon he'll probably have them too."

"Women's fixin's?" Donovan asked, puzzled. "I don't need no women's fixin's."

"Could be," the sheriff shrugged. "But I guess your whore does, maybe."

"My whore? What whore?"

"Hell, boy, the whore you won from Ike Vance. As far as I recollect, her name's Nancy an' she always gives value for money honest and true. Now, I must say in bed she ain't the most enthusiastic dove in the world or the prettiest, but all in all, I reckon she's conscientious enough."

Stunned, his voice catching in his throat, Donovan gasped: "But . . . but I thought I'd just won a lay."

The lawman shook his head. "Son, the more I talk with you, the more I figure you fer a goddamned pilgrim. Who the hell, in his right mind, pays two months' wages to get laid?"

"But . . ."

"Hell, boy, you didn't just win a piece of ass—you won the whole whore!"

"I'll give her back," Donovan protested, spreading his hands helplessly. "I don't want her."

"Damn it, boy, there you go again," the lawman said, a hard edge creeping into his voice. "Listen here to me. The same thing applies to the dove as to that fancy French watch. You try to give the whore back, Ike will take it as a deadly insult and kill both her and you. But that ain't going to happen—"

"—in your town. Yeah, I know," Donovan interrupted testily.

The lawman nodded. "Just so you got it right. Now get ready; you're leaving."

Realizing that further argument was useless, the

young gambler quickly swapped his worn but fancy frock coat, frilled shirt and checked vest and pants for range clothes, a pair of sturdy jeans and a blue woolen shirt.

Donovan folded his gambler's outfit carefully in the carpetbag; then under the watchful eye of the sheriff and his two silent vigilantes, he walked across the street to the general store where the unsmiling old man Fenton stood behind a counter piled high with shirts, pants, canned goods and a red Elgin National big wheel coffee grinder.

Irritated at being wakened so early, Fenton was surly and uncommunicative, barely glancing at Donovan as he gave the sheriff and the vigilantes a quick nod.

"Damn gamblers," the old storekeeper muttered under his breath. "String 'em all up I say an' good riddance."

At that moment, in less than a good mood himself, Donovan fought down the urge to make a sharp reply, figuring he was in enough trouble already.

Aware of the limitations of his skill with a Colt, he bought a .44 Henry rifle and a box of shells. Then a sheepskin coat that more or less fitted him and would keep out the winter wind that was already blowing iron hard and cold off the Medicine Bow Mountains to the west, promising snow. He stomped into a pair of low-heeled work boots, placing his elastic-sided shoes in the carpetbag. He tried several hats, liked none of them, and decided to stick with his own battered plug. That hat with its narrow brim wasn't much for shading a man from the sun or sheltering him from the rain but at least it fit comfortably.

Coffee, a tin coffeepot, flour, bacon and canned beans completed his purchases, and Donovan winced when Fenton totaled it all up. The old man charged top dollar for everything and it put a big hole in his money.

Arms full, the sheriff and the vigilantes stepping warily close beside him, Donovan walked across the street toward the livery stable. He glanced in the direction of the saloon where an oil lamp hung in an iron bracket from the wall. Ike Vance stood near the lamp, its flickering, yellow light outlining his huge, threatening bulk. He was talking to someone even bigger than he was, a long-haired man made even more enormous by the shaggy bearskin coat he wore, and the Winchester rifle cradled in his arms.

Two other men stood close by and Donovan knew their kind. Lean and hard-eyed, they were professional gunmen who would sell their services to whoever had the money to pay, no questions asked and no mercy given.

"Ike Vance sure has no end of expensive friends," Donovan thought bitterly. "For a man who's flat broke and on his uppers."

But for hired gunmen such as the three standing with Vance, Donovan's big American stud, palouse packhorse, guns, saddle and gear would be payment enough for a killing they must surely figure stacked up to be quick and easy.

That was a worrisome thought and it troubled Donovan greatly as he reached the livery stable and stepped inside. The sheriff and his two hard-faced vigilantes stayed close by. Bearded and eagle-eyed, the vigilantes were not long on conversation but seemed mighty short on temper.

A sallow-faced old man in a dirty red vest and suspenders brought Donovan his sorrel and then helped him load his supplies on the packhorse.

The young gambler saddled his stud and shoved the Henry in the boot, replacing the Winchester he'd sold six months before when times were tough.

"Brung you your whore," the sheriff said, stepping into the stable, Nancy trailing angry and resentful behind him. "She'll need a pony, I reckon."

Donovan gave an annoyed shake of his head. "Hell, Sheriff, I don't have a horse for her."

"Then buy her one, sonny."

Donovan's dove had exchanged her ill-fitting saloon finery for a gray cotton traveling dress and a heavy wool coat, much worn and mended. She carried a small bag, the top drawn together by a leather string, and a tattered white parasol. And that, plus a cheap silver ring on the middle finger of her left hand, was the sum total of what she owned.

The young gambler, defeat hanging heavy on him, sighed and asked the livery stable oldster, "What do you have by way of horses?"

The man nodded, his eyes suddenly sly. "Back here."

Two horses stood hipshot in their stalls, a mean-eyed little buckskin mustang that probably weighed less than 800 pounds and a good-looking paint with a lot of Morgan in him.

"I'll let the buckskin go for fifty dollars an' throw in a saddle and bridle," the livery stable owner said. "If'n you want the paint, I wouldn't take anything less than an even hunnerd an' another twenty-five for the saddle."

"That would just about break the bank," Donovan said, his eyes bleak. Then he nodded, anxious to get this over with. "I'll take the buckskin."

"No, you won't." Nancy stepped beside him. "I want the paint."

"Listen," Donovan snapped, flushing, "I'm not putting no two-dollar whore on a hundred-dollar hoss."

The dove shook her head at him. "Listen to me and listen good," she said. "Ike Vance aims to kill you and take back his watch. He'll kill me too, either because I'd be a constant reminder of his disgrace or to keep my mouth shut."

Donovan tried to protest, but Nancy forged ahead. "Either way, if he catches up to us we're both dead and that buckskin"—she pointed her parasol at the horse—"has two bowed tendons. He won't get a mile from town before he breaks down."

The dove stepped closer to Donovan and looked up at him, her eyes flashing. "Now, you may own me, but I'm giving it to you straight. We got to put distance between ourselves and Ike. God knows alone he's bad enough, but he's got friends. You saw them Texas killers. The big man with the long hair and bearskin coat is another Texan, goes by the name of Hack Miller, and, Mister Gambling Man, he's hell on wheels with his fists or a gun."

Donovan had heard of Hack Miller. A skilled and pitiless gunfighter, he was said to have killed a dozen men and rumor had it that there were many more if you counted women, children and Mexicans. Miller was trouble with a capital *t*, a man best left strictly alone.

Suddenly, with sickening certainty, Zeke Donovan realized he hadn't outrun his unlucky streak, not by a long shot. It had dogged him all the way from Texas and was now perched on his shoulder, a cold-eyed buzzard waiting patiently for him to stumble and fall.

Swallowing hard, fear spiking at his belly, the young gambler choked, "I'll take the paint."

"Thought you mought," the livery owner said dryly.

A few minutes later the sheriff helped Nancy onto the paint and Donovan gathered the packhorse's lead rope and swung into the saddle.

"Just afore you go, I got some advice for you, Donovan," the lawman said.

The gambler looked down at the sheriff and shook his head. "Don't want to hear it. I'd say you've given me enough already. Sheriff, you don't shape up like much as lawmen go, but I reckon you're a hard, unforgiving man."

"Well, maybe so, but this is my town and I'll have my say.

The sheriff stepped closer to Donovan and his dove, making sure they both heard him.

"Donovan, you do like your whore says and put plenty of daylight between you and Ike Vance." The lawman studied Donovan's handsome, rigid face, his eyes turning cold. "See, the way I feel about it, you and Nancy there, you don't plant corn and you don't raise cattle. You don't run a store or a bank or drive a stage or a steam engine. You just prey on them as does.

"You and your dove, boy, you're two of a kind, damned parasites when all's said and done. And if Ike Vance and his hired guns catch up to you and kill you both, well, there ain't nobody going to shed a tear, including the law.

"Donovan, you're what's known around these parts as a member of the lily-fingered class. You never toil or spin, never do an honest day's work, yet you're always attired in fine linen fresh from the tailor's iron and now you're wearing a gold watch. After Ike Vance kills you, there ain't nobody going to grieve for you and nobody will even bother to read the words over your grave."

The lawman laid a hand on Donovan's knee. "You get my drift, boy?"

Donovan jerked his leg away from the lawman's hand. "I guess you laid it out for me clear enough."

"Just so we get it straight."

The sheriff slapped the rump of Donovan's big stud. "Now, git, and don't ever come back. We don't want your kind around here."

3

Zeke Donovan and Nancy rode north, approximately parallel to the Cheyenne and Black Hills stage route. This was rough and broken country, mostly low-lying buttes crowned with pine and alpine fir surrounded by lush grasslands cut through by narrow creeks carrying runoff water from the Laramie Mountains.

The wind blew long and cold, spattering both riders with icy drops of rain, and Donovan's stud tossed his head, bit jangling irritably, annoyed at being dragged from the warm livery stable and into this dark, blustery morning.

A vague plan was forming in Donovan's mind. He'd head toward Lance Creek but keep it well to his west until he reached the Cheyenne River. Once at the Cheyenne he'd turn due east toward booming Deadwood and its gaming tables, where he'd heard there were plenty of miners and rubes with more gold than card sense.

Although fleecing rubes was his stock in trade, Donovan did not consider himself a tinhorn, nor was he talked of as such by his fellow gamblers. He had the reputation of playing a straight game and usually won by calculating the odds, not by relying on a cold deck.

Luke Short once told him after he'd asked if cheating should be part of his game, "Zeke, sure you can use a cold deck or deal from the bottom. Almost any person, with a little practice, can do that. But to perform that feat undetected while several pairs of keen eyes are concentrating their gaze on your fingers requires an amount of coolness and nerve possessed by maybe one man in a million."

The gambler's cold, blue eyes had studied him closely, then he'd added, "You're not that man. Play it straight, boy. Play honest poker."

Luke had been right. Over the years Donovan had known tinhorn gamblers who could perform miracles of manipulation with a deck of cards—until it really counted. Most times when they got into a game under the sharp eyes of their fellow professionals their courage melted and they were forced to play honest poker, becoming what they were all along—very poor players who lost their stack of chips almost as soon as it was set before them.

Unlike most gamblers of that time, Donovan's skills had not been learned on the Mississippi riverboats or the maturing towns in California or the big cities of the east coast.

He had learned the hard way, mostly by trial and error, winning sometimes, losing more often than not across the gambling tables of cow towns like Abilene, Hays, Wichita, Dodge and Ellsworth. It was the losing hands that had been the best teachers, and their lessons, so expensively bought, had not been forgotten.

Donovan had also gained much from other professional gamblers, studying the way they handled the cards, how they carried themselves at the table, how they kept their faces still, their eyes shuttered, no matter which way the pasteboards fell.

It had been a difficult and sometimes dangerous apprenticeship but he'd learned well and once he'd taken on the mantle of professional gambler he'd prospered—on those occasions when Lady Luck had smiled on him.

That she was frowning now, there was little doubt, and as Donovan rode his black mood matched the clouds, unseen in the darkness, that were forming towering citadels above his head.

The young gambler rode steadily for two hours, studiously ignoring Nancy, who was matching his pace, then splashed across a shallow branch of the Niobrara River. A few cottonwoods spread their limbs along the banks and his horse started as a trout jumped at an early flying insect.

He turned a little ways east and joined the main stage trail, rutted by the passage of wheels and churned into mud here and there by the hooves of many horses.

As night shaded into a gray dawn the rain started in earnest, a steady, pelting downpour. In the distance, maybe twenty-five miles to the east, lay the mighty wall of Pine Ridge, its steep slopes dotted here and there with tall firs and an occasional stand of aspen. Beyond the ridge and further to the north were the Black Hills and among them, snug in its muddy gorge, the roaring, blazing, wide open city of Deadwood.

Donovan saw no sign of life, animal or human, and the only thing that moved in that majestic but lonely landscape were the tops of the pines along the buttes, rustling their branches, whispering to each other about the fool who would be abroad on a morning such as this.

Around him lay a vast and endless vista, a wild immensity of soaring mountains and great prairies where the buffalo roamed in herds that numbered in the thousands and hundreds of thousands, the dust of their passing in the dry summer months blacking out the sun.

Had an eagle been flying high overhead at that moment he would have seen Donovan and his dove as tiny dots lost against the magnificence of the landscape. The restless lives of men, the dreams they harbored and the stories they told, were reduced by the seemingly endless ground they crossed to total insignificance.

The sheriff had told Donovan and his dove that they were parasites, nothing more and maybe a lot less. In that, he'd been wrong. In their own way, they were helping to shape and tame this brawling, violent and unforgiving land just as much as the farmer, the rancher, the cavalryman and the storekeeper. They were here, in the West, and thus a living, breathing part of the country, and in the end, like the others, they would become one with its legend.

Had you been there, at that time and place, and asked Zeke Donovan if he thought about it now and then, about being part of history, he would have looked at you in genuine puzzlement, no such thought ever having crossed his mind, even for an instant.

"I survive," he'd have told you. "Day by day, I do whatever I can to see another tomorrow. That's all there is and I reckon that's all there will ever be."

But surviving took strength and its allied virtue of courage. Life was cheap in the West of those days, and thus it was very much a place for the enduring young.

There were old people to be sure, but harmless now, they kept to the shadows and smiled and watched and let youth have its way.

But a graybeard, shrewd enough, would have observed a strange brand of stubborn, if shifting, courage and strength in Donovan, virtues the young gambler would not and could not recognize in himself.

The wind was chill, driving hard from the north, giving a raw edge to the rain, but tired as he was, Donovan nodded in the saddle, jerking awake now and then as his dozing horse stumbled.

When he was three miles north of the Niobrara the dark night shaded into a gray and gloomy dawn and Donovan turned in the saddle and saw Nancy on his back trail about two dozen yards away.

He reined in his horse and cupped his hand to his mouth. "You get away from me!" he yelled. "I don't want you dogging me like this."

He rode on for a few minutes and looked back again. She was still there, doggedly maintaining the same distance.

Soaked, tired and angry, Donovan stepped out of the leather and threw his plug hat on the ground. "You, git!" he hollered, a frustrated rage rising in him. "I'm getting real mad at you. Now, go find yourself another trail."

The woman sat her horse, looking blankly at him, her white parasol opened over her head in a useless attempt to keep off the rain.

His anger flaring, Donovan looked around and found a rock. He heaved it at Nancy, missing her by a yard. He picked up another one, and this time his aim was better. The rock bounced off the young woman's shoulder and he saw her jerk in the saddle and wince in pain.

"Let that be a lesson to you!" Donovan yelled. "You keep the hell away from me."

He picked up his hat, angrily slammed it on his head and swung into the saddle.

He rode on, kicking his tired horse into a weary lope. When he looked back, Nancy was still following, her paint matching his stud's pace as she awkwardly held up her bobbing parasol against the teeming rain.

"Damn that woman," the young gambler whispered to himself. "She's hunting trouble for sure."

Donovan had planned to keep on riding through the day, but he was exhausted and more than anything else he needed sleep.

The odds were that Vance and his gunmen were already somewhere on the trail behind him and riding fast. He calculated, correctly, that he was holding a lousy hand and eventually would have to fold and face the consequences. Maybe it was better to do so sooner than later, when his horses would be too tired to go a step further and he himself would be so used up he'd be an easy target.

Peering through the shifting steel gray curtain of the rain, Donovan found what he was looking for. A thick stand of lodgepole pine stood atop a shallow hill, a jumble of ancient volcanic rock that at least promised some shelter from the worst of the keening wind scattered among their slender trunks.

Donovan swung his horse and cantered up the slope. It was better than he'd dared hope. A flat rock about ten feet across had fallen across two large boulders, forming the roof of a small, snug cave. Fresh water in the form of a stream, shallow and only a foot wide, bubbled around the base of the hill.

Dismounting, Donovan led his horses around to the slope hidden from the trail and staked them on some good grass, close enough to the pines if they needed shelter.

Weary as he was, he set about making the cave more rain- and wind-proof. He dragged over some fallen branches and brush to make a reasonably tight wall on either side of the flat rock and used more brush to cover the muddy floor.

Satisfied, the young gambler started a small fire inside his shelter. There would be little smoke from the dry twigs he'd gathered and what there was would be dissipated by the branches of the lodgepole pines, hardly visible to anyone passing on the trail below.

Donovan buttoned into his sheepskin, preparing for sleep, but suddenly realized he was needful of hot coffee. He grabbed the pot and left his shelter, slipping and sliding down the rain-slicked slope to the stream.

Nancy sat her horse at the base of the hill in the streaming rain, watching him stoically from under the rim of her parasol. The shoulders of the girl's coat had turned black from dampness and her hair hung wet and lank around her face.

Damn that woman!

If Ike Vance came this way he'd see her for sure and then there would be hell to pay. Out here, he'd be no match for four skilled gunmen.

Donovan filled the coffeepot, then straightened. He glanced over at the dove and his shoulders immediately slumped in defeat as he faced a harsh reality. He couldn't let Nancy stay out there, not with Vance maybe real close. Cursing himself for a fool, he beckoned to the woman. She didn't move.

With a deep sigh, Donovan stepped toward her. "You'll catch your death of cold sitting out there in this rain," he said, trying to keep his voice pitched reasonably gentle. "Better come on up."

Nancy shook her head. "I'll wait right here," she said, her voice cool and flat.

"Damn it, woman, Ike Vance could pass this way anytime. He'll see you for sure and then we're both dead."

"I'll wait right here," Nancy repeated stubbornly.

Donovan opened his mouth to speak, changed his mind about what he was going to say and snapped, "Oh, the hell with it. Stay out here in the rain if you want."

He turned to walk away but Nancy's voice stopped him. "You hit me with a rock."

Donovan shook his head and began to walk up the hill again.

"It hurt."

He stopped and looked down the slope at the dove, a small thin girl in shabby clothes, her eyes too large for her small pale face. Her wet hair lay over her forehead and rain dripped steadily from the rim of the parasol over her shoulders.

"What the hell do you want me to do about it?" Donovan asked.

"Say you're sorry."

"Okay, I'm sorry."

"Say it like you mean it."

Donovan gave an elegant bow. "I'm sorry I hit you with the rock. Please find it in your heart to forgive me."

Nancy smiled slightly. "That's better. Now I'll come up."

Despite his exhaustion, Donovan boiled coffee and broiled a few strips of bacon over the fire. After they'd eaten he and Nancy laid down side by side, their bodies carefully not touching, and within moments both were asleep.

The rain kept on falling from a lowering sky and once a young pronghorn buck warily stepped close to their shelter. Not liking the human smell, he bounded away on silent feet on ground carpeted with pine needles, disturbing a pair of yellow warblers pecking around the roots of a lodgepole.

The morning melted slowly into afternoon, the incessant hiss of the rain a counterpoint to the soft sound of the wind rustling among the pines.

Amid a confused dream that figured a scowling Ike Vance and gold watches with eyes that ran on spindly legs, Donovan woke with a start. He flipped open the case of Vance's watch. It was almost three. He urgently shook Nancy awake, then went down the slope and saddled the horses, catching up the packhorse's lead rope.

When he got back, the girl was standing outside the shelter, her useless parasol opened above her dripping head.

"I plan to ride the rest of the day and then through the night," Donovan said brusquely. "Less chance of being seen that way."

"What about me?"

Donovan shrugged. "That's up to you. You can come with me, I guess, if you can keep up."

"Donovan," she said, "just how far do you plan to run?"

"As far as it takes," the young gambler replied. "I reckon all the way to Deadwood. I have friends there."

Donovan studied the girl. He guessed she was about sixteen, old enough to have been married off by this time if she'd been raised by respectable, go-to-church folks.

A flicker of annoyance crossed Nancy's face. "Is that

all you can do? Run? Run from a streak of bad luck, run from Ike Vance, run from me, from everything?"

The gambler nodded. "Yes, that's about how she shapes up. I'm not the kind to wrap myself in the flag and go down fighting, if that's what you mean."

Nancy tossed her head and stepped to her paint, her nose in the air.

Donovan made a little exasperated yelp in his throat and gathered up the reins of his stud.

"Halloo, the camp!"

Donovan turned and saw six grinning riders in wide-brimmed hats and yellow slickers sitting their horses at the base of the hill, looking expectantly up at him.

He pegged them as passing drovers from one of the local ranches, but he held his Henry across his chest where it was handy.

"What do you boys want?" he asked.

The men rode slowly up the slope. They were young and tough, typical of the cowboys of that time, but their faces were good-humored and their eyes were alive with bashful excitement.

"Hell, man, we come to see your whore," one of the punchers said. "Ain't every day a man wins a whore with a full house over two pair."

Alarmed, Donovan asked quickly, "How did you find us?"

"Well," the puncher said, "the word about Donovan's dove got around mighty fast. The rain washed out most of your tracks, but we reckoned there's only a few places hereabouts where a man can take shelter if he has a mind to and this here Bear Medicine Hill is one of them."

The rider rolled a cigarette, keeping the makings close to his chest out of the rain. He lit his cigarette and said from behind a cloud of smoke, "I got to admit, we really didn't expect to find you. But, hell, here we are an' there you are."

"Ooh, lookee there, boys," another hand said. "There she is; there's Donovan's dove." He made a face, showing his disappointment. "Hell, I was told she had flaming red hair down to her waist and her name was Conchita. That little gal don't have red hair and I'm guessing her name ain't Conchita either."

"What's she doin'?" asked another rider.

"She's getting on that paint hoss."

"Well, I never seen the like in all my born days. A brown-eyed whore on a paint pony. Ain't that a sight to see."

"Look, look, she's getting down off the hoss again," another said. "Man, that's something."

"Hey, Donovan, how many times you done her so far?"

This from an eager young drover with a wispy mustache and corn yellow hair showing under his hat.

Knowing what the cowboys wanted to hear, Donovan dug the toe of his boot into the soft dirt and replied, "Aw, shucks, boys, no more'n a dozen times, on account of the rain and all."

"A dozen times," the young rider said, clapping his hands. "Man, I wish I'd seen that. It must have been a sight to see."

A thin man with a scar on his cheek nodded toward Donovan, rain cascading off the brim of his hat. "We heard you was wounded back to the saloon in town. You don't look wounded to me."

"What did you hear?" Donovan asked, letting them tell it.

"You mean you don't know what happened? Hell, man, you was there."

Donovan shrugged. "Tell me anyhow."

"Well," the thin man said, thinking about it, "we heard tell your whore was once a Spanish noblewoman who was kidnapped by a Chinee gang over to San Francisco way an' then sold into slavery. They say after you won her from Ike Vance, then you had to shoot your way out of the saloon. As I recollect hearin' it, you was a-holdin' your whore in your left arm and was blazin' away with your Colt in t'other."

Another puncher leaned forward in his saddle, both hands on the horn and said, "Way I was told it from them as were there, you killed two men and two more are so poorly they ain't expected to live."

Doubt shaded the man's eyes. "That was the way it was supposed to be. Ain't that the way it happened?"

A gambler played the odds and when he earned the reputation, deserved or not, as a cool gun hand, it had a way of acting in his favor when a man at his table combined losing with anger and too much whiskey and might just be inclined to reach for a handy Colt.

"That's exactly the way it was," Donovan lied smoothly, nodding. "Just like you heard it. 'Cept I gunned five of them Vance rannies, not four, and my whore is a Russian countess, not a Spanish lady."

The young gambler stepped back to his horse. "Now, boys, time is pressing and we have to be moving on. Will you give us the road?"

"Sure thing," the scarred cowboy said, "we got to be getting back to the ranch anyhow." He studied Donovan carefully for a few moments, then added, "I guess you know Ike Vance and three of his boys are on your trail? They left town at first light this morning."

"His funeral," Donovan said, smiling.

"Well, that's crackerjack!" the man exclaimed. "Mister, we'd be right proud to shake your hand."

One by one, Donovan took each cowboy's hand, then watched them ride away, excitedly talking to each other, through the shifting gray mesh of the rain.

"Okay," he said to Nancy, "mount up. We're riding."

The girl stood beside her paint and shook her head at him.

"No, we're not," she said firmly. "We're staying right here."

4

"What do you mean?" Donovan asked, an annoyed scowl on his face. "Mount up. We're wasting daylight."

"Not today."

Donovan shook his head, his irritation boiling to the surface. "Do like I told you or by God I'll hit you with another rock."

"I can't. It's my time of the month and I won't ride today and maybe not tomorrow."

The young gambler was stunned. "I don't want to hear stuff like that. I want no truck with female troubles."

"Listen, mister," Nancy snapped, her eyes angry, "when you own a woman, you borrow her troubles. And just in case you haven't noticed before, a whore is a female and a female has her time of the month. It's a fact of nature."

Donovan opened his mouth to speak but no sound came out but a strangled squeak. He tried again and this time succeeded. "I don't own you. Since the War Between the States nobody owns anybody else."

"You won me from Ike Vance, fair and square, remember?"

"Then I free you. This here is what you might call my Whore's Emancipation Proclamation. From this day forth you are no longer a slave. Now, go in peace and freedom."

Donovan gathered up the reins of his horse. "Me, I got to be moving along. Hey, it's been real swell, but it's time for us to say *hasta luego*."

"You're leaving me here alone?" Nancy asked, eyes blazing.

"You're a free person now," Donovan said, swinging into the saddle. "You've got to go your own way, take your own road. I think maybe some day you'll make your mark or you'll marry a right nice feller and have kids an' stuff."

"Ike Vance will find me and kill me for sure," Nancy said bitterly.

Donovan looked down at her. "He won't kill a woman. You'll be safe enough, maybe."

"I want you to stay with me. It's only for a day or maybe two. Probably not two."

The young gambler smiled. "No deal. Maybe Vance won't shoot you, but he'll kill me. From where I sit, that's a stonewall certainty."

Nancy shook her head at him. "Ike and his boys will ride right on by this hill. He knows you're a runner and he'll have studied on things by this time and reckon you're ahead of him. He won't expect for a single moment that you'd be dumb enough to stop and shelter from the rain."

"Too thin," Donovan said, ignoring Nancy's pointed reference to running. "Way too thin. I'm leaving right now and I have to ride fast and far."

"Go then, but don't expect any kind of warm welcome in Deadwood. You heard those cowboys; most everybody has been told the story of Donovan's dove by this time."

"So what?" Donovan asked uneasily, a small seed of doubt growing in his mind like a noxious weed.

"Just this. If you ride on out of here without me, folks will hear that you abandoned your dove to be murdered by Ike Vance. They won't cotton to that. They'll figure that any man who runs out on a woman in her time of need, leaving her to the hungry wolves, has got to be pretty low-down and not to be trusted.

"Mister Gambling Man, folks have long memories. With a reputation like that, you won't dare show your face at a gaming table in a western town again and maybe not in an eastern one either."

Suddenly Donovan felt like a trapped animal. He frantically threw Nancy's words around and around in his head, seeking a way out. There was none that he could see.

"You're a whore," he tried desperately. "You heard that hick sheriff back there. Ain't nobody cares about a two-dollar whore."

Nancy just stood there, looking at him, her raised, skeptical eyebrow saying a lot more than mere words could.

"Right!" the young gambler snapped, tasting defeat bitter in his mouth. "This here is a cold camp. No fires. No hot food. No coffee. None of the comforts of home. You think you can survive that?"

"I can if you can."

Nancy led her pony to Donovan and handed him the reins. "Now, be about your business while I attend to mine."

Donovan started to lead the horses back to the other side of the hill. But he stopped, turned to the woman and said with narrowed eyes, "I never thought winning a gold watch and a whore could land a man in so much trouble." He shook his head, leading the horses again. "It's sure a sight easier to borrow trouble than it is to give it away."

Two hours later, as Donovan and his dove huddled cold, wet and miserable in their shelter, Ike Vance and his three hired guns rode past the hill in a pelting rain, scarcely giving its pine-covered crest a second glance.

Time passed slowly, Donovan and his dove sitting in silence, busy with their own gloomy thoughts. As the long day shaded into night, Nancy hugged her drawn-up knees and shivered, her thin dress and coat sodden with rain.

Donovan glanced at her, looked away quickly, then, shaking his head at his own foolish weakness, took off his sheepskin coat and spread it over her shoulders.

The girl hugged the coat closer to her and gave him a grateful look. Donovan, embarrassed, said brusquely, "I think maybe we can chance a small fire. At least long enough to boil up some coffee. I don't reckon even a crazy lobo wolf like Ike Vance is riding in this weather."

As the coffee boiled, the rain was joined by thunder. Lighting flashed among the hills like the unfurling of terrible banners and the night birds sought refuge in the pines, scared black eyes blinking against the flickering glare.

Donovan and Nancy sat close together in their leaky shelter, each drawing warmth from the other, toes curling and uncurling near their feeble hatful of fire.

As he drank his coffee, Donovan opened Vance's watch and let the tinkling notes of "Beautiful Dreamer" float like tiny silver moths around the circle of the firelight, scarcely heard amid the racketing fury of the storm.

Nancy began to sing in a pleasant husky voice and Donovan, after his initial surprise, joined her, his light high tenor harmonizing above her own.

> *Beautiful dreamer, wake unto me,*
> *Starlight and dewdrops are waiting for thee;*
> *Sounds of the rude world heard in the day,*
> *Lulled by the moonlight have all passed away.*
> *Beautiful dreamer, wake unto me.*

The girl smiled, tilting her head to one side as they sang, ignoring the crashing thunder and the angry serpent hiss of the torrential rain.

> *Beautiful dreamer, queen of my song,*
> *List while I woo thee with soft melody;*
> *Gone are the cares of life's busy throng,*
> *Beautiful dreamer, awake unto me!*
> *Beautiful dreamer, awake unto me!*

Suddenly annoyed at himself, Donovan snapped shut the watch, the rest of the song stillborn in Nancy's throat.

"Time to bed down," he said sharply. "We got a long trail ahead of us tomorrow."

As he'd watched the girl's face as she sang, Donovan had felt something, an emotion he didn't recognize and couldn't explain. Somehow, in the glow of the fire, Nancy had looked almost beautiful and very vulnerable. He wanted to reach out and hold her. He wanted to protect her from whatever evils lurked out there in the lightning-branded darkness, like one of those knights errant of old.

And now he cursed himself for being a thickheaded fool.

No knight errant ever set forth on a milk-white steed to save a two-dollar whore—even if she did ride a hundred dollar paint pony.

Later, as he lay awake staring at the slab above his head touched with orange and yellow from the last flames of the fire, he turned and propped himself up on his elbow.

"You awake?" he asked.

"No," Nancy replied, only the top of her head showing above the collar of Donovan's sheepskin.

"How'd you get into the whorin' profession in the first place?"

"Ask me that tomorrow."

"Suit yourself. I was only asking."

Nancy sighed and turned to face the young gambler.

"Whorin' is like cowboyin'. It's something you do when you can't do anything else."

"Well, I've been a drover and there's some truth in what you say. When I was a boy I came up the Goodnight-Loving Trail from Texas to Colorado. I made that drive twice, then figured it was time to get into another line of work. Beef and beans and thirty a month just don't cut the mustard, not for eighteen hours in the saddle, seven days a week. That was hard, dirty and dangerous work and for what? A three-day drunk at the end of the trail, a hangover that would kill a mule and empty pockets."

"Me, I was an orphan and I was raised by a God-fearing farm couple who applied scripture and the switch with equal enthusiasm," Nancy said. "Soon as I was old enough, I ran away, met Ike Vance in Ellsworth and went into the whorin' profession."

She turned over, pulling the sheepskin coat around her. "Okay, I've told you my life story, Donovan. Now maybe I can get some sleep."

They took the trail at first light the following morning.

The thunderstorm had passed but it was still raining hard and the stage road was a winding river of oozing mud, stretching away into an endless gray horizon.

Nancy rode with her useless parasol over her head, her wet hair plastered to her face in dark, straight tendrils.

After thinking it over as he lay awake in the thundering night, Donovan had decided to head south, away from Ike Vance and his riders. Deadwood could wait for another time.

"By the time they figure they've missed us and doubled back, we'll be across the Platte and well on our way to Cheyenne," he told Nancy. "They'll never catch up."

Nancy nodded miserably, her slumped shoulders telegraphing her exhaustion. "Whatever you say, Donovan." Then, her voice flat and emotionless, she added, "Whatever you say."

The sun was hidden by a thick layer of gray cloud and the morning was slowly shading toward a bleak noon as Donovan and his dove rode past a low bluff crowned by juniper, a thick stand of yellow and scarlet aspen on its lower slope, broken up here and there by darker arrowheads of spruce.

Head down against the driving rain, Zeke Donovan didn't even hear the rifle shot from the aspens that blasted him clear out of the saddle.

5

Donovan hit the muddy ground hard, rolled over and lay still. Blood from his wounded head poured into his mouth and eyes and when he tried to move his arms he couldn't. He was conscious, aware of the rain, his surroundings and the terrible pain in his head, but he was completely paralyzed.

"Eeeeowsa! I got him, Paw! My ol' .56 damn near blew his head clean off!" Through half-closed eyes Donovan looked up and saw a young towhead looking down at him. The man was grinning, showing yellow, rotten teeth in a loose, ill-defined mouth. The vile stench of him was a living thing that clutched at the throat and violently assaulted the nostrils.

From somewhere an older, rougher voice said, "You fetched him sure enough, son. Damn it all, Ephraim, your sainted mama would be proud of you if'n she was stilt alive."

The older man's face swam into Donovan's line of vision, the features an exact copy of his son's except that the teeth were fewer and even more rotten, and the washed-out blue eyes were red-rimmed and fevered with greed and the hot, triumphant aftermath to a killing.

Both men wore shabby bearskin coats, tied at the waist with string, and each carried a rifle and wore a canvas belt of ammunition around his hips.

Donovan had seen their type before. They were small-time but vicious predators who killed from ambush, sure-thing robbers who preyed on the old, the weak, the sick and the unwary.

And, he thought bitterly, like any wide-eyed pilgrim, he'd let them bushwhack him.

Men like these two were descended from immigrants who'd traded the poverty-stricken and stinking stews of European slums for the greener and pine-scented poverty of the Tennessee hills.

They were the product of generations of relentless and mindless inbreeding, raised on hardscrabble dirt farms where a girl remained a virgin only as long as she could outrun her brothers.

There were good, hardworking mountain folk in Tennessee and Donovan had known and liked a few. But he recognized these two as part of a shiftless, no-good breed who had drifted west to murder and steal rather than walk behind a plow.

Donovan felt the younger man go through his pockets, taking his money and the gold watch. Then he stripped off the sheepskin coat and saw the holstered .45.

"Lookee here, Paw," Ephraim said, "he got one of them aces under his armpit. Must be he's one of them gambler, gunfighter fellers we hear so much about."

"Take that gun off'n him, boy," Paw said. "If he is a gambler, his card sharper days are over."

Donovan saw Paw's face come closer, studying him.

"You got him right through the head," he grinned evilly. "You're a credit to me, boy. I always said you was golden."

Ephraim stripped off Donovan's boots then picked up the plug hat and slammed it on his head. "Look at me, Paw," he said, dancing a little jig in the mud. "I'm one of them big city fellers."

"Enough o' that," the older man said sternly. "We got his woman to attend to."

Out of the corner of his eye Donovan saw Nancy sitting her horse. She'd closed her parasol and now held it loosely in her right hand.

Paw stepped closer to the girl, grinning, his eyes fevered with lust. He turned his head slightly in his son's direction without taking his eyes off Nancy for a moment and said, "Me and you, boy, we're gonna wear this bitch out an' then throw away what's left, an' that won't be much."

Ephraim let out a wild whoop. "We're wasting time! Let's get at her, Paw!"

The older man walked to Nancy's paint and looked up at her. "Come here, you," he said roughly, reaching out a hand to pull her from the saddle.

Donovan managed to turn his head very slightly, enough to see Nancy's pale, frightened face and the grinning man beside her.

It happened very fast.

The girl brought up the parasol and jabbed its sharpened steel end hard into Paw's right eye. The parasol pike was a well-known whore's weapon, a last-ditch defense against drunken clients who might seek perverse sexual pleasure with fists or a knife, and Nancy had used it well.

The bushwhacker shrieked like a wounded animal

and stepped back, thick scarlet blood mixed with something viscous and white running down his cheek.

Nancy swung her horse around and kicked it into a gallop, gobs of mud flying from the paint's hooves as it stretched out its neck and ran.

"She blinded my shootin' eye, boy!" Paw screamed. "Kill her."

Ephraim raised his Spencer to his shoulder and fired. Donovan could no longer see Nancy but he heard a loud thud as both horse and rider went down hard.

"I got her, Paw!" Ephraim yelled. "I done for her."

The boy ran to where Nancy had fallen. He returned a few moments later with something red and gory in his hand.

"Brung you something, Paw," he said. "Couldn't get that ring off'n her, so I brung you this."

Now Donovan saw what Ephraim carried. He held Nancy's bloody, severed finger, the cheap little silver ring still around it.

Paw was moaning softly, his destroyed eye a horrible welter of crimson gore.

"You want I should put another bullet into the gambler feller, just to make sure, Paw?" his son asked.

"Nah," the older man replied. "He's dead as a rotten stump. But are you sure you kilt that bitch, boy?"

"Done shot her right through the back, Paw. She's as dead as this one."

"Let's gather up their horses an' traps. I got to get some attention for this eye."

Donovan heard Ephraim whisper uncertainly, "Paw, your eye ain't there no more."

"Don't you think I know that already, you idiot?" the older man snapped. "You real sure you kilt that bitch?"

Ephraim raised his rifle and fired.

"Now I've kilt her for you twicet, Paw," he said.

Donovan tried to raise his head but still couldn't move. The effort cost him a shocking, red-hot spike of pain and then he was falling, tumbling headlong into a black pit that had no beginning and no end. . . .

6

The day faded. Shadows formed among the hills and ravines as time turned and the land grew darker. A branch fell among the aspens, unheard. The hour of sleep arrived for wild things, heralded by an owl that questioned the night, then paused, patiently awaiting an answer.

A hungry coyote trotted warily from the pines and sniffed the air, scenting blood. On cat feet, the little animal silently closed the distance between itself and the body of the man lying faceup in the rain.

Closer now. The coyote paused, its instincts clamoring. It heard the man groan and move slightly, a foot churning the mud.

The coyote turned tail and ran. A dead human meant food. A live human, or even one just half-alive like this one, could only mean trouble.

Donovan groaned and opened his eyes to a world of darkness and rain. The pain in his head pounded like a hammer on an anvil and he felt nausea curl in his belly like a green snake.

He moved his leg and felt his socked foot bury itself in the mud. Slowly he tried moving his arms, then both his legs. He was no longer paralyzed. The bullet that had cut across his head had made him lose the power in his limbs, but only temporarily.

He rose to a sitting position, held his head in his hands and tried to remember what had happened.

Bit by bit, like the pieces of a child's picture puzzle fitting together, it came back to him.

He had been bushwhacked and Nancy . . .

Nancy!

Donovan tried to rise, but the effort was too much for him. His head swam and he fell back into the mud. He lay still for a few moments, then rose once again to a sitting position.

He looked off to his right, where he'd heard Nancy's horse fall.

There was an indistinct shape lying in the rain, maybe a hundred yards away. The shape was too small to be the horse, so it had to be the girl.

Not trusting his legs, Donovan crawled on all fours toward the dark, motionless bundle. It took him about ten minutes of painful crawling across the muddy, rain-slicked ground before he reached her.

She was lying on her side, her lips slightly parted, her face deathly pale. Donovan lifted the girl and held her in his arms. The rain was falling steadily and he thought he saw her eyelids flicker as drops fell on her face.

He pressed his ear close to Nancy's chest. There was a heartbeat, faint and irregular, but it was there.

She was still alive.

A quick examination of the girl's body revealed that she'd been shot low in the back. The bullet seemed to have struck bone then ranged off to the right, emerging from her waist just above her hip. Ephraim's second bullet had merely nicked her left arm, but the middle finger of her left hand was gone, chopped off by the man's bowie knife.

Nancy was weak from loss of blood. She needed rest and medical attention, but neither was to be found in this vast, untrammeled wilderness.

Unsteady and fevered from his own wound, Donovan rose slowly and painfully to his feet. The hot pounding in his head was relentless, thought crowding on thought so that there was no separating them and the whole became jumbled, meaningless.

Well, he would carry her. Carry her all the way across the Platte and then to Cheyenne where there were doctors.

How many miles? Two hundred maybe?

It had to be done.

The watch, Donovan thought. If he had the watch he could play "Beautiful Dreamer." It would be his marching tune. But he didn't have the watch. Who took it? He scowled, trying to remember. Ike Vance. Yes, it had to be Ike Vance.

Zeke Donovan bent over and lifted Nancy in his arms. Hell, she was no bigger than a nubbin and weighed hardly anything.

He stumbled forward, carrying the girl into the darkness and the rain. How far to the Platte?

Maybe Ike Vance had stolen the Platte. Could a man steal a river? It could be done. But a man sure couldn't carry it in his hip pocket.

Hip pocket! Donovan laughed so hard he tripped and fell. He picked up Nancy again and asked her if he'd told her about the river Ike Vance stole. It was a good joke and she should be laughing. Why wasn't she laughing?

The young gambler staggered on, the fever now burning inside him like a fire.

The night parted, allowing his stumbling passage, then closed in around him again like a dark shroud, and the ceaseless rain hissed at him with mindless venom, pelting into his face, mocking his every step.

"Mine eyes have seen the glory of the coming of the Lord . . ." Donovan roared his song to the uncaring hills and silent prairie. "He is trampling out the vintage where the grapes of wrath are stored . . ."

In his arms Nancy stirred and moaned quietly but Donovan wasn't aware. Now stern old Charlie Goodnight was talking to him, telling him he had a herd to move and to get back to the goddamned dust of the drag where he belonged.

And Luke Short. What was Luke doing out here on a cattle trail?

Luke was standing in front of him, shaking his head at him, his mild blue eyes amused. "Now you've done it, boy," he said. "Now you've really hit rock bottom. You played a lousy game, Donovan, and you're plumb out of chips."

Then Charlie Goodnight was gone, and then Luke. And once again there was only the forever of the night stretching out across the endless miles ahead of him.

Later Donovan would have no clear memory of how long and how far he carried Nancy. He would not recall how many times he stumbled and fell, how many times he picked up the girl and kept walking, how often he lifted his head and roared his anger and pain at the unheeding sky.

It was close to one o'clock in the morning when he saw a light ahead of him in the darkness, the faint orange flicker of an oil lamp behind a window.

He struggled forward, the girl now heavy in his weakening arms.

When he was about fifty yards away, Donovan could make out a low, sod cabin and what appeared to be a barn and a good-sized corral in the back. A windmill towered over the cabin, creaking slightly in the wind.

The cabin lay at the foot of a tall bluff crowned by scattered pine that showed evidence of being logged, and a stunted willow grew close to a dry creek that curved around the front of the cabin and then ran behind the corral.

It seemed to take an eternity of walking before Donovan reached the door of the cabin. He stood outside for a few moments, then hammered on the door with his cut and bleeding right foot, his sock now hanging in tatters.

He heard voices whisper inside, then the sound of a bolt being drawn back. The door swung open and a bearded man stood there, a Winchester in his hands.

Donovan, Nancy in his arms, took a single step forward, then stumbled inside . . . and into oblivion.

Zeke Donovan woke to sunlight.

A man with a thick red beard and green eyes was looking down at him, a concerned expression on his face.

"Where . . . where am I?" Donovan asked.

The man laid the back of his hand against the young gambler's forehead then replied, "Ah, your fever has gone at last, I'm thinking."

"Where . . . ?"

"You're at the O'Brien's Bluff stage station and I'm Patrick O'Brien. And you're in my barn, though it surely shames me to tell you that."

"Nancy?"

"If it's the girl you're talking about, she's back in the house with me missus. It's against the policy of the directors of the Cheyenne and Black Hills Stage Line to have overnight guests at any of their stations. But isn't the girl lying quiet as a mouse on a pallet at the foot of our own bed, so who is any the wiser?"

"How long have I been here?" Donovan asked, trying hard to find his memory again.

"Three days, and most of that time crazy as a loon as ever was."

Donovan struggled to a sitting position. His hand went to his aching head and his fingers found a thick bandage.

"You have a nasty wound there, but the missus treated it for you, and you out of your mind with the fever the whole time." O'Brien said. "Did somebody hit you with a rock?"

"No, somebody hit me with a .56 Spencer."

Donovan tried to rise but sank down again, surprised at how weak he felt.

"I have to see Nancy," he said desperately. "I'm"— he hesitated, then added finally—"responsible for her."

"Later," O'Brien soothed. "She's asleep right now and there's nothing you can do for her that hasn't already been done. For a while there I thought we'd lose her, but she's young and strong and if her wounds don't get infected, she'll recover."

O'Brien rose to his feet. "Wait there. I'll bring you something to eat. It will give strength to you and help put some meat on those poor skinny bones."

The big Irishman returned a few minutes later carrying a plate piled high with antelope steak, potatoes and half a dozen fried eggs.

Donovan didn't realize how hungry he was until he smelled the food, and he ate ravenously and in silence until the plate was scraped clean.

O'Brien had watched Donovan eat with quiet approval, and when the young man was done, he said carefully, "That young girl, Nancy, now, she's been shot and she's lost a finger."

Irish he may have been, but O'Brien had lived long enough in Wyoming to have acquired the Western man's reluctance to probe too deeply into another man's troubles.

"It's just an observation, you understand," he added quickly. "I may be no better off for knowing the why and wherefore of it."

"My name is Zeke Donovan," the young gambler said, by way of introduction.

"That I guessed already," O'Brien nodded. "I heard from some passing riders that Nancy there is really a German baroness and that you saved her from a heathen Chinee gang down Cheyenne way." The big man shook his head angrily. "Damn pigtailed Hindoos, cutthroats every one of them."

Donovan smiled, determined to be truthful with this man as a way of repaying his kindness and hospitality. "Well, Mister O'Brien," he said, "it didn't quite happen that way."

In as few words as possible and without embellishment, the young gambler described his card game with Ike Vance and his subsequent flight north. Then he described how he and Nancy had been bushwhacked and left for dead by a man named Ephraim and his paw.

"The rest you know," Donovan concluded. "I saw your light and walked toward it."

"And just as well you did," O'Brien said, his kindly

face concerned. "You were both very near to death as far as me and the missus could tell."

O'Brien mused in silence for a few moments, then said, "Ike Vance I've heard of, but I don't know the man personally and I can't put a face to him. The two who bushwhacked you are a different story.

"I'd say you ran afoul of Jeb Louper and his boy. Now Ephraim is said to be a bit touched in the head, but he's just as poison mean as his paw. The two of them are wolfers and scalp hunters and they've turned to murder a time or two, but nothing could ever be proved. They don't leave witnesses, man, woman or child.

"Jeb and his boy have a dugout cabin back in the hills to the south of the Cheyenne near a place called Lost Nugget Creek. I've always said we should organize a posse of vigilantes and go up there and clean them out, but I guess all the boyos I spoke to were married men because nobody seemed too keen to go up against Ephraim's rifle. He's a crack shot, or so I'm told."

Donovan nodded. "I guess his shooting was a mite off when he bushwhacked me, or I wouldn't be sitting here talking about it."

"Ah, Saint Patrick must have been looking out for you, Mister Donovan, and that's a fact. And maybe even the blessed Lord himself."

Donovan rose to his feet. The food had done him good and he felt stronger. He was in the loft of O'Brien's barn and narrow beams of dust-specked sunlight were slanting through the green planks.

"O'Brien," he said, "I need a gun and a horse."

"Whatever for?" the big man asked, surprised.

"I'm going after Jeb and Ephraim. I intend to get back what is mine."

"Jesus, Mary and Joseph, you'll do no such thing!" O'Brien exclaimed. "And you nearly dead on your feet."

"Nevertheless, I will go."

It never occurred to Donovan for even an instant to ask O'Brien to come with him. In the West a man was expected to fight his own battles and there was no room for discussion on that point.

Donovan winced as the pain in his head spiked briefly. "Do you have a rifle?" he asked.

"That I have, but it's the property of the Cheyenne and Black Hills Stage Line and the directors say it is not to be loaned out to anyone or used for hunting."

"A horse?"

"Only the six mustangs you see here in the barn. They're a fresh team for the next stage and not one of them is broken to the saddle."

Donovan felt defeat crashing in on him and his shoulders slumped, something noted by O'Brien, who was at heart a compassionate and feeling man.

The big Irishman shook his head. "It is that I'm cursing myself for my own foolishness," he said, "but I have a Colt .36 Navy, loaded and capped and ready to go. As for a horse, I have a mule but no saddle. Neither gun nor mule is the property of the directors of the Cheyenne and Black Hills Stage Line and you are welcome to borrow one or t'other or both."

Donovan nodded, relief evident on his face. "Thank you kindly. I'll take you up on your offer and borrow both." He hesitated, then added, "I'll return them, have no fear on that score."

"Never entered my mind that you would not," O'Brien said.

When Donovan walked to the cabin, Mary O'Brien,

a plump, motherly woman told him Nancy was asleep.

"And that's just as well," she said, "for that's how nature heals the body." She shook her head sadly. "Poor thing, she's as skinny as a rail and it's obvious she's had a hard life and not much by way of love and care."

"Can I see her?" Donovan asked, suddenly feeling guilty, though precisely for what, he did not understand.

"Well, perhaps just for a moment."

As O'Brien had told him, Nancy lay at the foot of his huge wooden bed on a pile of blankets. She was breathing easily and in her sleep she looked very young, little more than a child.

Donovan stood there for a few moments looking down at the girl, conflicting emotions he didn't comprehend pulling him this way and that. Finally, his face bleak, he turned on his heel and walked out of the bedroom and into the main cabin.

Ten minutes later, wearing a pair of O'Brien's shoes and his spare coat, both items several sizes too big for him, the Navy Colt stuck into the waistband of his jeans and a bony, ill-tempered mule under him, Donovan rode from the stage station toward the foothills of Laramie Peak.

He was still far from well. But he had a job to do.

7

When night fell, Donovan gratefully climbed off the mule's back and made camp in a stand of cottonwoods and willows beside a narrow creek. He staked the mule on a good patch of bluegrass studded here and there with buttercups and opened the sack Mary O'Brien had given him.

She hadn't stinted on his supplies.

There was a small tin coffeepot, coffee, sugar, some sliced beef, a slab of bacon and a loaf of sourdough bread.

Donovan gathered some greasewood brush from under the cottonwoods and made a small fire to boil coffee while he ate a thick sandwich of beef and bread.

Patrick O'Brien had given him extensive and exacting instructions on how to get to the Louper dugout and thanks to the mule's distance-eating stride, he figured to arrive there some time the next day's afternoon.

As to what his plan of action was going to be once he confronted Jeb and Ephraim he had no idea.

The Navy had five loaded cylinders and there was

no spare. That didn't give him much firepower and—
him not being an accomplished marksman—very little
margin for error.

After he drank his coffee, Donovan rolled himself in
his blanket, for the night was chill. He lay on his back,
looking up at the stars. They were very close and it
seemed a man could reach out and sweep up a handful of them.

About forty yards out there was an outcropping of
eroded red rock. A wolf tiptoed along its flat top, then
stopped, regarding Donovan with interest.

The young gambler idly watched the wolf, thinking
of Nancy.

Perhaps when tomorrow was over and he had his
horses and guns back, he would just keep on riding,
maybe all the way to Deadwood. The O'Briens were
good people and they'd take care of the girl until she
was well enough to travel. Nancy had to make her
own way sooner or later. She must realize she had no
future with a gambler, a man who had to travel fast
and light, never staying in one place long enough to
push his luck lest the run of the cards change in his
disfavor.

Donovan watched the wolf test the wind, gray muzzle raised, learning more about this country from that
single sniff than even an Apache could discover in a
month of scouting.

Donovan smiled. It was decided then. He would
keep on riding. This time next week, if he lived that
long, he'd be in Deadwood.

When he looked at the rock again the wolf was
gone, vanished like a puff of woodsmoke.

Still smiling, the gambler closed his eyes and let
sleep take him.

*   *   *

A few minutes after noon the next day Zeke Donovan rode past the dugout on Lost Nugget Creek without seeing it.

After an hour of riding he doubled back—and this time the dice rolled his way.

He had just crested a shallow, spruce-covered hill when below him he saw a man on a paint pony ride toward a point on the hillside opposite, where a thin tendril of smoke tied faint gray ribbons against the blue of the sky.

Donovan dismounted and led his mule a ways down the hill. He then bellied up to the crest again and watched the man as he rode toward the smoke. The man climbed off the paint, then led it up the hill.

Now that his eyes were becoming accustomed to the distance, Donovan saw what he'd missed before. There was a wooden door on the hillside, painted green, almost invisible against the surrounding grass. This must be the front of the Louper dugout, cut right into the side of the hill.

The man led the pony toward the door, then turned and disappeared behind the dugout.

There must be a flat area back there, Donovan guessed. And maybe a corral or even a small barn.

Donovan studied the hill carefully. The cabin wasn't a true dugout. It looked like the floor had been cut into the hillside, then four sod walls had been raised to a height of maybe seven feet. The roof was flat and it too was covered in sod, much of it sprouting bluegrass and even a few wildflowers. A narrow iron chimney stuck up from one end of the roof, presumably attached to a stove of some kind.

A single window, unglazed but covered by a piece of canvas, gazed blankly to the front. Donovan guessed the presence of a door at the back of the cabin that would be opened during the day to provide light and fresh air.

There was no way to rush the cabin. Donovan knew that if Ephraim Louper was even half as good with a rifle as O'Brien said he was, he'd be cut down before he even got halfway up the hill.

If he'd had his Henry, he might have been able to lie up here and snipe at the cabin. But those thick sod walls would stop a bullet and the Loupers could hole up there for days if need be, and maybe longer.

Donovan bellied backward and once clear of the crest of the hill he stood and walked around its base. Beyond this hill lay about fifty yards of flat, open ground and then the elevation rose slowly, becoming a low saddleback that curved around the far side of the cabin.

If he could get across that open ground unseen, he could approach the cabin from its windowless side, hidden by the saddleback. And maybe, if he was lucky, take the two bushwhackers by surprise.

There was no other way. He would have to chance it.

Donovan gripped the walnut butt of the Navy Colt, settling the revolver more firmly in his waistband.

Fifty yards.

Even sprinting at his top speed, he'd be in the open for maybe six seconds—long enough to be picked off by a marksman from the cabin.

Gulping a breath of air, Donovan lowered his head and ran.

Now he was sprinting in the open, every nerve jangling, expecting at any moment to feel the sledge-hammer blow of a .56 bullet.

It never came.

Donovan covered the last couple of yards by throw-

ing himself headlong behind the rise of the saddleback, landing among a thick carpet of late blooming
forget-me-nots and larkspurs. He lay there on his back,
panting, blessing his lucky stars he hadn't been seen.

A few minutes later he crested the top of the northern-
most rise of the saddleback and saw the side of the cabin
about twenty yards away.

Donovan drew his Colt. Crouching low, he closed
the distance between himself and the cabin and
reached the low sod wall undetected.

Slowly, watching where he trod in his oversized
shoes, the young gambler made his way to the corner
and looked around.

There was a small corral behind the cabin where his
big sorrel and Nancy's paint stood with two other
horses. Beyond the corral, hogs wallowed in a pen and
Donovan heard the shrill squeals of piglets. Close to
the pig pen there was a narrow outhouse and even
from where he stood, the vile stench of it hit him like a
clenched fist.

A door opened, and Donovan ducked back his
head. When he glanced around the corner again he
saw Ephraim slam the cabin door shut, then walk toward the outhouse, slipping his suspenders off his
shoulders. He was unarmed and was carrying what
looked to be a Sears and Roebuck catalog under his
arm.

Donovan waited until the outhouse door closed,
then paused a few seconds longer. A fly buzzed
around his head and he waved it away from his face
with his hand.

He slipped off O'Brien's shoes and tiptoed silently
past the cabin door, stopping a few feet away from the
outhouse. He studied the outhouse door, calculating
where Ephraim would be sitting, then cut loose with

the Colt, slamming three quick shots through the thin pine.

A surprised, agonized scream came from inside. Then a loud thump. Then silence.

Donovan, his heart pounding, ran to the other corner of the cabin and ducked out of sight. He heard the cabin door open, followed a few moments later by Jeb Louper's harsh roar of grief and anger.

When he glanced around the corner, Donovan saw Jeb pulling his son out of the outhouse by his legs. The younger man's filthy, stained underwear rode down around his ankles and the front of his equally filthy vest was splashed vivid scarlet with blood.

"Ephraim, they've kilt you!" Jeb roared "They've kilt my boy!"

Donovan stepped out from the cabin and walked on silent bare feet to Jeb's side. He touched the man on the shoulder.

"Hi, Paw," he said. "Remember me?"

Jeb quickly snapped his head around. The man's one good eye widened in recognition and then terror as Donovan placed the muzzle of the Navy Colt against Jeb's forehead and pulled the trigger.

The .36 caliber ball hit hard, blowing the front of Jeb's head apart in a scattering fountain of blood and brain, and he collapsed on top of his son.

Donovan, his hands trembling, looked down at the two dead men.

"I gave you the same chance you gave me," he said finally, his voice hard and unforgiving. "You boys dealt the cards and I could only play out the hand I was given."

A pine-scented wind blew the sparse hair on Jeb's head and his single eye was wide and staring. Under him, Ephraim gasped once then was silent as death finally took him.

Donovan shook his head and shoved the Colt into his waistband. He stepped through the open door of the cabin and looked around. The place, as he'd expected, was filthy and smelled terrible. Holding his breath, he quickly found his carpetbag, watch, guns, sheepskin coat and boots and gratefully stepped outside again.

After he'd shrugged into the coat and stomped into the boots, the young gambler entered the cabin again. He spent a few minutes searching for Nancy's ring but couldn't find it and stepped outside again.

He walked over to Jeb's body and saw the ring on the little finger of the man's left hand. Donovan kneeled and tried to wrench it off the man's finger, but he couldn't get it over the knuckle.

"Sorry about this, Paw," he said. He took the old man's bowie from his belt and hacked off the finger just above the ring. It slipped off the bloody stump easily.

Donovan stepped over to the horse trough and washed off the ring, then shoved it into the pocket of his coat.

A few minutes later, astride his sorrel, hazing the mule, Nancy's paint and the Louper horses in front of him, Donovan rode down the hill away from the cabin.

He didn't look back.

Donovan had thought to keep on riding, but it came to him then that he owed it to O'Brien to return his gun and mule as he'd said he would.

Was that really his motive, or was it something else? Was it because he didn't want to leave Nancy alone?

As he rode, Donovan shook his head, angry at himself for even thinking such a thing.

No, it wasn't Nancy. He was going back only because he'd given his word to O'Brien.

It was just that and nothing else.

"Jesus, Mary and Joseph and all the saints in heaven help us and preserve us, are you telling me you shot a man while he was squatting in the shitter?"

Patrick O'Brien's face was stiff with shock, his blue eyes wide and unbelieving.

Donovan nodded. "I had to even the odds somehow."

"But . . . but you gave him no chance," O'Brien persisted, the old country's sense of fair play strong in him. "No chance at all and him a-reading of the Sears and Roebuck catalog."

"The ladies' corsets pages."

"Ah, the ladies' corsets pages was it?"

"I had the drop on him and I gave him the same chance he gave me," Donovan said, his smile tight. "And you're right, O'Brien, that was no chance at all."

"Then for mercy's sake, don't be tellin' the missus," the Irishman said. " 'Tis my thinking it's something she wouldn't understand."

O'Brien, although mildly critical, was not passing judgment. Getting the drop on somebody was a thing he himself knew and understood well. Later generations raised on Western myth would believe that getting the drop on another man meant you were able to slap leather, draw your sixgun faster and gun him down.

It meant nothing of the kind

You had the drop when you were able to shoot an enemy, preferably with a scattergun, when he least expected it—in the back, while he was asleep, when he was unarmed or even while he was kneeling, lips moving in an odor of sanctity, at his holy prayers.

Winning a gunfight was everything, mainly because there was no future for the man who finished second best.

But gunning a ranny while he sat at his business in an outhouse, Sears and Roebuck catalog in hand, opened to the ladies' corset page, was a new twist for O'Brien, and the big Irishman had trouble wrapping his mind around that and its implications.

The two men stood in O'Brien's barn, Donovan having ridden directly there with the horses and mule, swinging wide of the cabin.

"How is Nancy?" Donovan asked, quickly changing the subject, amazing himself that he felt genuine concern.

"She's young and strong. I'm thinking she'll be on her feet in a week or maybe two."

"A week or two! I can't stay here that long."

Donovan thought for a few moments, then nodded toward the corral where the Louper horses stood with the stage company mustangs.

"You can keep the horses and saddles, O'Brien," he said. "They'll pay for Nancy's keep. Me, I got to be riding on."

O'Brien's face stiffened. "It is not for me to be asking payment for an act of Christian charity," he said, his voice touched by annoyance. "The girl can stay here until she's better and 'tis myself that won't be asking a penny for it."

Donovan realized he'd offended the Irishman, one of a race with a notoriously touchy pride and a belligerence to match.

"I know that, O'Brien," Donovan said smoothly, trying to put a patch on their rapidly fraying relationship, "but I'd feel better if you took the horses. Call it my way of thanking you and your wife for all you've done for Nancy."

"It was no bother at all," O'Brien said, slightly mollified. "And as for the Louper horses and traps, I'll sell them and split the money with you. Where can I reach you when the time comes?"

"Deadwood," Donovan said with finality. "I had thought to go to Cheyenne, but I've just now changed my mind. Give the money to any stage driver. He'll know where to find me."

"You have friends there?"

Donovan nodded. "A few. Mainly a feisty little gambler called Doc Holliday and another man who goes by the name of Colorado Charlie Utter. They both owe me a favor or three."

O'Brien nodded. "I've heard tell of them, though little of it good." He studied Donovan closely for a few moments, then said, "Well, good luck to you, and now I have to be getting the team ready for the stage and then help the misses with the 'taters and bacon for the passengers."

"I'll help you with the team," Donovan said, seeking to put yet another patch on their relationship.

"You shouldn't be botherin' yourself," O'Brien said. "Them mustangs are only half-broke and they'll kick you or take a bite out of your britches if they get half a chance."

Donovan smiled. "I've worked with mustangs before. They don't scare me none."

8

"Well, best as I can tell, it isn't broke, but you'll be laid up for a spell," Patrick O'Brien said, his face concerned as he studied the massive bruise on Donovan's right thigh.

The young gambler winced, pain spiking at him as the big Irishman probed the wound with thick, blunt fingers.

"If it was broke, I think I'd be able to feel the bone all splintered and shattered and terrible," O'Brien said.

Donovan shook his head, his lips a thin, tight line. "Thanks," he said. "That makes me feel a whole heap better."

"Didn't see it coming, did you?" O'Brien asked. "I told you those mustangs are only half-broke. They're full of mischief and deviltry, they are."

"Damn thing turned on me and kicked out with both his back legs," Donovan said, still scarcely believing that it had happened. "He could have killed me."

He sat in O'Brien's cabin, his leg propped up on a

three-legged stool. His right thigh was puffed up to twice its normal size and O'Brien had split his jeans to accommodate the swelling.

Three stage passengers were crowded into the small cabin, two of them bearded miners, rough-looking men in lace-up boots and plaid shirts, revolvers strapped around their waists. The third man was a drummer in ladies' undergarments who smelled of whiskey and had the pale, peaked and perpetually on-edge look of a henpecked husband.

One of the miners, thick black beard spilling over the front of his shirt, finished eating, clanked his fork onto the tin plate on the table before him and rose to his feet.

"Let me take a look at that leg," he said.

Donovan regarded him warily. "Are you a doctor? You don't look like a doctor."

The man nodded. "I'm a qualified physician, graduate of the University of Pennsylvania School of Medicine, class of '70."

Donovan was still unsure. "You look like a miner to me."

The man nodded. He was several inches over six feet and his thickly muscled shoulders were an ax handle wide. "I am a miner. I had me a time in Cheyenne until my poke ran out, and now I'm headed back to the diggings."

"How come you aren't working as a doctor?" Donovan asked, still wary.

The big miner sighed. "I can't stand sick people. I hung up my shingle in Boston town back in '71 but it didn't pan out. Seems like everybody who came to see me was down with something. I saw rashes I didn't want to touch and heard coughs I didn't want anywhere near me and finally I'd had enough. I threw the shingle on the fire, then headed west."

The man spread his hands helplessly. "Don't get me wrong. Being a physician is to be a member of a fine profession—so long as you don't have to deal with sick people. They kind of ruin it for everybody."

O'Brien shook his head in agreement. "It's true indeed that folks with a misery are a trial to be around."

"Amen, brother," the miner said, nodding. "They're a whining bunch to be sure." He shivered. "And you've got no idea of the kind of horrible ailments they come up with. Why, I've seen stuff that would make your blood run cold and disturb your sleep o' nights, let me tell you."

The miner took a step toward Donovan. "Now, let me take a look at that leg."

"Thought you didn't like sick people?" Donovan asked, trying to smile.

"If your leg's busted, you're not sick, just broke."

With surprising gentleness, the big man bent and examined Donovan's thigh, probing around the huge, black and blue bruise and the open skin where the mustang's steel-shod hoof had hit hard. Then he clucked his tongue and straightened up. "O'Brien here is right. It's not broken. But I'd stay off it for at least a week until the swelling goes down."

"I was planning to ride out of here today," Donovan said, disappointment shadowing his face. "I've got to ride fast and far."

The miner shook his head. "I don't advise it. You put too much pressure on that leg and it could become infected. I've seen it happen. You could end up losing the limb."

Defeated, Donovan's chin sank to his chest. "Damn

that mustang," he muttered. "And damn my own bad luck. Then I'm stuck here."

"Bad luck, now, that has a way of riding a man until he's mighty weary of it," the miner said, smiling faintly.

"Don't I know it," Donovan agreed, his eyes bleak.

After the stage left, carrying the miners and the drummer to Deadwood, Mrs. O'Brien stepped out of the bedroom and walked over to Donovan.

"Nancy is awake," she whispered, as people do around the sick. "She's asking for you."

Donovan nodded. "I'll go see her, if you can help me to my feet."

"Wait," Patrick O'Brien said, "I've got something that will help."

He stepped out of the cabin and returned a few moments later, a crutch in his hand. "This belonged to a passenger," he said, handing the crutch to Donovan.

"How come he left it here?" asked the young gambler.

"Oh, he was a very old man, bless his heart," Mrs. O'Brien said, "and he's got no more need for it. He passed away right here at the station, not a three month ago."

"Pegged out right about where you're sitting, Donovan," O'Brien said. "He just upped and died and his face fell right into his beans and bacon."

Donovan nodded. "Figures. All in all, this has been a real happy day."

With the help of the O'Briens, Donovan struggled to his feet, jammed the crutch into his right armpit and hobbled to the bedroom door. He swung the door open and hopped his way inside.

Nancy, pale as death, her brown eyes huge in her

thin face, was sitting up, an empty bowl that had once held chicken soup lying beside her.

"What happened to you?" she asked weakly, looking at his swollen leg.

"I got kicked by horse. It isn't broke."

Nancy held up her bandaged left hand. "Donovan, they took my finger."

The gambler nodded. "I know." He frowned in thought, then said, "Wait just a minute."

He hobbled back into the main cabin and found his sheepskin coat. He searched in the pockets, then found what he was looking for.

Donovan hopped back into the bedroom and held up the silver ring. "I got this back for you."

"Those two men," Nancy said, "where—"

"They're dead," Donovan said. "I done for them both. I shot the younger man, the one who cut off your finger, while he was sitting in the shitter. O'Brien says I shouldn't ought to have done that, I mean shooting him while he was in the shitter looking at ladies' corsets in the Sears and Roebuck catalog."

Nancy shrugged her thin shoulders. "Those two weren't men, they were wild animals. Beasts like that, you kill any way you can." Her eyes reddened. "They took my finger, Donovan. Can I still work in the whoring profession with just nine fingers?"

Donovan smiled, trying to make the girl feel better. "Sure you can. Who's going to notice that a whore is missing one of her fingers? Hell, I wouldn't."

"Are you sure?"

"Sure I'm sure. Anyhow, you're Donovan's dove, remember? Men will be lining up to pay you top dollar for a lay."

Nancy eased back on her blankets. "I've been a lot of trouble to you, haven't I, Donovan?"

"Nah," the gambler replied. "I like having you around. Why else, when O'Brien told me I should be riding on, would I have told him right sharp that I planned to stay here until you got better? Does that sound like you're a lot of trouble?"

"Is that the truth?" Nancy asked. "Did you tell him that?"

"Sure did. Told him a lot more, besides. I told him that I knew we were a burden to him but if he wanted me to leave without you to go right ahead and shoot me because I'd rather be dead than leave you behind."

"Where are we going, Donovan?" Nancy asked, her young face suddenly alight with hope.

"Deadwood. I've got friends there." He smiled and with considerable difficulty squatted on the floor beside her, his injured leg sticking straight out in front of him. "Give me your hand."

Nancy held out her bandaged left hand.

Donovan shook his head and smiled. "No, the other one." He slipped the little silver ring on her middle finger. "There, now you have your ring back."

The girl spread out her fingers, studying the ring. "I'm going to get better real soon so we can ride out together, Donovan," she said finally.

"That suits me right down to the ground." Donovan hesitated for a few moments, then said, "Now, once the swelling goes down in my leg, you may see me ride on out of here." The girl opened her mouth to protest, but the gambler held up a hand. "All I'll be doing is scouting the trail ahead, to make sure Ike Vance and his gunmen are nowhere around." He smiled. "I'll curve on back for you and then we'll head for Deadwood."

The girl nodded, swallowing the lie. "I'll be waiting, Donovan."

She closed her eyes. "I'm very tired. I think I'd like to sleep for a while."

"Good idea. You take a little nap."

Donovan waited until the girl was asleep. With her eyes closed she looked very young and vulnerable. He leaned over and his lips came close to her cheek. But he thought better of it and struggled to his feet, beads of sweat popping out on his forehead from the effort.

The young gambler stood, looking down at the sleeping girl for a few moments. Then he hobbled out of the bedroom and back into the cabin.

Over the next week, Donovan paid for his keep by helping out the O'Briens as much as he was able. He stayed clear of the mustangs but helped Mrs. O'Brien prepare food for the passengers and he washed dishes and mopped floors, hobbling around awkwardly on his crutch.

Stages came and went, and once an eight-man cavalry patrol stopped at the station and the sergeant in command warned O'Brien to keep a close watch, since there were Cheyenne in the area.

"Just yesterday, they burned a settler cabin five miles south of here and murdered the farmer and his wife and their three children," the sergeant said. "There are about a dozen of them, young renegades that broke out from a reservation in the Montana Territory, and I fear they plan more mischief."

O'Brien asked for a couple of troopers to help guard the station, but the sergeant, a grizzled man with a great walrus mustache, said he'd none to spare. "You must see to your own defenses," he said, before galloping away.

Donovan brought his Henry into the cabin from the barn where he slept, and O'Brien took his Cheyenne and Black Hills Stage Line company Winchester from its hook on the wall and kept it close to hand.

Another four days passed with no sign of Indians and both Donovan and O'Brien began to relax a little, though they remained alert and watchful.

Although pale and weak, Nancy was back on her feet and with the resilience of the young, her wounds were healing rapidly.

On the fifth day, a stage rolled up to the station in a pelting rain, a dead guard up on the box and a passenger inside who was gutshot and could not be expected to live.

The swelling in Donovan's leg had gone down considerably and he was able to get around without the aid of the crutch. He helped O'Brien hitch up a fresh team because the driver was on edge and anxious to leave.

The dead guard they laid inside the coach, the wounded man alongside him, since he needed more doctoring than O'Brien could provide. The only other passenger was a profane and bearded bullwhacker on his way to the goldfields who elected to ride shotgun on the box.

"If you've got a lick of sense, you'll get out of here with us, O'Brien," the driver, a man named Ronson, said. "Them Cheyenne hit us just as we were slowing to make the grade across Red Wall Gulch, an' there was a passel of them."

Ronson, a small, sun-wrinkled man in greasy buckskins, kept looking over his shoulder through the shifting wall of the rain as though the Indians were about to attack at any moment.

"Did you get any of them?" Donovan asked.

The man shook his head. "Nary a one. Ol' Clem

there, he was killed in the first volley and all I could do after that was make a run for it."

Ronson climbed up on the box, took the lines in his hands and nodded toward O'Brien, rain cascading from the brim of his hat. "Pack a carpetbag, Patrick, and come with us. There's room inside and on top for all four of ye and time is a-wasting."

O'Brien shook his head. "Donovan here and his dove can go and my missus, but I must stay. It is the policy of the Cheyenne and Black Hills Stage Line that station employees must remain on the premises at all times unless otherwise instructed by a director, superintendent, officer or other senior and duly authorized representative of the company."

Mrs. O'Brien, who had been listening closely to this exchange, said, "As for me, I'll stay with my man and don't you go telling me to do anything else, Charlie Ronson."

The driver shrugged. "Your funeral." He turned to Donovan. "Are you and your woman ready to go?"

Donovan hesitated. He realized he owed O'Brien and his wife a great deal, yet gratitude had its limits, especially when squared off against a war party of Cheyenne. Hostile Indians were bad news and he wanted no part of them.

"Give me a few minutes to saddle up our horses," he said finally. "We'll ride with you."

"We ain't got a few minutes," Ronson said impatiently. "Leave what you have and climb up right now or I'll be on my way and be damned to ye."

Nancy appeared at Donovan's elbow, her white parasol opened above her head, and Donovan whispered to her urgently. "Climb up on the stage. We're getting out of here."

He stepped to the front wheel and put a foot on the

hub, then pulled himself up on the box where the big bullwhacker slid over on the seat, making room. Donovan turned, extending his hand, expecting to find Nancy waiting for him. But she hadn't moved, looking at him with eyes that held a mixture of contempt and pity.

"Let's go!" Donovan yelled, anger flaring in him.

Nancy stood her ground. "You go. I'm staying here to help the O'Briens. I owe them."

"Hell," Donovan snapped, "this isn't our fight. We don't work for the goddamned stage company."

Nancy nodded. "That's right. But I owe the O'Briens."

"Time to go," Ronson said. He snapped the lines and the mustangs shambled into a short-coupled trot.

Donovan turned his head and glanced behind him. Nancy and the O'Briens stood in the hammering rain looking after him, three lonely and vulnerable figures, dwindling smaller and smaller against a vast backdrop of gray sky, green hills and tall pines.

"Oh, hell," Donovan swore bitterly. He turned to Ronson. "Stop the stage. I'm getting off."

Limping slightly, he trudged back to the station along a trail rapidly turning into a sea of mud.

Nancy stood still, arms folded across her breasts, watching him come, and when he was close she said, "Forget something?"

"Yeah," he said, his smile thin, voice dripping sarcasm. "I forget what Indians look like." He nodded to the crest of a hill about two hundred yards to his south. "But it seems to me, if I recollect rightly, that they look like that."

Nancy and the O'Briens turned and all three saw the Indian at the same time—a Cheyenne warrior, rifle in hand, sitting a spotted pony in the pelting rain. He was gazing down at them intently, wet war paint running down his cheeks in tangled streaks of crimson, blue and yellow.

The Cheyenne wore the red and green sash of the Dog Soldier and Donovan was well aware of all that implied. This man, and no doubt the others with him, was a warrior elite. The Dog Soldier sash could only be worn by proven men who had taken a sacred oath never to retreat, never to beg mercy or grant it and to never turn their back on an enemy who was still undefeated and bearing arms.

Donovan turned to the big Irishman, his eyes showing his concern. "O'Brien," he said, his voice unsteady, fear thickening his tongue, "this ain't going to be easy."

9

Patrick O'Brien ushered the women into the cabin and Donovan followed. The Irishman pulled wooden shutters across the two windows to the front and the one to the back. A rifle slit had been cut into each shutter and although it gave limited visibility, it offered a measure of protection for the defender inside.

"O'Brien, we can't cover all three windows," Donovan said, his unease making his voice pitch higher. "They'll come all at once and hit us front and back."

Mrs. O'Brien walked to a battered cupboard to the right of the stove, reached behind it and produced the Spencer Donovan had taken from the Louper dugout.

"It is myself who'll be guarding the window to the back," she said, holding the rifle steady in her hands like she'd been born to it.

Despite himself Donovan was impressed by the woman's quiet courage.

"You'll do, Mrs. O'Brien," he said.

Nancy stepped beside Donovan, her eyes calm.

"My place is here with you," she said, her determined tone making it clear that she'd brook no argument.

Now that his initial fear had passed, to be replaced by a fatalistic acceptance of whatever was to come, Donovan nodded. "Glad to have you." He reached into his coat and drew the short-barreled Colt. "You know what to do if it gets real bad and they get inside here?"

The girl smiled slightly, taking the gun. "I know what to do."

Like drops of water from a leaky faucet, the big railroad clock on the wall ticked slow seconds into the quiet of the cabin.

An hour passed. Then two.

Mrs. O'Brien and Nancy fried salt pork and made thick sandwiches with sourdough bread that the men ate at their posts behind the windows.

After he'd eaten, Donovan stepped to the door, pulled back the wooden bolt and opened it a crack, peering outside into the rain-lashed afternoon.

Nothing stirred.

The pines tossed their branches in a freshening breeze, the slight rustle of their needles unheard against the steady dragon hiss of the downpour. The clouds hung so low in the sky, they covered the crests of the surrounding hills like a thick fog, and the soaked spruce and lodgepole pines stood like obsidian arrowheads against the lighter green of the slopes.

In the distance, Donovan saw a jay flutter from one pine to another, the bird soon lost among the branches and the slanting steel needles of the rain.

"See anything?" O'Brien asked, his voice tinged with anxiety.

Without turning, Donovan shook his head. "Not a damn thing."

"Think maybe they've passed us by? Maybe they think we ain't worth the bother."

"Could be. Indians are mighty notional. You expect them to do one thing and they do another. But I wouldn't bet my last chip on them passing us by."

Donovan studied the sky. "Be dark soon," he said. "I reckon we'll be safe until sunup."

"How come?" Nancy asked. Her face was very pale in the gathering gloom of the cabin.

"Indians won't fight at night," Donovan replied. "The Cheyenne and other tribes believe if a warrior gets killed after sundown, his soul is doomed to wander forever in eternal darkness."

"Never heard that before," Nancy said.

"Well," Donovan said, "it's a natural fact. Heard it my ownself plenty of times."

The Cheyenne attacked an hour later—in full darkness.

There were twelve of them, and as far as Donovan could determine in the brief, flickering glimpses he got of the Indians, all wore the Dog Soldier sash. The Cheyenne rode past the cabin, firing as they came, whooping wild war cries as orange flame blossomed from the muzzles of their rifles.

Donovan heard O'Brien fire and a split second later he too squeezed off a round, aiming at a fleeting image of a horse and gaudily plumed rider.

"Get him?" O'Brien yelled.

"Nah. You?"

"Missed."

A bullet slammed into the shutter where O'Brien stood and the big Irishman yelped, the right side of his face suddenly bloody, covered in wood splinters like a mess of porcupine quills.

Donovan spared the wounded man a brief glance, then he fired into the darkness and fired again. He wasn't aiming because there was nothing to aim at, just momentary, flashing glimpses of yelling, hard-riding horsemen.

"They're after the horses!" Mrs. O'Brien yelled. The Spencer roared and the woman screamed, "Got one of them heathens! That's one less damned Hindoo to be bothering us."

Donovan ran to the back window. He stood close to Mrs. O'Brien and looked out on the corral and barn. He saw a warrior hazing the horses from the corral and he fired. Missed. He fired again. Another miss.

A bullet slammed into the shutter, banging it violently on its hinges, and Donovan heard Mrs. O'Brien yell, "Jesus, Mary and Joseph and all the saints in heaven preserve us!"

"O'Brien!" Donovan hollered. "They don't want us, they're after the horses."

The big Irishman, his face a welter of blood, the splinters sticking out from his cheek like cat whiskers, shook his head. "No! Those horses are the property of the Cheyenne and Black Hills Stage Line. I will not allow them to be taken without authorization from an officer or duly appointed representative of the company."

"Wait!" Donovan veiled. "Don't go out there."

It was too late.

O'Brien, his eyes wild, slid back the bolt on the door and rushed outside into the flame-streaked darkness.

10

Donovan, his Henry ready, stepped quickly to the door.

He saw O'Brien run toward the warrior who was hazing the horses, his arms waving above his head. "Stop, ye bloody heathen!" he howled. "Those animals are the property of the Cheyenne and Black—"

He never saw the Cheyenne who killed him. The warrior was coming at a fast gallop on a paint pony, his rifle spitting flame.

The bullet hit the Irishman in the chest and staggered him. Another warrior fired and O'Brien went down on his knees, gasping for breath, bright blood bubbling sudden and scarlet over his lips.

Donovan drew a bead on the Cheyenne who'd fired the first shot as the warrior wheeled his pony away. He fired and the Indian was knocked off his horse, splashing heavily into the mud where he rolled once, then lay still.

Donovan fired at the second warrior but missed, the man galloping fast into the shifting curtain of the teeming rain. Fear riding him hard, the hair at the nape of his neck standing on end, Donovan cranked a round into the chamber of the Henry and looked around for another target. There was none.

The Cheyenne had disappeared as fast as they'd come, fading into the storm-lashed night like ghosts.

Mrs. O'Brien rushed past Donovan's elbow and ran to her husband. She kneeled in the mud and cradled O'Brien's head in her lap.

"Oh, Patrick," she sobbed, "have they done for you at last?"

But the big Irishman was beyond replying. He was beyond anything. He was dead.

Donovan stood beside Mrs. O'Brien for a few moments, his hand on her shoulder. Nancy stepped beside him and he nodded toward the sobbing woman. "Help her," he said. "Do what you can."

Nancy kneeled beside Mrs. O'Brien and put her thin arm around the older woman's plump shoulders, saying nothing, but trying to comfort her with the closeness of another human being.

Donovan walked to the Cheyenne he'd shot. Now more and more of the mature warriors were being killed in their futile and losing battle against the Army, and this man was young, no older than sixteen.

But he wore the sash of the Dog Soldier and that meant he'd ridden on successful war parties and served a probationary period to see if he was worthy to join such an elite military society. He'd probably been preparing to be a Dog Soldier since he was about twelve and likely had only been recently initiated into the society.

The Indian's smooth, beardless face was peaceful in death, eyes open, upturned to the pelting rain, the paint on his cheeks running in streaks over his ears and braids.

Donovan left the dead warrior and checked the corral. All the horses were gone, including O'Brien's mule.

A blood splash on top of a corral post, rapidly melting away in the teeming rain, confirmed that Mrs. O'Brien had hit one of the warriors. But there was no sign of the man's body, so he might only have been wounded.

Rain streamed down Donovan's face, plastering his hair against his forehead, and he shook his head more in sorrow than in anger.

The Cheyenne had gained ten horses and a mule and snuffed out the life of a big, laughing Irishman. But it had cost them one warrior dead and another wounded.

Would they think it had been worth it at a time when their numbers were dwindling fast?

Donovan had no answer for that, nor did he seek one.

His gambler's fatalism took over, telling him what was done was done and there could be no changing of it, now or ever.

Swallowing hard, he walked back to Mrs. O'Brien and Nancy.

There was a burying to be done.

"Carry him into the house, Mister Donovan," Mrs. O'Brien said, getting to her feet. "I'll wash him and lay him out proper and say the rosary over his poor martyred body. It is a shame we have no priest, but God knows, himself never committed a mortal sin in his life. Patrick O'Brien was a good man."

He was also a heavy man, Donovan thought ruefully, going two hundred and fifty pounds and maybe more.

Nancy grabbed the dead man's legs and Donovan took his shoulders and between them, slipping and sliding in the slick mud, they managed to carry O'Brien inside.

Mrs. O'Brien had cleared the dining table and after a titanic struggle, they hefted Patrick O'Brien's dead weight on top of it.

"Nancy," the grieving women said, her voice soft, "help me get him undressed and we'll be washing his poor body."

Donovan, not wishing to witness what was to come, walked to the barn and found a shovel. He would bury the dead Cheyenne among the trees away from the cabin.

But when Donovan returned to the spot where the warrior had lain, he was no longer there. The body had been spirited away in the darkness by Indians moving silently on moccasined feet.

Suddenly wary, fear and a growing panic spiking at him, Donovan looked quickly around, then threw down the shovel and walked back into the cabin, bolting the door behind him.

The Cheyenne were still in the vicinity and it could be they were planning to attack again. If that happened they would go straight for the cabin and this time, without O'Brien's rifle, he did not give much for the little group's chances.

The Irishman was laid out naked on the table, a candle burning at his head, and Mrs. O'Brien and Nancy were washing down his body with water from a basin. The two wounds in his chest, close enough to be covered by a man's hand, had stopped bleeding and now they looked like ugly open mouths just under his right nipple.

O'Brien's eyes were half open and when the washing was done, his wife closed them and laid silver dollars on the lids. Nancy brought a sheet from the bedroom and they covered the man, pulling it up to his chin.

Mrs. O'Brien knelt beside the body and began to pray, ivory rosary beads clicking like dice between her fingers.

"Hail Mary full of grace . . . Hail Mary full of grace . . . Hail Mary full of grace . . ."

Between the Catholic prayers she raised her eyes to the roof of the cabin, wailing and moaning deep in her throat, the beads still, giving voice to a timeless expression of grief wrenched from the depths of her Celtic soul, harking back to a dark, pagan time long past.

The clock on the wall ticked away the hours of darkness and when the gray morning came Donovan blew out the flickering candle, its melted white wax now spread across the table like gnarled tree roots.

He stepped beside Mrs. O'Brien and laid a hand on her shoulder.

"Woman," he said, "it's time. We must ready him so he can be taken on the next stage for burial in Deadwood."

Mrs. O'Brien looked up at Donovan, her eyes wild. "We'll do no such thing. I will not have him lie in foreign soil. Patrick must be buried here. At his post."

Suddenly calm, she touched the back of Donovan's hand lightly with her fingertips. "Mister Donovan, find a shady spot. Patrick with his fair skin was always one to burn up terrible bad in the sun."

Defeat hanging heavy on him, Donovan was silent for a few moments. Then he nodded and said, "I'll see to it."

He walked outside into the rain, carrying the Henry, slanting drops driven by the rising wind slapping against his face. O'Brien's passing had affected Donovan deeply and the young gambler felt sick and empty, wanting only to get away from this place of death.

Thunder rumbled in the distance and the branches of the pines tossed restlessly this way and that under a scowling sky as cold and gray as steel. The windmill's iron wheel revolved with agonizing slowness, screeching on its axle, and nearby the creek, now full of water, brawled over submerged rocks and carried along tumbling driftwood from somewhere back in the hills.

The sun had risen but was hiding his face and Donovan, soaked to the skin, shivered as he picked up the shovel where he'd dropped it in his panic and looked around at the surrounding landscape.

It took him half an hour to find a suitable burial place, at the bottom of a low, saddleback hill, the spot shaded by a single, stunted spruce, its trunk crooked, grotesquely shaped by the prevailing long winds from the north.

Donovan propped the Henry against the tree, ready for use, though he doubted very much that even Cheyenne Dog Soldiers, now that they had a mule to eat, would be abroad in this weather.

The roots of the spruce were tangled and went deep and Donovan spent two hours digging a hole big enough to accommodate O'Brien's large body.

When the work was done he returned to the cabin, his soft, gambler's hands covered in blisters and torn skin from the rough ash wood of the shovel. The sheet had been pulled over O'Brien's face and beside the body Nancy and Mrs. O'Brien stood, the older woman again busy with her clicking beads.

The grave site was almost two hundred yards from

the cabin, near where Donovan had last seen the Cheyenne.

Now that the body was naked, covered only by the sheet, Donovan knew it was going to be a chore carrying him there.

Mrs. O'Brien put the beads in the pocket of her apron and from the cupboard found another candle. This she lighted, leading the way toward the door.

"That won't stay lit in—"

Nancy gave him a warning glance and Donovan stopped, letting it go. The woman would find out soon enough.

He stepped to the dead man's head and nodded to Nancy. "Get his feet." The girl was pale, her eyes large and frightened. Her wounds had not fully healed and her left hand with its missing finger was still bandaged.

She shook her head at Donovan. "I don't think I can do this."

"You have to do it," he said. "We can't drag him." He shook his head. "Not with her watching."

Mrs. O'Brien opened the cabin door. She held the candle in her right hand, fingering the yellow beads with her left.

She stepped outside and the wind and rain immediately extinguished the candle, a thin tendril of smoke from the wick quickly snatched away. The woman didn't notice, still holding the candle upright as Donovan and Nancy struggled behind her, carrying O'Brien's huge body, slippery from lye soap and rain.

"Over there," Donovan gasped to Mrs. O'Brien, over the roar of the wind and rain and growing thunder. He nodded toward the lone tree at the foot of the saddleback. "That's the place."

He was walking backward, carrying O'Brien by the

shoulders. He slipped in the slick mud, landing on his back and the body fell heavily on top of him. Nancy, unable to hold on to the legs, let them go, but then she skidded in the mud and fell flat on her face.

Ahead of them, Mrs. O'Brien walked steadily on, holding the candle. If she heard the commotion behind her, she didn't let it show, not even turning her head in Donovan and Nancy's direction.

Panting from the effort, Donovan rose and held out a hand to Nancy. She grabbed on tightly and he pulled her to her feet.

Despite his exhaustion he smiled. The girl was covered in mud from head to toe, only her eyes white against her face's covering of sticky black muck.

"If it's any consolation, you look like hell," Donovan said.

"You don't look so hot yourself."

Donovan turned, his eyes seeking the stunted spruce. "Not far to go."

"Donovan, I can't make it. He's too heavy."

Donovan studied the girl closely. She was all in, her shoulders under her thin coat slumped in exhaustion. The bandage on her hand showed a small red stain over the stump of her missing finger.

The gambler nodded. He looked at O'Brien's body. The sheet had fallen away and he lay naked, his skin rapidly turning to a pale shade of blue. His eyes were open, staring at Donovan in blank accusation.

"Keep him well him covered up, especially his face, because he's spooking the hell out of me," Donovan told the girl. "I'll drag him the rest of the way."

Slipping, falling in the mud, usually with the dead man landing on top of him, Donovan managed to haul the body to the graveside.

Mrs. O'Brien stood by the open grave, the yellowed

ivory beads shuttling through her fingers, lips moving silently in prayer. The woman's eyes were tight shut and Donovan realized that, flirting with a complete mental breakdown, she'd retreated to a place where she could be alone with her grief, a place neither he nor Nancy could reach.

He laid out O'Brien's body at the edge of the grave then he climbed into the rough, rectangular hole and grabbed the dead man's shoulders, sliding him into the grave beside him. The legs followed, but landed halfway up the side of the hole, big feet sticking almost above the rim.

The hole was too short!

Donovan extricated himself from the upper part of O'Brien's body and stepped on top of him to reach the legs. The body was still supple and he managed to bend the knees, getting the feet lower, but the knees themselves were still much higher than the rest of the body.

It would have to do.

The young gambler stepped onto O'Brien's chest and hauled himself out of the grave. Nancy threw the sheet on top of the corpse and Donovan immediately grabbed the shovel and began to fill in the hole, worried that Mrs. O'Brien might open her eyes and see how inadequate the grave was and object.

But the woman stood stock still, eyes shut, oblivious to what was happening around her.

Blood from Donovan's blistered hands stained the handle of the shovel before his grim task was finished and Patrick O'Brien was finally buried under three feet of muddy Wyoming earth.

For a few moments he and Nancy stood, head bowed, beside Mrs. O'Brien. The wind and hammering rain plastered the wet skirts of the women against their legs and their hair streamed wild. Donovan had never been a praying man, so he concentrated on his own rain-soaked misery, his flayed, burning hands and the lightning that crashed and flickered above their heads, threatening all three of them with imminent destruction.

After what seemed like an eternity, Mrs. O'Brien opened her eyes. She looked at the grave and asked, "So, Patrick is laid under the sod, then?"

"He is," Donovan said. Then, trying to reassure her he added, "He'll rest content here."

The woman smiled. "Then we'll go back to the cabin. There's a bottle of good rye whiskey and we'll have a drink or two and sing the fine auld Irish songs that Patrick loved so well."

Without another word, she turned on her heel and walked back toward the cabin, Donovan and Nancy trailing behind her.

His eyes flat and expressionless, Donovan fell into step beside the girl and said, "I can't figure it out. No matter how I look at it, up, down, from the side, I still can't figure it out."

"Figure out what?"

Without expecting a reply, he said, "Where the hell my luck went."

Nancy smiled, rain streaking the mud on her face. "You're alive," she said. "That's lucky."

She turned her head, glancing over her shoulder. "You could be lying back there. Like him."

11

The stage from Cheyenne rattled up to the station the next day at noon, drawn by a team of six tired, mud-spattered mustangs.

Without embellishment, a slightly hungover Donovan told the driver, a man named DeVries, about the attack by the Cheyenne and O'Brien's death. DeVries, since there was no fresh team, decided to let his horses rest for a few hours before continuing on to Deadwood.

There was only one passenger, a slender young miner on his way back to the diggings, and both men stepped inside the cabin.

DeVries pulled off his hat and offered his condolences to Mrs. O'Brien. "I'll inform the company when I get to Deadwood," the man said. "They'll send out another manager pretty quick." He studied the woman closely, then added, "I can take you to Cheyenne on my return trip. Mrs. O'Brien, do you have kin anywhere?"

The woman nodded. "I have an unmarried sister.

She teaches school back east in Philadelphia." She smiled. "But I won't be leaving. My place is right here with Patrick."

DeVries was stunned. "But . . . but a woman can't run a station. That's strictly against company policy."

Mrs. O'Brien shook her head. "Nevertheless, company policy or no, I will not leave."

Cornered, DeVries gave up, muttering into his gray beard about obstinate women.

Nancy had prepared food and DeVries, the driver, and his passenger sat at the table where O'Brien had lain just hours before and ate.

For her part, Mrs. O'Brien refused all food and drink and had not partaken of the bottle of rye that Donovan and Nancy had finished between them during O'Brien's wake.

After the men had eaten, Donovan took DeVries aside and after a few moments' persuasion the driver agreed to carry him and Nancy to Deadwood.

"You helped defend this station against the Cheyenne and I'm sure the company would agree that it's the least I can do," he said.

The man smiled, his teeth stained from chewing tobacco, and dug Donovan in the ribs with his elbow. "Besides, I heard all about you and your dove and I'm glad to share in even a small part of such an adventure. Boy, the two of you are becoming real famous." Doubt clouded DeVries' leathery face. "Though I must say, she don't much look like a French princess to me."

Donovan nodded, smiling. "Oh, she's a princess all right."

And Nancy stuck out her tongue and made a face.

"I heard tell how she was kidnapped by a Chinee gang an' you rescued her," the miner said, eagerly picking up the tale. "They say you kilt a dozen of them pigtailed heathens afore you got her free."

"Something like that," Donovan said, refusing to look Nancy in the eye.

The miner shook his head. "Then what I don't understand is why Ike Vance is so hell-bent on killing you, him and them gun handlers of his. After what you done, I mean freeing the princess an' all, you'd think he'd be patting you on the back an' buying you a drink."

"Where did you hear that?" Donovan choked, the panic rising in him. "I mean that he plans to gun me."

"Hell, man, it's all over the place," the miner answered for DeVries. His face suddenly thoughtful, he added, "Here, now, was ol' Ike in league with them heathen Chinee?" The man shook his head. "Don't seem like his style."

"Well," DeVries said to the miner, "you ain't heard the whole story is all. The way it was tole to me, Ike tried to steal the woman from Donovan here after he saved her from the Chinee." He turned to the young gambler. "I heard you kilt three, four of his men down Fort Laramie way. Ain't that the truth of it?"

"Where is Ike Vance?" Donovan asked, ignoring the man's question, sudden fear tightening his throat.

DeVries shrugged. "Last I heard he was in Cheyenne, but then I was tole he was in Deadwood. So who knows? A man like Ike makes his own road and there ain't many who would care to step into his path."

The driver studied Donovan closely, his eyes shrewd. "Here, you ain't skeered of him, are you?"

"Nah," Donovan said, forcing a smile. "I ain't afraid of a ranny like Ike Vance."

DeVries nodded, smiling back. "Didn't think so. I hear tell you're hell on wheels with a gun."

"That's a natural fact," the miner agreed, nodding. "Heard that same thing my ownself."

"I get by," Donovan began modestly. But then he added, puffing up a little, "Though I reckon there ain't too many around who can shade me."

This time he caught Nancy's eye and the girl was looking at him steadily, one eyebrow raised in amusement.

Donovan had the good grace to look down at the floor and blush.

DeVries took out his watch and glanced at it. "I reckon the team has rested enough. We got to be rolling if we're going to make time."

Nancy turned to Mrs. O'Brien. "Why don't you come with us?" she asked. "We can get you settled in a hotel in Deadwood and maybe you can get in touch with that sister of yours."

"My dear, I'd be too much of a bother."

"You'd be no bother at all," Nancy said. "After all you and"—she hesitated a moment, then managed— "the late Mr. O'Brien did for Donovan and me, it's the least we can do."

Mrs. O'Brien smiled sweetly, her eyes faraway, vague and remote. "It's nice of you to be so concerned, dear, but my place is here with Patrick and here I'll stay."

Nancy hesitated for only a single heartbeat, then she smiled and kissed the older woman on the cheek. "I understand."

If Donovan was expecting to hear more, it never came.

Perplexed, he followed DeVries out to the waiting stage. The rain had stopped, at least momentarily, and when Nancy joined him she was carrying her parasol unopened.

Jutting his chin toward the cabin, Donovan asked, "Why won't she come with us?"

Nancy smiled. "She can't leave her husband."

"Hasn't she noticed one small fact—that her husband is dead? She saw him buried and she sang 'The Minstrel Boy' at his wake last night."

"I know," Nancy said, "but dead or not, she just can't stop loving him. They were together a long time."

"What will she do?" Donovan asked, trying desperately to understand.

The girl shrugged. "She'll stay here and just pine away. She won't eat and she won't drink. All the songs that were inside her she sang last night and now they're all gone. By this time next week or maybe the week after she'll be dead."

Donovan shook his head. "That's unnatural. It's . . . it's . . ."

"It's called love," Nancy said, brushing past him, her head high, before stepping into the coach. She settled in her seat, then turned, her eyes blazing. "Something, Mister Donovan, you apparently know nothing about."

It seemed the rain had really decided to stop. The clouds cleared and Donovan, caring little for Nancy's distant, icy civility, rode up on the box beside DeVries, his carpetbag with his gambler's finery between his knees, Henry rifle at his side.

They rolled through wide and broken country, the stage trail winding between tall hills and buttes covered in pine, thick stands of yellow and crimson aspen on their lower slopes.

Despite their tiredness, the team made good time and by two in the afternoon they'd reached the station at Cheyenne Crossing where the horses were changed.

DeVries handled the ribbons well and they crossed Dutch Flats and headed northeast, keeping Bald Mountain to their west, where the watery sun was already beginning to sink behind the craggy, 6,617-foot peak.

At the wide sandbar where Whitetail Creek met Deadwood Creek, DeVries gave the team a breather and allowed Nancy and the miner to get out and stretch their legs.

"Be in Deadwood just after dark," DeVries said, biting off a thick chew of black tobacco. "But day or night, it's all the same. Seems to me, ain't nobody ever sleeps in Deadwood."

Donovan and the driver were still sitting up on the box, but Nancy and the young miner had walked a distance from the stage, talking to each other in low tones and once the girl laughed softly.

Irritated without really knowing why, Donovan took his watch from his pocket and thumbed open the cover. It was almost four-thirty.

"Nice watch," DeVries said. "What's that tune it plays?"

" 'Beautiful Dreamer,' " Donovan replied. "It was written by a feller called Stephen Foster."

"Right purty."

Donovan snapped the watch shut. "I've got friends in Deadwood," he said, his irritation growing as Nancy laughed again. "A couple of gamblers, Doc Holliday and Colorado Charlie Utter. Have you seen them?"

DeVries nodded. "Know 'em both. Doc, he ain't in

Deadwood no more, but Charlie's there, though folks haven't exactly been cottoning to him recently."

"How come?"

The driver shrugged. "He wants to take a shovel an' dig up Wild Bill."

12

The miner got off near his diggings on Nevada Gulch and Donovan decided he and Nancy would do the same thing before the stage pulled into Deadwood, fearing to attract undue attention to themselves should Ike Vance be in town.

"I'd be obliged if you'd keep it under your hat, I mean about me and Nancy, her being a runaway princess an' all," Donovan said after he'd explained his plan to DeVries. "There could be Chinee about who might want to take her back," he added, lying smoothly. "And maybe Ike Vance his ownself."

The driver's face was sour, since he'd expected to roll into town at a spanking trot and announce to all and sundry the arrival of Donovan and his dove. Robbed of his moment and a chance to bathe in Donovan's reflected glory, DeVries was surly. "I thought you said you wasn't afraid of ol' Ike an' them Texas gunmen of his."

"I'm not, but right at the moment I'm in no condition to get into a shooting scrape," Donovan said, making it up quickly as he went along. "My leg is damn near broke and you saw the dove's hand. Hell, man, she's missing a finger."

DeVries' face cleared. "Did them heathen Chinee do that to her?"

Donovan nodded. "Sure did. But I killed them as done it."

Placated somewhat, DeVries nodded and grinned. "I just want to be around if you go after ol' Ike an' them. That will be a sight to see." He turned and sympathy showed briefly on his face. "I mean when you're feeling up to it."

"You'll be the first to know," Donovan said.

The driver completely missed the irony in Donovan's voice and grinned.

"Well, I'm right obliged to ye for that."

DeVries stopped the stage near a stand of cottonwoods on Strawberry Creek about half a mile south of Deadwood and Donovan climbed down and opened the door.

"We're getting out here," he told Nancy.

The girl frowned. "Why here? Donovan, I'm all in. I need a bath, a decent meal and a soft bed in a hotel." She paused for a moment, then held up her bandaged hand. "I also need to see a doctor for this and my other wounds."

"Not tonight," Donovan said. "Maybe tomorrow if Ike Vance isn't in town."

Nancy shook her head stubbornly. "I'm not leaving this stage."

From the box, DeVries hollered, "Donovan, I got to be going. If the dove wants to stay, then for Pete's sakes let her stay."

Exasperated, Donovan laid a hand on Nancy's knee. "Do you want to see me get shot? Is that what you want?" His voice took on a wheedling tone. "After all I've done for you, this is the thanks I get? Hell, I even got you your ring back."

Doubt clouded the girl's face. "You saved my life and I owe you for that," she said. Then, suddenly making up her mind: "Donovan, will you take me to a fancy hotel in Deadwood tomorrow with clean sheets on the bed and buy me a steak and then take me to a doctor?"

"Of course I will," Donovan said, his face bland. "You know I will. I've got friends in town and they'll see me and you are set up just fine and dandy. Snug as bugs in a deep pile rug—that's how we'll be this time tomorrow."

"Are you sure?"

"Trust me."

"Donovan, will you buy me a new dress and maybe a warm woolen coat? Sometimes, come winter, I get awful cold."

"Sure."

"And gloves?"

"Sure."

Nancy hesitated. "Donovan, you wouldn't lie to me?"

"Me? Never. Don't I always tell you the truth?"

"Then I'll stay with you. But it's only for tonight, right?"

"You got it," Donovan said. He extended his hand. "Now, let me help you down from there."

DeVries had lit the oil lanterns on either side of the coach, splashing yellow and orange light on the red and black paintwork. Donovan, Nancy at his side, looked up at DeVries in the gathering gloom and put a hushing forefinger to his lips. "Remember what I said, DeVries. Shh . . . not a word."

The driver nodded. "I'll be quiet as a deaf-mute's shadow. Ain't nobody gonna hear nothing from me." DeVries touched the brim of his hat. "Well, good luck to ye both."

He slapped the ribbons and hoorawed the team into motion and soon the stage was swallowed by the darkness. After a few minutes the rattling of the wheels died away and only the bobbing orange glow of the lanterns could be seen in the distance, until they too were finally lost against the myriad firefly lights of Deadwood.

Nancy stood with her small bag at her feet, her tattered parasol in her hand. She shivered as the wind sighed long and cold off the Black Hills, rustling the dry leaves of the cottonwoods. A crescent moon rode high in the sky, nudging scudding black and silver clouds with its horns, and a few frosty stars glittered low above a horizon formed by the dark bulk of the surrounding peaks.

The wind had the raw, iron taste of winter and whispered the promise of snow and of hard times to come. Soon the land would be covered in white and the creeks would freeze solid like brittle blades of steel and there would be no warmth and no place to shelter from the blizzards blasting icy and merciless from the north.

All this the wind promised. But not yet.

Tonight, as Nancy stood and shivered, there was just a bone-numbing chill and with it the implied threat of worse to follow.

"Donovan," the girl said, her teeth chattering, "I'm so cold."

Looking around him, Donovan decided that he could safely build a fire. Who in his right mind would be abroad on a night like this, forsaking the warm, amber whiskey and cherry-red stoves of Deadwood?

The gambler gathered enough dry wood from among the cottonwoods to get a small blaze glowing and Nancy sat close to its meager warmth, her chin on her knees, the wind-flickered flames reflecting red on her pale skin.

"Donovan, do you know what I'd like, I mean, right now?" she asked.

The young gambler shook his head. "No, what?"

"A plate of stewed rabbit, swimming in onions, and white potatoes with butter. And to drink, just coffee. Black and strong and boiling hot."

Donovan frowned. "Well, we don't have none of that."

"I'm hungry, Donovan."

"So am I, but we don't have any food. Unless you think I carry a rabbit stew in my back pocket."

The girl was silent for a few moments, then she asked, "Donovan, what are we going to do in Deadwood?"

Donovan opened his mouth to speak but hesitated.

He had a plan, as yet vague and half-formed, but Nancy was no part of it. Mainly, it involved borrowing a stake from Charlie Utter and trying his hand at the gaming tables in Deadwood's seventy saloons and sporting houses.

A gambler played the odds and Donovan figured the odds were his bad luck streak couldn't last much longer. He had survived a shooting scrape with the Loupers and an Indian attack, so the cards seemed to be finally falling his way.

Of course, there was the vexing matter of Ike Vance, but he might not be anywhere near Deadwood. For all

Donovan knew, the man could be back home in Texas by this time

As for Nancy, well, she had her profession to fall back on. She'd be all right.

Donovan told himself he had to stay loose, stay unattached and drift with the prevailing winds, no matter which direction they blew in. That was his way, the way of the gambler, and it left no room for a woman.

"Donovan, didn't you hear me?" Nancy said. "What are we going to do in Deadwood?"

Donovan smiled. "Oh, I don't know. That depends."

"Depends on what?"

"Depends on whether or not ol' Charlie Utter can stake me and how the cards fall. I figure to play poker and see what happens. I don't have a crystal ball to see the future, Nancy. Win or lose, I can only play the hand I'm dealt."

"Donovan, you wouldn't leave me there alone, in Deadwood I mean?"

The young gambler shook his head, his smile slow and easy. "Not a chance." He winked at the girl. "Now get some sleep. Tomorrow I'll head on into Deadwood and talk to Charlie. Once I see that the coast is clear and Ike Vance isn't around, I'll come back here and get you."

Nancy smiled her contentment and lay on her side, close to the guttering fire.

Donovan grabbed his carpetbag and said, "Here, put this under your head."

The girl did as she was told, then, her thin body shivering, said, "I'm freezing cold."

So was Donovan. But he shrugged out of his sheepskin coat and placed it over Nancy's shoulders. She snuggled into its warmth, pulling the fleece collar up over her neck.

"Donovan, you're so good to me," she whispered, "and I'm so darned ungrateful all the time. I didn't mean what I said back at the stage station, about you knowing nothing about love. I didn't mean a word of that. See, I never knew a man before who treated me the way you do. I never in my whole life met a man who was kind and gentle the way you are."

"Go to sleep," Donovan said, guilt sending a rush of blood to his cheeks. "And as for not knowing about love, well, there's plenty of gals on the line from Texas to Kansas who'd tell you Zeke Donovan knows plenty about loving." He nodded. "Yes, sir, they'd sure tell you a thing or two."

"Donovan," Nancy said drowsily, "will you stay awake for a while, just to watch over me?"

"Sure," Donovan replied, trying to keep his chattering teeth still. "Sure I will. Now, go to sleep."

"Good night, Donovan."

"Good night, Nancy."

Donovan edged closer to the fire. Somewhere back in the hills a cold and hungry coyote lifted his head and yelped his misery to the uncaring moon.

"You and me both," Donovan whispered under his breath, looking up at that same moon. "You and me both."

13

Night shaded into morning, and Donovan, sleepless, rose stiffly to his feet, settled his plug hat on his head and began to gather more wood for the dying fire.

Nancy slept on, eyelashes fanning over her cheekbones, her bandaged hand held high next to her face.

A cold mist clung to the slopes of the surrounding hills, drifting among the slender trunks of the pines and aspens like a gray ghost. The wind had dropped but overhead storm clouds were gathering, threatening more rain, and the weak fall sun had yet to lift its weary head over Bear Den Mountain to the east.

Donovan's breath smoked in the chill air as he tossed wood on the fire. He was needful of coffee and maybe a slow-burning and fragrant cigar to ward off the morning chill, but he had neither, a fact that did nothing to improve his foul mood.

Donovan had thought to dress in his gambler's finery, the better to impress Colorado Charlie Utter and perhaps give him the impression that he was not flat broke and desperately trying to buck a losing streak but merely a prosperous sporting gent temporarily out of funds.

But the tailored frock coat and frilled shirt, threadbare and shabby though they were, would attract too much attention in a town full of roughly dressed miners.

If Ike Vance was in Deadwood he could not fail to notice, especially since Donovan, vanity driving him, would wear the expensive Berthoud of Paris watch and chain, giving Charlie Utter an eyeful.

No, it would be too dangerous, like wading through quicksand over hell, and best left alone. He would remain dressed in the range clothes he stood up in, and that way melt, hopefully unnoticed, into the crowd.

Donovan shivered, badly wanting his sheepskin coat back.

What the hell time was it anyway? Nancy should be up and doing.

He pulled Vance's watch from his pocket and thumbed open the case. It was just seven, the tinkling notes of "Beautiful Dreamer" loud in the silence of the morning.

Nancy opened her eyes, looked at Donovan and smiled. "That's a nice way to wake a person," she said.

Donovan snapped the watch shut. "Well, it's time to get up," he said, his voice rough, refusing to be taken as sappy. "I've built the fire up so you'll stay warm when I take my coat back."

The girl shivered. "I wish we had coffee."

"Don't have none of that."

"And bacon."

"Don't have none of that either."

"Donovan, I want to come with you. I don't want to stay out here by myself."

"You'll be fine. Nothing's going to happen to you here."

Donovan thought for a few moments, then added, "If we're seen together, we'd attract too much attention. Remember, we don't know if Ike Vance is in town or not. We have to stay low and make no ripples, at least for a while."

He smiled. "I'll come back for you real soon, but in the meantime you stay as quiet as a little church mouse. Okay?"

The girl nodded. "I'll be quiet."

Donovan nodded, smiling. "Good girl, that's the ticket. Just remember, we don't want to attract any more attention to ourselves than we have to."

No sooner were those words spoken than Donovan jerked up his head, his smile fading quickly as he heard a sound in the distance.

"What the hell . . ." Donovan began. He looked toward Deadwood and what he saw made his heart sink all the way to his boots.

Marching toward them, playing "A Life on the Ocean Wave" badly out of tune, but *loud*, was the entire twenty-one-piece Deadwood City Brass Band, resplendent in uniforms of blue and silver, led by Mayor Solomon Star.

His honor walked arm in arm with the splendidly mustachioed Sheriff Seth Bullock and what looked to be around two thousand people. The mob was formed mostly of hard-rock miners plus a lively sprinkling of mounted punchers from the surrounding ranches, gamblers, soiled doves in short, frilled dresses, bearded sodbusters breaking their journey as they headed further west and with them the respectable businessmen of the town with their wives, all of them wearing the latest fall fashions from Dodge and Denver.

"What the hell . . ." Donovan whispered again, the words dying in his throat as the waving, yelling throng came nearer, the band, now that their objective was in sight, playing even louder than before.

The grinning horde reached the cottonwoods where Donovan and Nancy stood watching them come. The band surrounded the two of them on all sides and cymbals clashing, horns blaring, brought Epes Sargent's lively sea chantey to a thunderous if ragged conclusion.

The crowd applauded and cheered wildly as Mayor Star found a convenient sawn tree stump, stood precariously fighting for balance on its narrow, slanting top for a few moments, then raised his arms for silence.

"Welcome! Welcome to Deadwood!" the mayor hollered and the crowd cheered.

"Eh?" Donovan asked, deafened by the close proximity of the band, his ears ringing.

But Sol Star was hollering again, making his voice carry across the cold, misty morning so all could hear his words.

"Ladies and gentlemen, citizens of Deadwood, it gives me great pleasure to welcome the famous Zeke Donovan and his dove to our fair city."

The crowd cheered wildly and Donovan, his hand cupped around his ear, looked around in bafflement and said, "Eh?"

"It is," the mayor continued, amid much applause, "my humble duty—" Here he broke off and, in a barely subdued aside, added, "Yes, humble, I say, for who would not be humble, who would not willingly shed all worldly arrogance, who could remain aloof in the presence of this paladin of the plains, this prince of pistoleers, this living embodiment of all the manly virtues, this man we lesser mortals dare to call Zeke Donovan!"

The throng cheered themselves hoarse, and Donovan, still deaf as a snubbing post and having no idea what was going on, grinned and nodded, figuring that something mighty important was being said.

The mayor held up his arms for silence, and when the clamor had died down he continued, "As I said, it is my humble duty to ceremonially present to this gallant hero"—he paused for effect, then ended in a triumphant shout—"the keys to our fair city!"

Another cheer broke from the denizens of Deadwood, and the band, crowding even closer to Donovan, enthusiastically launched into a spirited and noisy rendition of "Yankee Doodle."

The tune thundered to its conclusion and Sol Star, small and thin and nimble as a mountain goat, hopped back on the stump.

He raised his hands in the air and the crowd fell silent.

"Over there," Star hollered, pointing at Nancy, "is a lass with blood as blue as the wide Pacific Ocean. Oh, she may not look like much, I agree, but, as Mister Donovan himself will tell you, she's a Portugee princess recently and cruelly torn from the royal bosom of her family by a cutthroat band of Chinee pirates."

"Boo! Boo!" the crowd yelled, and Donovan, confused, looked around wildly and said, "Eh?"

Again Star raised his arms for silence, then yelled, "Donovan, cutlass held in his teeth, swam to the Chinee pirate ship in the dead of night and rescued the pathetic princess. It was eighty against one, but Donovan slew seventeen of those heathen demons with his flashing blade ere he once again reached the shore, the swooning lady in his arms."

A cheer rose from two thousand throats and hefty hands slapped Donovan on the back, but, bells clamoring in his ears, he could only grin and say, "Eh?"

"Alas," Star continued, "it was not over. No sooner had Donovan reached shore, than a mighty and cowardly blow to the head dashed him insensible to the sand. Once again the princess was kidnapped, this time by the desperado Mike Chance and his band of Mexican outlaws."

"Boo! Boo!" the crowd yelled.

"Eh? Eh?" asked Donovan.

"Ladies and gentlemen," Mayor Sol Star went on, warming to his subject as he smote his breast dramatically, "I can hardly bring myself to recount what happened next." He pointed to Nancy, who was standing, eyes downcast, as befitted a tragic princess. "That fair example of European maidenhood, that nobly raised flower, was forced by the evil Chance into a life of prostitution and was despoiled time and time again by any sporting gent with two dollars in his pocket and a bulge in his pants."

"Shame!" the crowd yelled, the knot of soiled doves loudest of all.

"Shame, indeed, but all was not lost," Star exclaimed. "Once again our fearless fighter, our dauntless champion, Zeke Donovan, rode his famous white stallion, Thunder, to the rescue. Mike Chance, that pitiless pimp and gunman, was the first to fall under Donovan's bucking Colts. Then a Mexican desperado went down, then another and another until eight men lay dead on the saloon floor."

"Huzzah! Huzzah!" yelled the crowd.

Donovan nodded and smiled, hearing very little but ringing bells.

"Once again," Star concluded, "the brave little princess who had become, by tragic circumstance, a soiled dove, was free!"

"Huzzah!"

"As we see her here today!" the mayor yelled, apparently deciding that some additional information was needed.

"Huzzah!"

Bottles of Mumm's were opened, corks popping, and people crowded around Nancy and Donovan, grinning miners slapping the young gambler on the back, women hugging Nancy close and some of the respectable matrons hugging Donovan even closer.

The band launched into "Dixie," the cymbals again clashing dangerously close to Donovan's ear, and Mayor Star was heard to declare to Sheriff Bullock that, despite the early hour and the morning chill, "a good time was being had by all."

"Dixie" roared to its conclusion, the last notes from the trumpets and French horns getting badly tangled, and Mayor Star again called for silence.

"Sheriff Bullock," he yelled, "will you now do the honors?"

Bullock, huge in a buffalo coat, grinned and produced two large keys from behind his back. Each key was about three feet long and had been hurriedly cut from the thin wood of a tea chest, then painted silver. They were tied together with white ribbon and Bullock held them stiffly out in front of him as he walked toward Donovan.

The young gambler, having little idea about what was going on, took a step backward in alarm, but the miners pushed him toward the towering Bullock with

much back-slapping and cries of "True blue!" and
"Brave fellow."

"It gives me great pleasure to present to you, Mister
Donovan," the sheriff declared loudly, "the keys to our
fair city of Deadwood."

The crowd cheered, the band played and Donovan,
hearing nothing and understanding less, took the keys
and grinned foolishly.

Bullock turned and yelled, "Bring on the chariot."

A spring wagon, draped in red, white and blue
bunting appeared from the midst of the crowd, pulled
by a dozen eager volunteers.

"Up you go, Mister Donovan," Bullock yelled, "you
and your Portugee princess dove."

Brawny miners cheered and raised Donovan and
Nancy on their shoulders and they were none too
gently deposited in the bed of the wagon. Donovan's
carpetbag and rifle were tossed in beside him.

"Onward!" Seth Bullock hollered to Donovan above
the heads of the crowd. "Into the city that is now
yours!"

"Huzzah!" the crowd yelled.

The volunteers dragged the wagon toward the
muddy gulch that was Deadwood, the cheering
throng and brass band, now badly playing selections
from Gilbert and Sullivan's recent box office smash
HMS Pinafore, following close behind.

Donovan, baffled, sat close to Nancy on the lurch-
ing, bouncing wagon and whispered in her ear, "What
the hell just happened?"

The girl smiled, pulling Donovan's sheepskin coat
around her shoulders. "You're a hero."

"Eh?"

"You're a real big hero!" This time louder.

Donovan shrugged. "Can't hear you." He looked

around. "This is obviously a case of mistaken identity."

"I'll say," Nancy said. But again Donovan didn't hear.

They were almost on the outskirts of town, the unflagging energy of the miners pulling the wagon propelling them forward at a spanking pace.

Tents lined both sides of the road, a canvas shanty town hurriedly erected by miners who'd expected to strike it rich at the diggings real quick and then head back east. Woodsmoke from hundreds of iron stoves hung blue and pungent in the air and stray dogs roamed around the tents in packs, hungry and sly as outhouse rats.

Donovan rammed his plug hat tighter on his head as the wagon rocked along the rutted road, then looked quickly at Nancy as her fingers dug hard into his arm.

This time he didn't need to hear her.

He followed her horrified gaze to the edge of the crowd where four horsemen sat their mounts, watching the procession go past.

Donovan's eyes met those of a big man on a roan horse who was studying him intently, his face black as thunder. The man's eyes were blue and hard and full of anger.

It was Ike Vance.

And he looked like he was in the mood for a killing.

14

The wagon was pulled through Deadwood's muddy main street to the IXL Hotel, where it lurched to a halt and immediately the band struck up again, this time badly mangling George Frideric Handel's "Hail the Conquering Hero Comes."

The proprietor of the hotel, a self-important little man named Adams, stepped onto the boardwalk outside his hotel and puffed up a little as he stuck his thumbs into the vest of his broadcloth suit and smiled broadly at the crowd.

"I am honored," he said, when the band had straggled to a halt, "to welcome Donovan and his beautiful dove to my hotel."

The crowd cheered and Adams held up his hands for silence.

"To mark this auspicious occasion, I will provide, completely free of charge, two nights' lodging for the hero and his princess."

Another wild cheer went up and Adams beamed

and continued, "Not one, but two rooms, mind you, so that all the necessary proprieties may be observed."

"Huzzah!" the crowd yelled, and the members of the band hefted their instruments and inflated their cheeks, getting ready to play again.

But Deadwood was spared another musical rendition, because at that moment the rain that had been threatening all morning, heralded by a few scattered showers, started in earnest. A torrential downpour fell from an iron gray sky and thunder bounced and rumbled like a massive boulder between the sheer sides of Deadwood Gulch, long shorn of its sheltering timber.

The crowd and the band quickly scattered and Donovan and Nancy found themselves alone on the boardwalk outside the hotel. Rain cascaded off the narrow brim of Donovan's hat as he retrieved his carpetbag and rifle from the wagon and followed Nancy into the hotel lobby.

Adams handed each of them a key and said, beaming, "And let me tell you both once again what an honor this is."

"Eh?" Donovan asked.

But Nancy dropped a quick little curtsey and said, "Thank you kindly." She grabbed the perplexed Donovan's arm and pushed him toward the stairs leading to the second floor.

Their rooms were adjoining and Donovan opened his own, Nancy stepping inside after him.

The young gambler threw his bag and rifle on the bed, then turned to Nancy, his face puzzled. "What the hell was all that about?"

"Can you hear?"

"Eh?"

Louder: "Can you hear me?"

"You don't have to shout, I'm not deaf." He took off

his hat and slapped the side of his head. "Damn cymbals."

"They think you're a hero," Nancy said.

"A what?"

"A hero."

"Why?"

"Because they think I'm a princess and that you rescued me from Chinese pirates and then from Ike Vance, though they got the story so mixed up the mayor called him Mike Chance."

Donovan shook his head. "Hell, this tale just grows and grows like it has a life of its own."

"It does have a life of its own." Nancy smiled. "People need a hero and, unlikely though it may be, that hero is you."

"Ike Vance doesn't think I'm a hero," Donovan said. "You saw him out there. He hasn't forgotten or forgiven a thing and I fear he means to kill me."

Nancy sat on the edge of the bed. "Donovan, what are we going to do?"

Donovan shrugged. "Hightail it out of here tonight."

He reached into his pocket and threw some crumpled bills and change on the bed, then quickly sorted through the money. "Just over eighty dollars. It's maybe enough to buy a horse."

"We're going to ride double?"

"Nancy, you're not coming with me. I have to ride fast and far."

"If you leave me here, Ike will kill me."

Donovan shook his head. "He won't, not here in Deadwood. Any man who'd harm a woman would find himself strung up real quick."

"It won't wash, Donovan."

"What do you mean, it won't wash?"

"I told you this once before. But now it's even worse. I've become part of your legend, story, whatever you want to call it. If you run out on me, you'll never be able to show your face in a Western town again. You'll no longer be considered a hero because folks will look at you and hiss and boo and call you a low-down, yellow dog."

Donovan's face was stricken. "Yeah, you told me that once before, and then, like right now, I felt trapped. It's not a good feeling."

He took his short-barreled Colt from the shoulder holster and spun the cylinder, checking the loads. He eased the hammer back onto the empty chamber, slid the gun back into the holster and said, "Okay, let's hear it. What are we going to do?"

"There's one thing you can do, Donovan," Nancy said quietly.

"What's that?"

"You can dress up in your fancy gambling duds, put on your poker face and start to live up to your legend."

"Hell, I'm no hero," Donovan snapped angrily. "I didn't do all those brave things they're talking about." He shook his head. "I killed them two Louper lowlifes, but that was hardly a fair fight. Hell, I gunned one of them while he was sitting on the shitter, a-reading of the Sears and Roebuck catalog."

"I know that and you know that"—she waved a hand toward the window and the street outside—"but they don't."

The girl sighed. "Donovan, you can't run any more. You've got to face up to Ike Vance and you've got to do it here, in Deadwood. Mister Gambling Man, you've reached the end of the line and there's no more level ground ahead to lay tracks. You can't hide because for some strange reason fate dealt the cards and made you famous. You can't just up and skedaddle because there's no place left to go. Anyhow, wherever you run, as long as Ike Vance has breath in his body, he'll follow. Can't you get that into that stubborn head of yours?"

Donovan stood silent, absorbing what Nancy had just said. Then came the slow, agonized realization that she was right. The world was closing in on him fast and he was trapped, trapped right here in Deadwood.

Without a word he made up his mind. He opened the carpetbag and laid out his frock coat, checked pants, frilled shirt and elastic-sided boots.

He thumbed open the watch. "It's early yet, but I can still buy you that steak," he said, surprised that his voice sounded so steady.

"I'm hungry enough to eat it," Nancy said. "Then we'll go see a doctor."

"Right, now, go get ready and I'll stop by your room for you in a few minutes."

The girl smiled. "But I am ready."

"That's all—" Donovan began, stopping himself before he said more.

Nancy nodded, reading his eyes. "This is all I have. What I'm standing up in right now."

Donovan tried to find his tongue, then after a few awkward moments said, "Well, go to your room anyway. I have to change."

The girl left without another word and Donovan dressed in his threadbare gambler's finery. He knotted a string tie around his neck and combed his wavy black hair into place. After a moment's hesitation, he picked up the watch and dropped it into his vest pocket, draping the chain with its wolf head fob across his lean belly. He badly needed a shave, but that would have to wait until later.

Donovan took a step away from the dresser mirror,

quite pleased with what he saw, a handsome young man who looked prosperous enough if you overlooked the patched frock coat, the frayed collar of his shirt and the down-at-heel boots.

Settling his plug hat on his head at what he hoped was a jaunty, devil-may-care angle, he stepped into the corridor and rapped on the door of Nancy's room.

"Before we eat, let's see if we can find a store that sells women's fixings," he said when she opened the door. He smiled, taking the sting out of it. "Can't have a princess looking like that."

"Let me see here, young man," the blond, middle-aged woman behind the counter of Madame Cherie's Ladies' Fine Apparel Emporium said, chewing on the end of her pencil. "I'll have to tote all this up."

Everything was expensive in Deadwood, and Donovan knew he'd been charged top dollar for each item Nancy had bought.

"Right," the woman said. "Shirt, three dollars and ninety-eight cents; skirt, nine dollars and twenty-five cents; drawers, frilled, eighty cents; chemise, one dollar; belt, sixty cents; hose, silk, two dollars and forty-seven cents and the English tweed coat is nineteen dollars and fifty cents."

She arched an eyebrow and looked at Donovan accusingly, as though half-expecting him to dispute the prices or confess that he couldn't pay. "That will be thirty-seven dollars and sixty cents, young man."

Donovan sighed and paid up, and Nancy threw her arms around his neck and said, "You're so good to me, Donovan."

"Yeah," he said. "I know." He nodded. "Right, let's go eat while I still have a few chips left."

"Not yet!" Nancy exclaimed, horrified. "I have to

change into my new clothes first. I've never had store
bought clothes in my whole life that weren't hand-me-
downs and I want to show them off to other women-
folk."

His stomach grumbling, it was in Donovan's mind
to tell the girl she could change later after they ate, but
as he looked at her shining, excited face, he thought
better of it.

"Okay, we'll go back to the hotel and you can
change," he said. Then, more roughly, lest he be
thought a sentimental fool, he added, "But make it
quick, mind."

The earlier downpour that had come on so suddenly had ended as quickly as it had begun, but the
clouds above Deadwood still hung low in the sky, an-
chored between the steep, confining walls of the gulch.

The town's main street was a sea of mud, churned
up by the ceaseless passage of heavy freight wagons
going to and from the gold diggings, profane, bearded
bullwhackers lifting their knees high as they trudged
beside their plodding, eight-ox teams. Muleskinners,
better paid and of higher social status, sat on sprung
seats on their wagons and cursed their big Missouri
mules or yelled, "Ho, there!" and "Make way there,
damn ye!" at the few adventurous pedestrians who
ventured from the boardwalks onto the street.

Husky youngsters who called themselves ferrymen
stood at intervals along the boardwalks, offering to
carry anyone across the black, oozing river of mud for
two bits. It was mostly women, careful of their long
dresses, who took advantage of the ferrymen's services, opening their parasols above their heads as they
were carried across the street.

That morning, as Donovan and Nancy walked back
to the hotel, the population of Deadwood hovered

around thirty thousand, overwhelmingly male, fertile ground for a rollicking prostitution trade.

Morphine and opium was widely used by the whores and their customers alike, often administered by hypodermic syringe. Venereal diseases were rampant, spread by needles that were used a dozen times by different people before being thrown away.

The insatiable Western thirst was quenched at more than seventy saloons, from lowlife, sod and tin roof dives to more opulent sin palaces like the Bucket of Blood, The Montana, Nuttall and Mann's No. 10 and the Green Front Sporting House, where bonded bourbon cost a dollar a shot and a good Havana cigar a dollar fifty.

Among the hundreds of false fronted buildings lining the street were the Gem and Bella Union theaters, both of them attracting famous—and high-priced—thespians from as far away as New York, Boston, Paris and London.

Deadwood was roaring day and night, brawling and boisterous, bursting at the seams, the banks handling a hundred thousand dollars worth of gold a day and predicting even more prosperous times to come.

The town was, Donovan decided, a place where a man's luck could change real fast—if he could find Colorado Charlie Utter and talk the dandified little gambler into staking him to a stack of chips.

And if he could avoid a revolver showdown with Ike Vance and his Texas gunmen.

All things considered, that was a mighty big "if."

Donovan sat in the hotel lobby and scanned a week-old issue of the *Black Hills Daily Pioneer* while Nancy went upstairs to change.

The paper was full of routine doings in and around Deadwood, mostly accounts of people arrested for minor offenses, everything from tooth and nail altercations between soiled doves to a knifing in Chinatown. There was the usual sprinkling of local politics and, Donovan noted wryly, a story about a child falling down a well, something that seemed to happen in Western towns with alarming regularity.

Donovan was about to throw the paper back on the table when an item caught his eye. It was under the fold on the back page and only ran two paragraphs.

He lifted the paper again and read the story. Apparently in the nearby town of Lead, a community much more straitlaced than Deadwood, Charlie Utter had had himself a scrape with the law.

Under the headline CHARLIE CORRALLED, the story read:

Charles Utter, nuisance, keeping a dance house. To Mr. Utter the court delivered a very severe lecture, condemning all such practices in unmeasured terms. But in consideration that Mr. Utter has now closed the place, Judge Moody sentenced him to one hour's confinement and a fifty dollar fine and costs.

It should be noted that after his stay in the calaboose Mr. Utter made a hasty departure for the welcoming bosom of Deadwood. Ere he forked his bronc, he told your humble reporter that he again wished to make it known that once he reached his destination no one would be allowed to enter his tent and lay down on his fine blankets. This, he declares, is a shooting matter with him.

Donovan smiled and nodded. So Charlie was in Deadwood and if the fifty dollar fine hadn't cleaned him out, he was in the chips.

After he ate, he'd call on Charles Utter, nuisance, and see what was shaking.

Donovan refolded the paper and Nancy appeared soon afterward. Dressed in her fine new clothes, she looked almost pretty this morning, Donovan decided, but the tweed coat with its high collar made her look very young and vulnerable.

"You look . . ." Donovan searched for the words. ". . . very nice."

Nancy smiled. "I feel like I look nice."

Donovan nodded and gave the girl his arm and they stepped outside onto the boardwalk. The rain was still holding off, but the wind blew a chill along the gulch and set the store signs hanging on their iron chains above their heads to creaking.

A load of logs had tumbled off a freight wagon, sinking without trace into mud of unfathomable depth, and the unfortunate bullwhacker stood beside his ox team and turned the air around him sulfurous with curses.

Luckily, since the Open Door restaurant lay only a short distance from the hotel on the same side of the street, Donovan and Nancy had no need to hazard a crossing of the road.

At this time of the morning, too late for breakfast and too early for lunch, the small eating place was empty. There were only four tables, each covered in a red checkered cloth, and Donovan ushered Nancy to one of them, taking the chair opposite her where he could keep watch on the door.

A man in a stained white apron stepped out from behind the counter. He had close-cropped iron gray hair and sported a dragoon mustache, and he had the look of an army cook about him.

Without asking what they wanted, he laid two cups

on the table and said, "I got sonofabitch stew an' she's almost ready, I reckon. Got some grease and flour dumplings too."

Donovan nodded toward Nancy. "The lady would like a steak."

The cook studied the girl for a few moments, realization slowly dawning on him. "You're the dove that was took by the Chinee gang, ain't you?"

Nancy blushed and looked down at the table, nodding a mute reply.

"And you must be Zeke Donovan, the pistol artist we've all been hearing so much about."

"That's me," Donovan said. Then trying to end it, he asked hastily, "Do you have steak?"

"Sure I do. I got elk steak, buffalo steak and beef steak. Take your pick. Got fresh eggs, if you like eggs."

Donovan and Nancy both ordered beefsteak and fried eggs and the cook poured them coffee.

Before the man left to fill the order, Donovan asked, "Say, I'm looking for a friend of mine, a gambling man called Charlie Utter. You know him?"

The cook nodded. "Sure I do. Feisty little feller, wears a mustache and an imperial. Some say he struck it rich a while back and maybe that's so. Saw him the other day a-wearing a Prince Albert coat and top hat and he had a two-foot watch chain acrost his belly made of ten-dollar gold pieces."

Donovan smiled. "Sounds like Charlie. Where can I find him?"

The cook shrugged. "He don't get up much before noon. Sometimes he'll partake of his morning bourbon and cigar at Madame Mustachio's place or Dirty Em's Sporting House. After that, well, there's seventy-eight saloons in Deadwood. Take your pick."

"I read in the newspaper he's living in a tent."

"Yeah," the cook said, "somewheres on the out-skirts of town." He paused, thinking, then said, "If'n I was you, I'd speak to Frenchie the Bottle Fiend. He knows everybody in Deadwood and it will save you a heap of walking."

"Why do they call him the Bottle Fiend?"

The cook waved a dismissive hand. "Long story. You'll find him in a tarpaper shack behind the Montana saloon and he'll tell you why his ownself."

The man went back to the kitchen and a few moments later Donovan heard the sizzle of steaks hitting a hot fry pan.

Nancy leaned across the table and placed the tips of her fingers on Donovan's hand. "I've been sitting here thinking, and I know how to get money so you don't have to ask Charlie What's-his-name."

"Utter," Donovan said, then suspiciously, "What do you have in mind?"

The girl's brown eyes were huge. "I can work at my profession. There's no shortage of men in town looking to get laid and you'd have yourself a stake in no time."

Donovan looked like he'd been struck. He opened his mouth to speak, closed it again, then managed, "Listen, I've done some mighty low-down things in my life, but pimping isn't one of them. I'd rather steal money, rob a bank, than live off the sweat of a whore."

Then, because Nancy had bruised his male ego, he wanted to hurt her. "Anyhow," he said, anger edging his voice, "there ain't nobody going to pay two dollars to screw a nine-fingered whore."

He sat back in his chair, expecting to see tears spring into the girl's eyes, but Nancy grabbed tight hold of the wrong end of the stick.

"Donovan," she said, sniffing slightly, "you're so good to me."

"What?" Donovan asked, confused.

The girl sniffed again and rubbed her nose with the back of her bandaged hand. "You just don't want me to go whoring any more, do you?"

Donovan didn't know how to reply. He opened his mouth to speak but was saved when the cook came out from the kitchen and placed the food on the table.

"The plates are hot, so be careful," he said. Then, as an afterthought, he added, "Name is Ned Lowery, by the way."

The steak was good, prime sirloin burned to the color and texture of old shoe leather in the Western manner, and Donovan and Nancy ate hungrily. Every now and then Donovan saw the girl lift her eyes from her plate and glance at him, an adoring look in her eyes that he'd seen before only in hound dogs.

"How's your steak?" he asked brusquely, squirming a little under Nancy's gaze.

"Just fine. And yours?"

Donovan didn't get a chance to reply, because suddenly the door was thrown open, banging loud on its hinges, and four men stepped inside, a blast of cold air and gusting rain following them.

There was no mistaking the man who led them, blond and cruelly handsome, huge in his fur coat.

Ike Vance stopped in midstride when he saw Donovan, and his thin mouth curled into a smile under his mustache. "Well, well, if it ain't the gambling man."

The smile slipped as Vance dropped his gaze to Donovan's belly, his blue eyes turning cold and ugly.

"I told you not to wear that watch," he said. "And I aim to kill you for it."

15

So it had come.

Donovan wiped his mouth with his napkin, vaguely surprised that his hands trembled only a little and the hard knot in his stomach was getting no tighter.

He rose slowly to his feet, aware of Nancy's frightened eyes on him as his chair scraped back loudly on the rough pine floor.

As he'd been taught years before by Luke Short, Donovan placed his left foot behind his right, upper body slightly turned toward his target. He had adopted the duelist's stance, hand inching toward his holstered Colt—movements that did not go unnoticed by Vance and his experienced gunmen.

Beside Vance, and even bigger than his boss, stood Hack Miller, long hair spilling over the shoulders of his bearskin coat. The coat was open, giving the Texas gunman access to his revolver in its crossdraw holster, and his mouth was a tough, tight line, fevered eyes betraying an eagerness to kill.

The two other gunmen behind Miller stood poised and ready. Familiar with such scenes, they'd wait to see how the cards fell, then they'd react.

Donovan knew both men would be certain, deadly and almighty sudden.

"Vance," he said, the fear gnawing at him husking his voice, making it sound weak, "you've been pushing me almighty hard and I want it stopped." He touched the pocket of his vest. "You can have this back. I never planned to keep your damned watch in the first place."

Ike Vance's voice was cold, flat and hard. "It's too late, way too late. Why just ten minutes ago a travelin' man stopped me on the street and said he'd seen a no-account gambler wearing my watch. The man said he'd recognized it right off on account of the wolf head fob, said he reckoned maybe good ol' Ike had fallen on hard times, parting with his watch to a low person an' all."

Vance's smile didn't reach his eyes. "He was lucky, that travelin' man. I only broke his jaw."

One of the gunmen behind Vance guffawed and slapped his thigh. "That's a natural fact, Ike. I reckon that ranny's gonna be eating through a tube for a six-month."

"See how it is, Donovan," Vance went on, "the word gets around. Now I have to stop it quick before I become a laughingstock all over the territory and beyond."

Donovan wiped his sweaty palm on his vest, tensing for the draw he knew would be the last chip he'd ever throw on the table.

But Lowery suddenly appeared from the kitchen, a wicked-looking meat cleaver in his hand and determination in his eyes.

"Here," the cook exclaimed, "this won't do. There will be no killing in my place." He pointed at Donovan. "That man has friends in Deadwood and there is duly appointed law here."

Vance nodded. "Yeah, so I heard."

The moment hung suspended and dangerous in the air, then quickly passed.

Vance turned to Lowery. "It's no matter, I never kill a man before breakfast anyhow. It's kind of a golden rule with me." He pointed a thick finger at Donovan. "The reckoning between us is still to come. By dawn tomorrow, or maybe the day after, the sun will come up over the rim of Deadwood Gulch, but it won't matter a damn to you because you won't see it." He smiled, thin and mean. "That's on account of how you won't be around no more."

Hack Miller laughed and slapped Vance on the back. "That's telling him, Ike!"

Vance nodded, smiling. "Hell, I'm all through talking to this ranny. Let's eat. My belly is so empty I'm gonna start echoing when I talk."

The gunmen crowded around a table, Vance staring fixedly at Donovan, predatory eyes glowing with hate and something else, a hint of an unholy obsession fast turning into madness.

The young gambler met those eyes, swallowed hard and turned to Lowery. "How much do I owe you?"

"On the house," Lowery said, "on account of how you and your dove have the keys to the city." He leaned closer to Donovan, whispering. "Now, get the hell out of here and take my advice—get out of Deadwood." Lowery's face was stiff, humorless. "Mister, I've turned a hand to a lot of things in my life, and one of them was a spell as a cow town marshal down the Texas Panhandle way. Over the years I knew a deal of slick revolver handlers and they came at me in a lot of different ways, wearing a lot of different faces, saying different things. But no matter what you tell folks, you really ain't one of them, are you?"

Donovan opened his mouth to reply, but Lowery held up a hand and shook his head. "You don't have to say anything because it don't matter a hill of beans what you say. I see what I see and I know what I know. Don't spit on me and tell me it's raining."

Donovan searched the man's eyes and they were gray and hard and eloquent.

"I get by," he said finally.

"Getting by ain't near enough." Lowery started to say something else, changed his mind and shook his head, dismissing the thought. "Just walk on out of here," he said, all at once sounding tired and old.

Taking Nancy by the arm, Donovan ushered her toward the door. Vance watched them go, his eyes taking in the girl's new coat, and he said, grinning, "Hey, Donovan, I got news for you. No matter how you dress up a two-dollar whore, she's still a two-dollar whore!"

The men around the table laughed and Donovan felt himself flush with anger. But he let it go. It was four against one, all of them named and deadly gunfighters, and there was no bucking those odds. He faced a stacked deck and he knew it, so he swallowed his pride, gulping it down, choking on it as it stuck in his craw like a tasteless, dry bone. Without turning his head, he stepped through the door and outside into the thin morning light and a merciless rain.

Nancy raised her parasol above her head and asked above the angry dragon hiss of the downpour, "Donovan, what are we going to do now?"

The rain beat a kettledrum rattle on Donovan's plug

hat. "We're going to talk to that Frenchie the Bottle Fiend feller, then we'll go see Charlie Utter and beg a road stake."

He looked down at the girl's pale, drawn face. "Don't worry, I'm taking you with me. That way nobody can say I ran out on you."

"Where are we going, Donovan?"

"Anywhere. Anywhere away from here."

"I'm frightened, Donovan."

"Hell, woman, so am I."

A freight wagon hauling a massive steel drill churned past through the mud, a soaked and miserable bullwhacker sitting on the wagon tongue, his whip cracking over the backs of the straining oxen. On each side, the rocky walls of the gulch rose sheer and treeless, the low clouds forming a sodden roof of iron gray and black.

Rain battered against painted signs outside stores and saloons and set them to creaking on their rusty chains, water cascading from their edges onto the boardwalks.

Deadwood was hemmed in solid, pounded by the hammering rain, squeezed in on itself so tight it had no room to move or breathe, a town slowly suffocating in a sea of black mud and close-packed, teeming humanity.

All this Donovan saw without joy. Like Deadwood itself, he found it difficult to draw breath, and the narrow, confining gorge and crowded, green timber buildings made him feel that he was being buried alive in a cramped coffin of rough-sawn pine.

"Donovan."

"Huh?"

"Donovan, before we go see that Frenchie the Bottle Fiend person, I have to let a doctor take a look at my finger." The girl's face was pained. "It hurts so bad, Donovan."

The young gambler sighed. "Later. I don't know where the doctors are in Deadwood. They come and go."

"Ask somebody, Donovan."

Protesting that there was nobody in sight, Donovan looked around and saw a soaked and obviously ill-tempered miner step out of a nearby saloon. The man was about to pass them on the deserted boardwalk when Donovan moved into his path and asked the whereabouts of the nearest physician.

"Across the street and to your left," the man said sullenly, broken red veins spread like spider webs on his cheeks, eyes dulled by a hangover to those of a dead fish. "And be damned to ye for stopping a man in such a rain."

"Right friendly town," Donovan muttered, watching the man stomp away.

"Donovan," Nancy said, "I can't cross all that mud. My new coat will get ruined."

"What do you want me to do?"

"You'll have to carry me, Donovan."

"I can't do that. Nobody knows how deep that mud is and we could both sink without trace. We'll go see a doc some other time, in a different town."

"My hand hurts, Donovan. You'll have to carry me across."

The young gambler made a frustrated, yelping sound in his throat. "You know, I read one time in a newspaper that there are fifty thousand whores west of the Mississippi. How come I had to win you?"

Eyes huge, rain plastering her dark hair to her forehead, Nancy said, "You'll have to carry me across, Donovan."

Donovan shook his head, his shoulders slumping in defeat. "When I finally get rid of you, and God only knows when that will be, I'll never have truck with whores again. That I solemnly vow."

"Are you ready to carry me, Donovan?"

Donovan cradled the girl in his arms and stepped off the boardwalk, immediately sinking to his knees in thick, odorous mud.

"Am I heavy, Donovan?" Nancy asked, holding her useless parasol above her head as the rain lashed at them both.

"You're no bigger than a nubbin," Donovan said, his temper short as he waded through the black and clinging ooze. "How the hell could you be heavy?"

The girl put her head on his shoulder and sighed. "You're such a nice gent, Donovan. You know exactly what to say to a woman."

Donovan made no reply, breathing heavily, intent on getting himself and his burden safely across the sluggish river of Deadwood mud.

Luckily, because of the downpour, there were few wagons in the street and with considerable relief he finally stepped up on the boardwalk on the other side. He let Nancy slide to her feet and then looked down at his checkered pants. They were black and muddy to the knees and when he walked his boots squelched with every step.

"Damnation," he muttered, "hell and damnation."

"What's wrong, Donovan?"

"I just remembered, we have to recross that damn street."

Nancy smiled and let her head rest on Donovan's wet shoulder as they walked. "You're so good to me, Donovan. You'll just have to carry me again."

*　　　*　　　*

The doctor's name was Shafter and he was young, keen and efficient. While Donovan waited, he took Nancy into his surgery and they reappeared fifteen minutes later.

"The finger is healing well," he said, "and I've put some salve and a lighter bandage on it." He looked hard at Donovan, an eyebrow lifting in annoyed accusation. "How did this girl get so shot up and mutilated?"

"We ran into bandits," Donovan replied, shifting his feet uncomfortably under the physician's relentless glare. "They wanted her ring."

The doctor relaxed just a little and said, "Say, now I remember. I heard about you. I was told that this young lady is descended from Polish royalty and that you saved her from Chinese pirates over to San Francisco way. Is that when she was shot and lost her finger?"

"Around that time," Donovan said. The doctor stood there, looking at him intently, waiting for more, but the young gambler said only, "How much do I owe you, doc?"

"Two dollars."

The physician, sizing up Donovan as a sporting gent and possible habitual sinner, took the money and pulled on his small, pointed beard, giving the young gambler a brief, newcomer's lecture on the perils of Deadwood's strong drink, lewd women and rampant social diseases.

Summing it all up he said finally, "While you're here, stay well way from whiskey and whores and you'll be all right."

Donovan nodded. "I seldom touch the first." He looked hard at Nancy. "As for the second, I recently made a solemn vow to have nothing to do with any of them."

"Good man!" Shafter said, beaming. "I wish some of my other patients thought that way."

It was still raining when Donovan and Nancy left the doctor's office and stepped onto the boardwalk.

Nancy raised her parasol and suddenly pointed across the street, her voice shrill. "Look, Donovan!"

Ike Vance and his three gunmen stood under the canvas awning of a general store, all of them looking in Donovan's direction, grinning.

Vance raised his right forefinger, sighted along it as he pointed at Donovan and brought down his thumb like the hammer of a revolver. Even at this distance, above the hiss of the rain, Donovan heard Vance's loud "Bang!"

The mocking laughter of Vance and his companions carried across the street as they finally turned away and strolled along the muddy boardwalk before stepping into a saloon.

"That man will not rest until he kills both of us," Nancy said, her eyes frightened.

Donovan nodded. "I know, but he'll have to catch us first."

He bent and scooped up Nancy in his arms. "Once I talk to Charlie Utter and borrow a road stake, we can be out of here before nightfall." He nodded, as though making up his mind about something. "Let's cross this damn street and go find Frenchie the Bottle Fiend."

16

Even at this early hour the Montana saloon was full of miners, assorted townspeople, hangers-on and idlers. A tinny piano tried valiantly to be heard above the roar of the men crowded along the bar, and as Donovan and Nancy passed, a woman laughed loudly and a man cursed his luck at a gaming table.

A narrow alley lay between the Montana and a rod and gun store and Donovan stepped into the muddy, garbage-strewn passage, Nancy following close behind him.

At the back of the saloon stood a wide, two-holer outhouse with a tin roof, a rare and expensive luxury at that time in the West, shaded by a single, spindly spruce. A trough and water pump lay too close to the outhouse, a breeding ground for the cholera that ravaged Deadwood from time to time, and beyond that a wood frame and tarpaper shack huddled, its roof sagging, close to the base of the gulch wall. A thin line of greasy smoke, straight as a string, rose from the shack's stovepipe chimney, defying the efforts of the teeming rain to disperse it.

A dozen pyramids of stacked bottles of all shapes and sizes, some as high as a tall man, crowded close to the shack. Hundreds of other bottles lay scattered over the ground like dead men after a ferocious battle.

"Now we know why they call him the Bottle Fiend," Donovan said dryly.

"Donovan," Nancy whispered, "I'm scared. Frenchie might be nuts. He could be dangerous."

"Of course he's nuts," Donovan said. "But he knows where Charlie is located." He smiled. "If it makes you feel any better, if he shapes up to be real loco and dangerous I'll plug him for you."

Donovan stepped up to the tarpaper door, guessed where the frame joist might be and rapped hard with his knuckles.

Silence.

"Maybe he's not to home," Nancy suggested, glancing hopefully around her.

Donovan rapped again, harder this time.

There was a few moments' pause, then a man's heavily accented voice from inside the door said, "Go away."

"Are you Frenchie the Bottle Fiend?" Donovan asked.

"Who wants to know?"

"I need to talk to you. I'm trying to find a friend of mine."

"Frenchie has many friends."

"Not your friend, my friend. Oh hell, man, open the damn door."

"Who is your friend?"

"A gambler feller. Goes by the name of Colorado Charlie Utter."

Another pause, then the door opened a crack and Donovan saw a single eye, black and bright as a bird's, peering at him.

"Are you going to shoot Charlie? Many people want to shoot heem I think."

"I told you, I'm a friend of his." Donovan moved closer to the door, trying to see inside. "Where can I find him?"

"Maybe Frenchie will tell you, but then again, maybe not."

The door opened slowly, hanging askew on its doubtful hinges. Donovan saw a small man in a celluloid collar one size too small and a patched frock coat three sizes too big standing in the doorway. His hair was thin and black, parted in the middle and plastered down with grease on both sides of his head, and a thin mustache smeared his upper lip.

His eyes slid past Donovan to Nancy, standing in the pelting rain, her dripping parasol above her head.

"Ah, I didn't know there was a mademoiselle. She is young but, alas, not pretty. But, pretty or no, Frenchie is always the gallant." He waved a gracious hand as though his miserable shack was a palace. "Please, please to step inside."

Donovan stepped into the shack, Nancy following him. The floor was strewn with bottles and the only furnishing was an iron cot that stood in one corner. An internal organ of some animal bubbled in a pot on the stove and, in the absence of windows, light was provided by a single oil lamp that hung, pungent and smoking, from the ceiling.

Frenchie made a little bow to Nancy and told her he regretted having no coffee to offer. "A temporary lack of funds makes coffee impossible." A sly look crept into his face and he tapped the side of his nose with a forefinger. "But soon Frenchie will have plenty of money and there will be coffee enough for all."

"How do you plan on that?" Donovan asked, instantly annoyed with himself for asking the question.

Frenchie nodded. "Ah yes, wouldn't you like to know."

Donovan shrugged. "It's your business. I didn't mean to pry."

The little Frenchman shrugged. "Maybe I will tell you 'ow I plan to, 'ow you say, strike eet rich."

"There's no need," Donovan said hastily. "I just want to know where to find Charlie Utter."

"How do you plan to get rich?" Nancy asked, oblivious to Donovan's annoyed glance.

"Let me show you something, mademoiselle," Frenchie said. He stepped to a dark corner of the shack and put his hand on the neck of a massive bottle Donovan hadn't noticed before.

"This is the largest of all champagne bottles," he said. "Eet is called the Nebuchadnezzar, named for a great king of Babylon. This once held the equal of twenty ordinary bottles of champagne and when eet was full weighed more than eighty pounds."

Nancy gasped. "That's a lot of champagne." She turned to Donovan, eyes wide. "Have you ever drunk champagne?"

Donovan nodded. "Sure, plenty of times when I was in the chips."

"I've never tasted champagne," Nancy said, her eyes suddenly wistful. "Is it good?"

"It's good," Donovan smiled. "Maybe one day I'll buy you a bottle."

Nancy sniffed and lightly touched his arm. "You're so good to me, Donovan."

"Ah, yes, the champagne, eet is made to go with

women and with love," Frenchie said. "But soon I
will buy one of these only for myself—the mighty
Nebuchadnezzar."

"Listen, Frenchie, about Charlie—"

"This one was brought all the way from Denver for
a miner who struck eet rich last year," the Frenchman
said, interrupting, warming to his subject. "He drank
the whole bottle at one sitting, right 'ere at the Montana." Frenchie shrugged. "He died of course, but I
made sure I got his empty Nebuchadnezzar."

The little man spread his hands wide. "Do you
know how many bottles of this size there are in this
country?" Without waiting for an answer, he said,
"Very few, maybe just six or seven."

"About Charlie," Donovan said, his exasperation
growing.

"So, one day Frenchie sits right here in his little
shack and thinks a long time about many things, but
especially bottles," the little man continued as though
he had not heard. "Deadwood has a big thirst and
every day eet uses and throws away thousands of bottles—champagne bottles, wine bottles, beer bottles,
whiskey bottles and plenty of the medicine bottles."
He studied Donovan closely, searching his eyes for an
answer. "Now, what ees the result of all that bottle,
'ow you say, throwing away?"

Donovan, bored, shrugged. "I've no idea."

"The result ees," the little Frenchman said tri-
umphantly, "that soon Deadwood will run out of bottles. Not only Deadwood, but the whole territory and
after that the entire nation. Because of the thirst of
thirty thousand miners, this country will soon face the
bottle shortage. And who will it turn to when it needs
more? Moi, Frenchie!"

The little man beamed. "I'm the best bottle man in

Deadwood and that is why I've cornered the market. Soon I will make, 'ow you say, the killing. I will be rich, rich beyond my wildest dreams!"

Donovan opened his mouth to speak, but Frenchie charged ahead, his eyes wild. He placed a fist on his right cheek and tapped his temple with his forefinger. "People say, 'That Frenchie he ees crazy,' but he's not so crazy, I think."

He raised an eyebrow and asked Donovan, "Do you think Frenchie, he ees crazy?"

"I've known some raving loonies in my time," Donovan said, flatly stating the fact without much emphasis, "and I reckon I'd put you right up there with the best of 'em."

"Ah, you too." The little man smiled. He looked shabbier all at once, and sad. "But you will see, soon Frenchie will ride in a fine carriage drawn by gray horses and drink only from the Nebuchadnezzar."

"Well," Donovan said, his patience wearing thin, "good luck to you. Now, about Charlie Utter."

"Ah, yes, Charlie." Frenchie nodded. "I will take you to heem."

Donovan shook his head. "You don't have to do that. Just tell me where to find him."

"*Non*, I will take you. It doesn't matter because rain or no, I have to make my rounds." He stepped to the cot and pulled a burlap sack from underneath. "Last night was Saturday and there was much drinking, much celebration. This morning Deadwood will be covered in bottles."

Frenchie fussily removed his bubbling pot from the heat and placed it on the side of the stove. "Perhaps when we return, we will dine together. This is ox heart. Mmm, eet is very good."

"We just ate," Donovan said, carefully not looking at the pot. "Maybe some other time."

The little man shrugged. "Then I fear you will miss a feast."

Frenchie ushered Donovan and Nancy out of the shack and into the rain. He carefully closed the door behind him and threw the sack over his shoulder.

"Charlie lives in a tent on the edge of town," he said. "We will find heem there eef somebody hasn't already shot heem." He glanced at the watch chain across Donovan's belly. "What ees the time?"

Donovan opened the watch, "Beautiful Dreamer" tinkling over the racket of the downpour. "It's almost ten."

"Then we will see a holy and wondrous sight," Frenchie said. "Eet is almost time for Charlie's bath."

It took Donovan and Nancy half an hour to reach the outskirts of Deadwood, mostly because Frenchie kept stopping at saloons to pick up discarded bottles. By the time the timber-built buildings petered out, his sack was bulging and heavy, clanking with every step.

The boardwalk ended at a general store and beyond lay a level, open stretch of ground, mostly mud, dotted here and there with clumps of struggling buffalo grass and a few stunted pines.

Among the pines, tents had sprung up everywhere, most of them with smoking stovepipes sticking out of their peaked, canvas roofs, and the air was thick with the smell of burning wood and frying salt pork.

"Thees way," Frenchie said, venturing off the boardwalk and onto the muddy level, bent over under his load. "Charlie's tent is over there to the right."

Donovan and Nancy followed the little Frenchman and his clanking burden, walking between rows of tents, some of them sagging badly as their pegs pulled out of the soft, ankle-deep mud.

A bearded man in suspenders and a stained undershirt stepped out of his tent and watched the trio curiously as they walked by. "Hey, ain't you—?" he yelled finally.

"Yes, I'm him," Donovan threw over his shoulder.

"Hey," the man yelled again, disappointment heavy in his tone, "that dove don't look much like no queen of Sweden to me."

"Her crown is all packed up," Donovan said. He grabbed Nancy by the arm. "Just keep walking."

"Over there," Frenchie said, quickening his pace, the out-of-tune chiming of the bottles on his back sounding like cracked bells. "We don't want to miss the bath."

Frenchie led the way to a tent whiter and larger than the rest. The flap was closed but Donovan saw the tent wall bulge slightly as someone moved around inside.

Despite the rain, a crowd of about three dozen people had gathered under a spruce near the tent. At the base of the tree a fire burned with more smoke than flame and a couple of buckets of creek water steamed on top of the coals. A pair of husky youngsters stood talking near the fire, one with a white sheet thrown over his shoulder. A zinc bathtub stood close to the fire.

"Come to see ol' Charlie's bath?" a thick-bearded man in miner's clothes asked Donovan, studying him up and down.

Donovan shrugged. "I come to talk to Charlie but not to see him take a bath. What's so special about a man taking his bath?"

"Hell, man," the miner said, his voice booming and

loud, "Charlie takes a bath every single day." He shook his head in wonderment. "It just ain't natural, I tell ye. A man should only take a bath when he's so dirty he can't stand hisself no more, an' that's maybe only onset or twicet a year tops."

He studied Donovan closely, then Nancy. "What's your opinion on that, young lady?" he asked the girl.

Nancy shrugged. "I always think it feels good to be clean all over."

The miner nodded. "Yeah, but not too clean. A man can kill hisself being too clean—to say nothing of the rheumatisms he can get when he don't have a coating of dirt to protect his joints."

"Oh, there he is!" somebody in the crowd yelled.

Colorado Charlie Utter appeared from the tent, a large white towel wrapped around him. His blond hair hung in gentle waves over his shoulders and he sported a carefully trimmed mustache and imperial. He was small and neat and thin, only his face and hands showing brown from the sun, and he had a slow, hesitant way of walking, like he thought about every single step he was about to take.

"Ain't he the purtiest man you ever did see?" the big miner asked, shaking his head in wonderment. Then, without waiting for a reply, he added, "Damn me if'n he ain't."

The crowd cheered and Charlie inclined his head and lifted a limp hand in acknowledgment, well-kept teeth flashing white.

The two youngsters, practiced and obviously hired regularly, moved to Charlie, one on each side, and carefully held up the sheet between them, shielding him from the view of the crowd.

When the sheet was dropped, Charlie was already in the bathtub and only the top of his chest, revealing a sparse triangle of hair, and his head and shoulders showed above the rim.

The onlookers gasped and somebody said, "He's in!"

One of the youngsters brought a bucket from the fire and Charlie leaned over and tested the temperature with his elbow. Satisfied, he nodded and the man poured the water into the tub. The second bucket followed and the other young man handed Charlie a huge bar of lye soap.

"Well, lookee there," a woman in the crowd marveled, "he's lathering hisself up all over."

"Ain't that a sight to see," someone else said.

"Hey, Charlie, don't fergit behind your ears!" the miner behind Donovan hollered and the crowd laughed.

Charlie's ablutions took the best part of half an hour, the crowd braving the pelting rain to take in the sight, something to tell their kids and grandkids about, a story they could improve upon with each telling.

Finally, for modesty's sake, one of the young men held up a towel as Charlie stood. The other youngster returned from the creek with a bucket of cold water and this he poured over Charlie's head. The little gambler gasped and hopped from one foot to the other, hollering loudly as the cold water hit him and the crowd laughed uproariously.

Finally, Charlie emerged from behind the sheet, again wrapped in his towel and a round of scattered applause followed him back to his tent, Charlie waving a lethargic hand the whole time in aloof acknowledgment, as if he reckoned he was receiving no more than was his due.

As the crowd broke up and began to drift away,

Nancy gave Donovan a slanting look. "He's going to be our savior?" she asked, her eyes uncertain and accusing.

Donovan nodded. "Charlie is strange by times. But right now he's our only hope."

"Donovan, the mayor gave us the keys to the city," Nancy said. "Maybe we could get a loan from a bank."

The young gambler shook his head at her. "I don't think the keys to the city included the keys to the banks. All those big keys meant was two nights at the hotel and nothing else. They're about as worthless as the stuff they're made from."

Frenchie the Bottle Fiend walked up to the tent and said loudly, "Charlie, you got eet?"

After a few moments a bare arm was thrust out of the tent flap, an empty whiskey bottle in hand. Frenchie took the bottle and touched his forehead with the neck. "Thankee, Charlie," he said. He waited. The hand reappeared and this time it dropped a silver dollar into Frenchie's open palm.

"Thankee again, Charlie," said Frenchie.

He threw the coin in the air, caught it and said to Donovan and Nancy, "Now we can have beer with lunch. The invitation still stands."

Donovan shook his head. "Maybe some other time." He fished in his pocket and brought out his own silver dollar. He spun the coin toward Frenchie and the little man palmed it deftly. "Thanks for your help," Donovan said. "And good luck with the bottles."

Frenchie tapped the side of his nose with a forefinger. "Soon I'll be rich. You'll see."

He grinned, then turned and walked away, bent over like a hunchback, the bulging sack clanking with every step.

Donovan watched him go, shook his head sadly, then said to Nancy, "Let's talk to Charlie."

Doubt writ large in her eyes, Nancy followed Donovan to the tent.

"Hey Charlie, Charlie Utter."

Donovan stood at the closed tent flap, his head inclined to one side, waiting for an answer.

"Who is it?"

"Me, Donovan."

"Who?"

"Zeke Donovan. Remember, from Denver and a few other places?"

"Can't be," Charlie said after a few moments hesitation. "You're dead. Ain't nobody told you yet?"

"Well, I'm talking to you so I must be alive."

The tent flap opened and Charlie's head appeared, damp hair falling over his forehead. "I heard you was shot dead in a saloon down Cheyenne way, then I heard you was scalped by Indians in the Montana Territory, then I heard you was chopped up by a Chinee gang over to San Francisco. With all them folks killing you, how come you're still alive?"

"Luck, I guess," Donovan said, "though mostly it's been all bad recently."

"A man makes his own luck," Charlie said, preachifying, "an' that's a natural fact. Anyhow, you was always a lousy poker player."

He looked at Donovan suspiciously, ignoring the young gambler's outraged yelp of protest. "What brings you here? And who's the girl?"

Deciding to say it straight out, Donovan swallowed hard and managed, "What brings me here is that I need a road stake, Charlie. I'm on the dodge."

"The law?"

"No. It's a lot worse than that, believe me."

Charlie thought this over for a few moments, decided not to press the subject, then asked again, "Who's the girl?"

"She's a dove," Donovan replied. "I won her in a card game about the time my luck ran out for keeps."

Charlie took his time absorbing this information, then he said, "You can come inside, but don't sit on my cot. That," he added grimly "is a shooting matter with me."

Donovan nodded. "I read about that."

Charlie hesitated, then added as though further explanation was needed, "I only made but one exception to that rule in my life and that was for Wild Bill Hickok. A man learned to step lightly around Bill, so I let him lay on my clean blankets." Charlie shook his head. "I always regretted it, so maybe I should have plugged him in his sleep."

"I thought he was your friend." Donovan said.

"He was, the only real friend I ever had, but there were times when he sore tried my patience." He looked at Donovan and then Nancy. "Well, come in out of the rain, but just bear in mind what I said about the cot."

Donovan stood, head bent, in Charlie's tent, Nancy beside him. For his part, Charlie, still wrapped in a towel, apparently didn't mind squatting on the cot himself, sitting cross-legged on blankets that were soft and spotlessly clean.

Close to the bed, on a pine nightstand, hung a double gunbelt, two long-barreled Colts in the black holsters. The guns were silver plated, embellished with gold engraving, the grips of fine, yellowed ivory. Charlie had killed his man in the past, and the flashy revolvers were not only for show.

"Okay, tell me," Charlie said, looking up at Donovan with cool eyes, seemingly unimpressed with what he was seeing.

"Tell you what?

"Your story. Everybody has a story to tell, especially a gambling man down on his luck, on the dodge and looking to tap an acquaintance he barely knows for a road stake."

For the second time that day Donovan choked down his pride and again it was hard and bitter, tasting like green bile in his mouth.

In as few words as possible he described his poker game with Ike Vance and his subsequent run-in with him that morning at the restaurant. He also told of his fight with the Loupers and the attack by the Cheyenne on the stage station.

"The bottom line is that Ike Vance means to kill me," Donovan said, winding it up fast. "And Nancy too. Charlie, we need that road stake real bad."

Charlie nodded. "Sure you do. There's a lot of Apache in Ike Vance and he's no bargain and Hack Miller is worse than him, maybe three times over worse. He's pure hell with a gun. Me, I don't give much for your chances."

"Neither do I," Donovan said. "That's why I'm here."

For the first time, Charlie looked at Nancy, studying her with growing interest, glancing her over slowly and carefully from head to toe.

"How much for a poke?" he asked. "After my bath I'm always in the mood."

Donovan was taken aback at this sudden turn in the conversation and opened his mouth to protest, but Nancy quickly stepped into the breach. She held up her bandaged hand. "Like Donovan told you, I had a finger cut off and I was shot a couple of times. I'm just not up for a man poking at me right now."

Charlie thought that over for a spell, then shrugged. "Well, if you're feeling right poorly it don't make no difference. I'm going over to Dirty Em's soon and I'll get me my morning poke there." He smiled. "When you get to feeling better, though, come see me. I pay top dollar."

Nancy nodded and said without much conviction. "I surely will."

"That Ike's watch?" Charlie asked Donovan, Nancy already forgotten and dismissed.

"Yeah, this is it," Donovan replied slowly, his eyes slanting to Nancy, who was looking down at Charlie without embarrassment and a commendable absence of rancor. He took out the Berthoud and thumbed open the cover.

Charlie sat for a few moments listening to the tune. He turned, looking up at Nancy. "You're a whore that doesn't like to poke. Can you sing?"

"Sure," Nancy said. She began to sing "Beautiful Dreamer" with the watch until Donovan testily snapped it shut, stopping her in midnote.

Charlie nodded. "Right pretty."

He turned to Donovan, his eyes flat and calculating. "Now, what do you want from me?

"Like I said earlier, I need a road stake. I mean money enough for two horses with some left over to take us to . . . well, wherever. This is not a matter that can wait. It's urgent, Charlie." Donovan paused. "Hell, you know I'm good for it."

Charlie Utter was beginning to grate on Donovan and he was rapidly starting to regret coming to him for a loan in the first place. Maybe he should say to hell with it and face up to Ike Vance and his killers. But as

soon as that thought entered his head, he dismissed it.
It would be like committing suicide and he wasn't
ready to die just yet.

Charlie was talking again and Donovan fought
down his irritation and listened. "You ever hear tell of
a town called Tombstone, down to the Arizona Territory?" Charlie asked.

Donovan shook his head. "Can't say as I have."

"Well, things are snapping down there on account
of the tons of silver they're pulling out of the Dragoon
Mountains. Tombstone is wide open and fortunes are
being made by smart operators off the backs of the
miners."

Interested now, Donovan paid close attention as
Charlie continued. "There's an acquaintance of mine
down there, a gambler feller and sometime lawman
named Wyatt Earp. Ever hear of him?"

"Name doesn't ring a bell."

Charlie looked vaguely disappointed. "Lived a
sheltered life, Donovan, haven't you? Well, anyhoo,
Earp and his brothers Morgan and Virgil have the
gambling concessions in Tombstone locked up tight as
Dick's hatband and they're doing some goldbricking
and pimping on the side. Those boys are all good Re-
publicans and true blue and they're making money
hand over fist. The last I heard they were looking to
run the law down there and really clean up."

Donovan was confused. "Why are you telling me
this, Charlie?"

"Because the Earps could find work for you and
your dove. All you have to do is mention my name.
They owe me a favor or three from way back."

"That's going to take money," Donovan muttered,
half to himself. "Arizona is a fair piece from here."

Charlie nodded. "It certainly is, but I'm holding

right now so I'll be happy to stake you. Hell, Donovan, I always said your credit was as good as gold. I told Luke Short that very thing one time, sure as I'm sitting here." He smiled, waving a dismissive hand. "Pay me back when you're in the chips."

"I'm beholden to you, Charlie," Donovan said earnestly, rapidly revising his opinion of the little gambler.

"Think nothing of it," Charlie returned. He hesitated for a few moments, then, a crafty look creeping across his face, said, "But, now when I study on it, there is something you can do for me in return."

"Anything. Just name it, Charlie."

Charlie Utter nodded, his face suddenly unsmiling and serious. "Help me dig up Wild Bill." He paused for effect. "Tonight."

17

Zeke Donovan was taken aback.

"Charlie," he managed after a long and expressive silence, "how come you want to dig up Wild Bill? I mean, that hardly seems natural."

"You didn't know Bill, did you?" Charlie asked, refusing to dab a loop on Donovan's question.

Donovan shook his head.

"Well, when Bill was alive, he never settled for second best," Charlie said. "That applied to horses, guns, whiskey and women and anything else you care to mention. And that's why we have to dig him up, because I know he isn't resting content in his grave like a man should."

"Is he in a second best grave then?" Nancy asked, the sarcasm in her voice as pointed as a stiletto.

If Charlie noticed the girl's tone, he didn't let it show. "That's exactly the case," he nodded, smiling. "Little lady, you summed up the whole thing real good."

"I don't get it," Donovan said, taking off his plug

hat, running his fingers through his hair like he was trying to massage life into a suddenly petrified brain. He settled the hat back on his head and added, frowning, "A grave is a grave and there isn't any second best to it. Hell, by its very nature being dead is second best."

"Maybe so," Charlie agreed, "but I don't reckon Bill sees it that way."

"All right," Donovan said, "if we dig him up, and that's a big if, then what?"

"Why, we plant him in a better grave."

"I still don't get it," Donovan said, totally mystified, but desperately groping for some understanding.

"It's really quite simple," Charlie said, slowly, like he was talking to a child. "See, Bill is buried on the other side of town at the Ingleside Cemetery, a nice enough place as boneyards go, but it doesn't compare with Mount Moriah."

"What's that?"

"Hell, man, that's the brand new cemetery they've laid out on the slope above town. It's pretty small right now but it's beautiful up there, all nice shady trees and marble columns and iron gates.

"But the mayor and the other idiots in this burg want to leave Bill right where he is. They say Ingleside is good enough for him and they told me if I try to dig him up it could be a hanging matter, mostly on account of how folks around here don't cotton to me much, anymore than they did to Bill."

Charlie searched Donovan's face. "Now do you understand? Bill won't rest content knowing there's a brand new, first class cemetery in Deadwood and he ain't a-lying in it.

"Like I told you before, he never settled for less than the best when he was alive and that's why I can't leave him where he is now he's dead. I swear, he'll come back and haunt me if I don't move him to Mount Moriah, hangman's rope or no."

"How, I mean—" Donovan began, but Charlie cut him off.

"How do we get him up there? That's easy. I'll hire a spring wagon and a mule and we just lay ol' Bill in the back and that's how we'll get him up there. Hell, Donovan, you don't even have to dig a new grave. I've got a couple of husky young fellers will do that."

"I'm not good at graves," Donovan said, defeat lying heavy on him. "I tend to make 'em too short." He looked at Charlie with gloomy eyes. "I'm also not big on getting hung."

"Don't you worry none about that," Charlie said. "The men I've hired are experts and we'll have Bill planted afore anybody in town even notices the ol' switcheroo."

He studied Donovan's face. "Well, are you in?"

"I don't know. It isn't exactly my line of work."

Charlie rose and stepped to a chair close to the bed. The gambler's fringed buckskin coat, bright with Indian beadwork, hung over the back of the chair and he reached into a pocket.

He brought out a small leather bag, pulled together at the top with rawhide, opened it and counted out five gold coins.

"A hundred dollars on account," Charlie told Donovan. "Take it, it's yours. Once the job is done and ol' Bill is sleeping snug as a bug in Mount Moriah I'll stake you another hundred." He smiled. "Deal?"

"Do I have a choice?" Donovan asked, knowing full well he didn't.

"Not that I can see," Charlie said, confirming it for him. "Unless of course you want to stay in Deadwood and face up to Ike Vance and Hack Miller and them."

Donovan sighed and opened his palm and Charlie dropped the five double eagles into his hand. "Meet me here tonight," Charlie said. "I'll have the wagon and the shovels and everything else we need. Coal oil lanterns too, on account of how we'll need light."

"What time?"

"You got a nice gold watch. Say, fifteen minutes before midnight."

Donovan nodded, his eyes bleak. "Now I'm a grave robber. I'd say I've come a long way since Denver."

"A man can only play the cards the way they fall, Donovan, even if he's plumb out of aces," Charlie's smile was thin. "Them's words of wisdom." He picked up his pants. "Now, get the hell out of here, I'm already late for Dirty Em's."

Donovan and Nancy trudged back toward the boardwalk at the edge of town. The sky was so heavy, it lay on the rooftops of the taller buildings like a gray mist and the steely rain beat on their faces, cold and vindictive.

"What are we going to do, Donovan?" Nancy asked, holding her parasol directly in front of her as a shield against the wind-lashed downpour. The girl's eyes were haunted. "Wild Bill's been dead for almost two years. He could be all moldy and horrible."

"Don't worry about that," Donovan said, his face grim. "We're not digging up Bill Hickok or anybody else, not tonight, not any night."

"What are we going to do, Donovan?"

"We're buying a horse and getting out of town."

"But—but you took Charlie's money."

"I'll pay him back. When we get to Tombstone and I'm in the chips again, I'll wire him the hundred dollars." He looked down at Nancy, rain pouring off the narrow, curled brim of his hat. "With interest. I reckon that Wyatt Earp feller will see us all right."

"But it doesn't seem the proper thing to do, Donovan. I mean, taking Charlie's money and then running out on him."

Donovan nodded. "No, it isn't the proper thing to do, since you put it that way. But Charlie himself told me to play the cards where they fall and he hit it right on the button when he said I was all out of aces." His face set and determined, he added, "I'm also out of options. We're buying a horse and getting out of Deadwood. That's how I'm playing this lousy hand, aces or no, and that's something Charlie will understand. Eventually."

"Donovan," the girl said, "suppose Ike Vance sees us leave?"

"That," said Donovan, "is a chance we'll have to take."

At the hotel, Donovan left Nancy in her room, then returned to his own and quickly changed into his range clothes. He folded up his gambler's suit and carefully laid it in the carpetbag, then he picked up the bag and his Henry rifle and rapped on the girl's door.

Nancy was waiting, standing in the middle of the floor, her parasol in her bandaged hand, her small bag in the other. To Donovan she looked damp and forlorn, her eyes way too big for her face, a homely, church social, apple turnover kind of girl who should be married, if not lovingly at least contentedly, to a somber and bearded farmer. In fact she should be anything else but a soiled dove about to flee with a down-on-his-luck gambler across wild and unforgiving country, chased by vengeful gunman in a teeming and seemingly endless rain.

The marks of a hard life, speaking of much harsh

treatment and little of even the smallest kindnesses, were on her, easy to see, and that morning she looked older than her sixteen years.

Touched, in spite of himself, Donovan asked, more gently than he intended, "Ready?"

Nancy nodded.

Then, ashamed of his weakness, he said brusquely, "Okay, let's go."

The bored desk clerk gave them only a passing, uninterested glance as Donovan and Nancy left the hotel and stepped onto the boardwalk. Main street was still quiet, a single, ox-drawn wagon churning slowly through the thick mud, but the saloons were busy as men sought to stay dry on the outside and wet on the inside.

Thomas J. Bearden's livery stable stood at the edge of town behind a general store and blacksmith's shop. It had been one of the first buildings in Deadwood and was made of pine logs that had been hewn from the then forested walls of the gulch.

The peaked roof, however, was of canvas, stretched across a timber frame and the corral behind the stable was built of timber planks, all of them warping badly.

Bearden was a tall, lanky man with a humorless face and the look of the hardscrabble dirt farmer about him and he stepped suspiciously out of his tiny office when Donovan and Nancy walked into the barn.

"What can I do for you folks?" he asked, with no friendliness in his voice.

"I need a horse," Donovan said.

"You came to the right place. I got two for sale," Bearden said. "Got a nice palouse mare and a little hammer-headed grulla."

"I've only got a hundred dollars and change," Donovan said.

"Then I got one horse for sale, a hammer-headed grulla," Bearden said, the momentary interest in his eyes shutting down fast to be replaced by impatience, like he was angry with Donovan for wasting his time.

"Let's see the grulla," Donovan said, feeling that no good was about to come out of this transaction.

Bearden led them to a stall in the corner of the barn, where a small, mouse-colored horse stood hipshot, tail twitching lazily at a late season fly.

Donovan looked the grulla over and said, "Isn't much, is he? He can't go over eight hundred pounds."

Bearden shrugged. "He's a hoss. Beats walking."

"How much?"

"You said you got a hunnerd, so the price is a hunnerd even."

"I need a saddle and bridle."

"Got an old McClellan and an even older bridle I'll let go for another twenty. Throw in a cavalry boot for your rifle. She's dry and cracked some, but she'll get the job done."

"That will just about wipe me out," Donovan said bitterly, seeing his five double eagles about to vanish like smoke.

"Well," Bearden said, "you got a choice to make, don't you?"

Donovan smiled without humor. "Mister, I'm all out of choices. I'll take the grulla."

"Thought you mought," Bearden said, his smile thin, and Donovan heard the echo of the same words used by another livery owner in a different place and time, a time that seemed like a hundred years ago.

The young gambler paid for the horse, took the bill of sale and folded it into the pocket of his coat. He led the grulla out of the barn and tied him to the hitching rail outside the general store while he and Nancy stepped inside.

Donovan, his face stiff and unsmiling, dug deep into his pants pockets and bought a two dollar coffeepot, a pound of Arbuckle coffee for thirty-five cents, and, unable to afford bacon at twenty-five cents a pound, settled on a greasy, twelve-cent slab of salt pork.

There were thirteen .44 rounds in his Henry and five loads in his Colt. He had no money to buy more ammunition and would have to make out with what he had.

Ten minutes later, in a hammering rain, Donovan rode the grulla out of Deadwood at a careful walk, Nancy behind him, sitting astride, her parasol opened above her head, new bloomers showing frilly and white under her dress. Leaving the town behind, they headed into open country, the broad miles stretching long before them under a lowering gray sky.

"Do you think Ike Vance saw us, Donovan?" the girl asked as they splashed across rain-swollen Strawberry Creek, keeping Whistler Gulch, half-hidden behind a gray curtain of rain, to their east.

Donovan shook his head. "I doubt it. Who else but poor, hunted fugitives like us would be riding out on a day like this?"

Nancy nestled her cheek between Donovan's shoulders. "You always say wise things, Donovan. I think I'm beginning to feel real safe when I'm with you."

"And you should." Donovan nodded, agreeing with himself. "Damn right."

But despite his bravado, Donovan's finely honed gambler's instincts were clamoring. He couldn't shake the uneasy feeling that someone was looking over his shoulder, reading his cards—someone who now knew just how weak was the lousy hand he was holding.

18

Zeke Donovan had no definite plan in mind except to put as much country between him and Ike Vance as possible.

He would head southwest toward Ruby Flats and then swing west and cross Icebox Gulch at Cheyenne Crossing.

After that, there was the Platte and beyond the river Laramie or Cheyenne or maybe even Denver, a whole new and better world opening up in front of him. He figured that his luck was due to change soon and the cards would finally start falling his way—if Ike Vance didn't catch up with him first.

Donovan and Nancy rode through open grass country, aspen- and pine-covered hills and tall mesas rising on either side of them, cut up here and there by deep, blue-shadowed ravines and gorges.

As they neared Ruby Flats they scattered a small herd of antelope, and once a jackrabbit bounded up between the front hooves of the grulla and quickly bounced away from them in a panic, zigzagging this way and that across the soaked buffalo grass.

Clouds lay low and heavy on the hills, so low the arrowhead tops of the lodgepole and spruce pines were lost in a mist and the air was chill, made even more so by the incessant hammering of the icy rain.

The grulla, small and ugly and shabby as he grew his winter coat, was tough and strong and he moved out willingly enough though his gait was close-coupled and choppy. The McClellan saddle, built to favor the horse, not the rider, was no bargain either and by the time they'd crossed Icebox Gulch and reached the northern edge of Ruby Flats, Donovan was already stiff and sore and Nancy was beginning to complain.

The shoulders of Donovan's sheepskin coat had turned black from the rain and his plug hat offered little protection, cold fingers of water trickling down the back of his neck.

"Donovan," Nancy said for the third or fourth time, talking over the hiss of the downpour, her mouth close to his ear, "let's shelter for just a few minutes. I have to stretch my legs or I'll die."

Donovan reined up the grulla and looked around. This was broad, wild country and on every side he saw no sign of life, just the endless, rolling miles. Once this land had belonged to the Indian and the buffalo but they had left no mark, only the occasional wallow carved out of the earth by huge bulls, now long overgrown with grass.

To Donovan's left, about half a mile away, a thick stand of aspen grew along the base of a lopsided mesa, their leaves a golden yellow canopy studded with scarlet that offered promise of at least partial shelter from the cloudburst. He swung the horse around and loped toward the trees, Nancy bouncing behind him, her parasol swinging this way and that above her head.

Suddenly Donovan reined up, stopping the little horse so short the girl's head thumped hard against his shoulders.

"Donovan, what—" Nancy began.

"Look!" the young gambler interrupted. "Over there by the trees."

Nancy put her chin on his shoulder as her eyes scanned the aspen. "Five riders. Donovan, it can't be Ike Vance and them. Ike has only three men with him. They must be drovers from one of the ranches hereabouts."

Donovan shook his head. "It's Vance and his boys all right. I'd recognize that bearskin coat of Hack Miller's anywhere. Ike must have picked up another no-account killer in Deadwood."

"What are we going to do, Donovan?"

"Ease on out of here before they see us, is what we're going to do."

Donovan swung the grulla around and kicked the horse into a fast lope. A split second later, a bullet whined above his head, then another round kicked up an angry exclamation mark of water and mud just ahead of him.

"They've seen us!" Donovan yelled. "Hold on!"

He kicked the grulla into a run, swinging south onto the flats.

But Vance and his men had anticipated that much and rode hard to cut him off. The grulla was game enough, but burdened by two people he was much slower than Vance and his well-mounted riders.

Donovan saw his route across the flats was blocked and swung north again, the little horse straining, neck stretched; as Donovan urged him into a faster gallop.

Bullets buzzed angrily around him and Nancy, Vance and his men firing as they rode.

Ruby Flats fell away behind him, and Donovan saw the rugged bulk of Sugarloaf Mountain ahead, its pine-covered foothills cut through with deep, rocky canyons that already echoed to the racket of Vance's relentless rifle fire.

If he could reach the mountain he could lose his pursuers among the hills. If he was lucky. Very lucky.

But it seemed that in some diabolical way Ike Vance was reading Donovan's mind.

Strung out in a line, the new man in the lead, Ike's riders were moving to cut Donovan off from even the doubtful sanctuary of the Sugarloaf.

Vance's men were closing the distance fast, too fast, and Donovan knew with sickening certainty that he wasn't going to make it. He'd have to ride through Vance and his riflemen to make the foothills and that was a dead man's play.

He reined up, yanking so hard on the grulla's bit that the little horse's hindquarters hit the ground, his hooves throwing up great clods of mud and dirt, and Nancy clung to Donovan's waist for dear life.

Quickly Donovan jerked his Henry from the boot, cranked a round into the chamber and fired at the leading horseman, a tall man wearing a black hat and brick-colored mackinaw.

A clear miss.

He fired again and this time the man jerked in the saddle. He rode bent over the horn for twenty yards or so, then very slowly toppled from his mount's back and thudded onto the sodden ground.

Ike Vance, Hack Miller close behind him, ignored the fallen rider and galloped on, working their rifles, firing again and again, their bullets kicking up dirt around the grulla's hooves.

His plan to disappear among the hills thwarted, Donovan had no option but to head his flagging horse north.

Vance and the others followed, keeping their distance but firing steadily, their bullets hemming him in on all sides.

"Damn it, they're herding us!" Donovan yelled at Nancy. "Vance could have killed us any time. He wants us back in Deadwood."

"We'll be safer in town than out here." Fearfully, Nancy glanced over at Vance and his men. "Just do as he wants, Donovan. It's our only chance. If we try to escape from Ike he'll kill us for sure."

Reluctantly Donovan accepted Nancy's inescapable logic. He shook his head in frustration and swung the grulla in the direction of Deadwood, kicking the animal into a tired lope. Vance and the others immediately fell in behind, alert but keeping their distance.

There was killing to be done and Ike Vance badly wanted to make the play.

But why in Deadwood? Why not out here in the wilderness where there were no witnesses?

Donovan shook his head, clearing his thoughts.

He did not have answers to those questions. But Nancy was right, he had no other choice. At least he might have a fighting chance in Deadwood. And there was law in town, such as it was.

"Donovan," Nancy said, her chin on his shoulder again, "what are we going to do?"

"Do what Colorado Charlie paid me to do I guess." Donovan took off his hat and wiped sweat and rain from his forehead with the back of his hand, his shoulders slumping in defeat.

"Ride back to Deadwood, then get a damn shovel and go resurrect Wild Bill."

19

Ike Vance, leading the dead man's horse but leaving the body where it lay, closely followed Donovan and Nancy back to Deadwood. The four gunmen sat their horses in the pouring rain outside the livery stable as Donovan led the grulla inside, startling Bearden who stepped quickly out of his office.

"Hell, I figured you'd be halfway to Cheyenne by this time," Bearden said, his face sour.

"So did I," Donovan replied. He handed Bearden the reins of the grulla. "He needs a handful of oats and some hay and a chance to rest up, but I got no money to pay for his keep."

Bearden looked past Donovan's shoulder to the small sack tied behind the saddle. "What you got in your poke?"

Donovan shrugged. "Not much. A new coffeepot, a sack of Arbuckle and a stab of salt pork."

The livery stable owner nodded, eyes greedy. "I'll take that as payment for two days feed an' a dry stall."

"Real horse trader, ain't you?" Donovan asked, his dislike for Bearden growing.

Bearden shrugged. "Take it or leave it, it's all the same to me."

"I'll take it," Donovan said, realizing bitterly that this was just another small surrender in a long, depressing string of such capitulations.

"Thought you mought," Bearden said, his mouth widening in a triumphant grin.

The man led the grulla to a stall, unsaddled him and tossed him some oats and hay.

Donovan watched for a few moments, then nodded to Nancy, and they both stepped to the door of the stable where Ike Vance, Hack Miller and the two other gunmen still sat their horses in the pelting rain.

"You going somewheres?" Vance asked, his smile thin and humorless.

"Back to the hotel," Donovan answered. "Like it's any of your business."

"It is my business," Vance said. He studied Donovan with unforgiving eyes. "You killed one of my men today and we'll be burying him later. He was the brother of Clint and Les here." He waved a hand toward the two unsmiling Texas gunmen. "And we all took his passing mighty hard." He jabbed a finger at the young gambler. "The miners will be in from the diggings tonight come seven o'clock. Be in the street. I'm plumb desirous to get this thing settled."

Realization dawning on him, Donovan said, "That's why you didn't kill us out there on the flats. You want the whole town to see."

Vance nodded, his smile wide but without warmth. "You know, for someone as stupid as you are, Donovan, you're quick on the uptake. Sure I need the whole town to see. I don't want it getting around that Ike

Vance didn't settle the score. Tonight, after you're dead, I want folks to be talking about it, telling each other what I done an' how I done it."

His nerves were frayed, yet a reckless anger was growing in him. Donovan took the watch from the pocket of his sheepskin coat and thumbed open the cover, vaguely aware of Bearden stepping beside him.

As "Beautiful Dreamer" chimed above the sound of the rain, he said, "It's gone three. Why wait that long? Let's settle it right here and now."

Donovan saw Vance tense, and Hack Miller's eyes were hungry and eager. He gave nothing for his chances, but this had gone on too long and now, suddenly, he realized he didn't give a damn.

But the moment passed and it was Bearden who ended it.

"Hey, Ike, ain't that your watch, the one everybody talks about?" the man asked, seemingly ignorant of what was happening. "How did this ranny get aholt of it?"

"You shut your trap!" Vance snapped, his handsome face flushed. He turned to Donovan, his shoulders slowly relaxing. "No, I'm not going to draw down on you, not now. It's too soon. I want plenty of people around when I take that watch off your dead body."

"Ike, why don't you just go away and leave us alone?" Nancy asked, stamping her foot. "We mean you no harm. Donovan will give you back the watch." She looked at young gambler. "Won't you, Donovan?"

If it was in Donovan's mind to reply, he never got the chance. "You keep out of this," Vance said. "This is a discussion between Donovan and me and I don't want no cheap, nine-fingered tramp butting in on my business."

Hack Miller laughed. "Hell, she's got to be cheap,

Ike. Ain't nobody gonna pay full price for a right homely whore with nine fingers."

Vance nodded. "Well, after tonight she won't have to worry about that." He looked at Nancy. "Your whoring days is coming to an end real soon, little lady." Vance sneered. "It's not like it will be a great loss. You were always a lousy lay anyhow."

"Ike Vance," Nancy said, tears starting to redden her eyes, "you're a filthy pig."

"You heard that, Bearden?" Vance asked.

The livery stable owner nodded. "Sure did. She called you a filthy pig, Ike."

"I know what she called me," Vance snapped, his eyes ugly. "You got no call to repeat it. Woman," he said to Nancy, "you just gave me another reason to kill you."

Donovan took a step toward the gunman. "I don't think folks in this town will take kindly to you killing a woman, Vance. They'll string you up right quick."

The big man shrugged. "They'll take it. They may not like it but they'll take it." He glanced over his shoulder at the others. "Won't they, boys?"

"Damn right," Miller yelled, slapping his thigh. "It will take more than a bunch of miners and a hick sheriff to stop us riding out of town."

"And speaking of riding," Vance said, putting his slipped smile back in place, "you ain't thinking of forking that grulla bronc and running out on us again."

"I don't aim to," Donovan said, his anger again elbowing aside his better judgment. "I'll be here if you're looking for me."

Vance shook his head. "You don't get it, Donovan. That wasn't a question. It was what you might call a statement. I said you ain't running from us again, not on that hoss."

He turned to Miller. "Do it, Hack."

The big man smiled and urged his horse through the livery door. Donovan watched Miller ride up to the stall where the grulla stood munching on hay. The gunman drew his Colt, extended the gun at arm's length, aiming just behind the horse's left ear, and pulled the trigger.

The little grulla's head jerked under the impact of the bullet, then he crashed to the floor of the stall, dead when he hit the ground, hay spilling from his mouth.

"Like I said, Donovan," Vance said after the roar of the shot had died away, "you ain't going nowhere. Not on that bronc, you ain't."

Hack Miller, laughing, rode past Donovan and it was then that the young gambler's patience snapped. Heedless of the danger he was facing, he reached up and grabbed Miller around the waist, yanking him from the saddle.

Miller, taken completely by surprise, thudded onto the dirt floor of the stable, slamming his head hard. Dazed, he struggled to rise and Donovan stepped in quickly, swinging a powerful kick to the gunman's face with the toe of his right boot.

Miller's nose burst apart, spraying a bright fountain of blood, and the gunman screamed and crashed onto his back.

Donovan heard the sound of pounding hooves to his left and he turned, clawing for his holstered Colt before a horse slammed into him, sending him sprawling.

Donovan lay stunned for a moment, then rose unsteadily to his feet, only to meet a tremendous straight right from the now dismounted Ike Vance. The punch exploded on Donovan's jaw and he reeled, arms cart-wheeling, three or four steps backward. His shoulders came up hard against a timber post supporting the roof and he steadied himself. Lights flashed like fire-crackers in his head and he could not focus.

Through a misty gray haze he saw Vance step toward him, a strange brightness in his eyes, and for the second time that day the realization crept into Donovan's dulled brain that this man was not only dangerous—he was insane.

Donovan quickly measured the distance between him and Vance and threw a looping left. Vance, a sea-soned street fighter who before now had killed men with his hands, easily brushed aside Donovan's fist and drove another right to his chin.

This time Donovan didn't stay on his feet. He crashed onto his back and lay there, still, struggling to avoid the deep pit of unconsciousness that suddenly opened up black before him.

A few moments later he felt strong hands grab his arms and he was hauled to his feet, spitting blood from a shattered mouth.

Vance's Texas gunmen pinned Donovan's arms to his side and Vance, grinning, drove a fist hard into his belly. Donovan gasped in pain and the gunmen let him fall. He landed face down on the dirt and retched un-controllably, the taste of green bile burning like vile acid in his mouth.

Somebody, probably Vance, laughed and kicked him again and again in the ribs and Donovan heard Nancy scream.

"Get that son of a bitch to his feet."

This time there was no mistaking the voice. It was Hack Miller.

"He's had enough, Hack," Vance said "We got to leave what's left of him to kill tonight."

"He broke my dose, Ike," Miller said, blood bubbling in his mashed nostrils.

"Yeah, well you can put the second bullet into him after mine. How's that set with you, Hack?"

Donovan moved slightly and saw Miller shake his head. "I want to break his dose, Ike."

Vance turned that over in his mind for a few moments, then said, "Well, I guess that's fine by me. But don't kill him, mind."

Again Donovan was dragged roughly to his feet. He caught a glimpse of Miller's crazed, bloodshot eyes as the man drew back a fist. A split second later hard, bony knuckles smashed into his nose and he felt the crunch of breaking bone, agony stabbing at him like a red-hot knife before darkness took him.

He woke to pain.

Nancy was bending over him but she was looking up fearfully at Ike Vance, who stood straddle-legged and arrogant a few feet away.

Donovan saw the big gunman mockingly touch a hand to his hat and it seemed like he was talking from the end of a long tunnel. "Well, until later then," he said. "I'll see you two lovebirds tonight, depend on it."

Donovan opened his smashed mouth to speak, but again darkness took him and he heard no more.

"Are you all right, Donovan?"

Donovan opened his eyes and saw Nancy's, pale, concerned face swimming above him.

"Yeah, I'm just peachy," he mumbled, the words coming thick through battered lips. He struggled to a sitting position, his head reeling. "Help me back to the hotel."

"You're all beat up, Donovan," Nancy said. "And your nose is broke."

Donovan raised a wary hand to his nose and touched it with his fingertips. It was swollen to twice its normal size and when he dropped his hand away his fingers came away bloody.

"Hack Miller did that, Donovan," Nancy said. She was trembling from fear and shock and her eyes were wide. "You broke his nose and then he broke yours."

Donovan nodded, a movement that made the pain in his nose flare. "I know who did it. I was here, remember?" He lifted his left arm. "Help me to my feet."

Donovan was almost a dead weight and Nancy had to struggle mightily to get him up, but after a few tries she succeeded and Donovan stood, swaying, the livery stable spinning around him.

"Young man, you better go see Doc Shafter. That beak of yours needs shoved back into shape." Donovan managed to get his eyes back in focus and saw Bearden, his head cocked to one side, studying him with much dislike and little sympathy. "Then you best see about dragging your dead hoss on out of here."

Two streams of blood from Donovan's nose trickled down his chin and he rubbed them away with an unsteady hand.

"Bearden, my horse was shot on your property," he said, breathing hard, his nostrils bubbling noisily. "That makes it your responsibility."

"The hell it does."

"And you owe me a hundred dollars for the loss of an animal while it was in your care."

"The hell I do."

Donovan let out an angry yelp from deep in his throat and his hand moved toward the Colt still holstered in his armpit.

Bearden, alarmed, threw up his arms. "Here, there's no cause for that. We don't need gunplay."

"Mister," Donovan said, "I've been roughly handled and I'm a mite tetchy. Like I told you, the horse is your problem."

Bearden thought that over quickly and said, "I'll have the horse dragged away. I reckon Frenchie the Bottle Fiend will eat it. But my responsibility for the animal ends right there."

Donovan was too far gone to argue. He nodded wearily, then turned to Nancy. "Help me back to the hotel."

Nancy put a supportive arm around Donovan's waist and they walked unsteadily toward the door of the stable.

Behind them Bearden groped around deep inside himself and found his uncertain courage. He called out loudly after them, "I'm making a full report of this to Sheriff Bullock. I won't be threatened with a gun in my place of business by a no-account gambler. Sheriff Bullock will not take kindly to a man being threatened . . ."

Donovan and Nancy stepped onto the rain-lashed boardwalk, Bearden's voice trailing into silence behind them.

"Donovan," Nancy said, "it seems to me we're making more and more enemies in Deadwood and mighty few friends."

"That thought," Donovan said, wincing against the pain in his nose and ribs, "had already occurred to me."

20

The desk clerk, a man with bushy black eyebrows that crawled halfway up his forehead like hairy, long-legged spiders, studied Nancy and Donovan closely as they walked into the hotel. He noted Donovan's smashed nose and puffed, cracked lips and his interest was roused.

"What happened to him?" he asked.

"Kicked by a horse," Nancy said, helping Donovan to the bottom of the stairs.

The clerk nodded. "They'll do it to you every time if they get half a chance."

The man gave Donovan one last, lingering look, then shrugged and went back to his newspaper, any momentary interest he had in the young gambler's plight gone as quickly as it had come.

Panting from the effort, Nancy got Donovan upstairs and into his room and, groaning in pain, he lay gratefully on the bed.

"I'm going for Doctor Shafter," Nancy said, looking

down at Donovan with concerned eyes. "He can fix your nose, Donovan, maybe."

Donovan shook his head. "You can't cross that street. You'll sink into the mud and never be seen again."

"There's no other way, Donovan."

Weakly, Donovan's hand moved to the pocket of his jeans. "Wait, I've got some money I think. Hire a ferryman to carry you across."

Tears sprang into the girl's eyes. "You're so good to me, Donovan."

But Donovan's hand came up empty. "I don't have any money."

Nancy laid tender fingertips on his shoulder. "Don't worry about it, Donovan. It's the thought that counts and the fact that you care about me so very much."

Donovan nodded, lying smoothly. "I sure do, a whole heap." But even as he said it, he realized just how hollow it sounded, and he waved a weak hand, hoping Nancy wouldn't eagerly latch on to the lie as she had an unsettling habit of doing. "Now, go get that damn Doc."

The girl stepped toward the door, hesitated a brief moment and then turned. "Donovan, when you get right down to it, we only have each other. It seems to me that nobody else in this whole wide world gives a damn about us."

Despite his pain, Donovan managed a slight smile. "Except for them as wants us dead."

Nancy thought this through, then said, "We'll make it. Won't we, Donovan?"

"Sure we will."

"We'll go to Tombstone together, won't we?"

"Sure enough."

The girl nodded, her eyes bright. "I'll go get the doctor."

After Nancy left, Donovan stared at the ceiling. The run-in with Vance and his gunmen convinced him it was time to face some home truths, unpleasant and hard to swallow though they might be.

Tonight, after he transplanted Wild Bill Hickok and got the other hundred dollars from Charlie he'd make tracks out of Deadwood before Ike Vance caught up to him. Maybe he could hop the Cheyenne stage or even steal a horse. But no matter how he did it, Nancy would only slow him down. Hell, she was a woman grown, she could fend for herself. As for destroying his reputation when word got around that he'd run out on her, well, he'd have to take his chances. Anyhow, those pimping Earp boys didn't seem the type to hold it against him.

His mind made up, Donovan closed his eyes.

He felt as though a great weight had been lifted from his shoulders.

Nancy returned with the doctor fifteen minutes later.

The girl was soaked to the skin and mud clung to her coat from the hem to her waist. Even her parasol was spattered with mud, and a blotch as big as a dime clung to her left cheek.

Doctor Shafter, used to the mud of Deadwood, seemed cleaner, though he'd crossed the same street as Nancy had.

The young physician sat on the edge of the bed and studied Donovan's nose for a few moments.

"Mmm," he said, "strange. This is the second one of these I've treated today, though my previous patient, having a much larger proboscis than you, presented more of a challenge."

The doctor opened his bag, took out a swab and alcohol and, with surprising gentleness, cleaned the dried blood from Donovan's nostrils.

"Now I'm going to perform what we doctors call a closed reduction," Shafter said. "And all that means is that I'm going to push the bones of your nose back to their original position." The physician smiled. "It will hurt, but then a man like you who goes around fighting Chinese pirates and saving wayward princesses won't care about that."

Donovan tried to force a smile but produced only a frightened grimace.

"How bad will it hurt, Doc?"

Shafter shrugged. "Let's find out, shall we?"

It hurt.

"Like hell, that's how it hurt, Doc," an outraged Donovan said after the procedure was completed, answering Shafter's solicitous question.

His face professionally sympathetic, the doctor nodded. "Yes, I thought so. I knew we were in considerable pain."

"Not we, Doc, me!"

The physician smiled and dug into his bag again, coming up with a roll of white surgical tape. "I'll use this and some bandage to stabilize the fracture," he said. "Luckily it was a quite straightforward break." He held up the tape. "This is zinc oxide tape and unfortunately it's been known to cause some minor skin irritation."

"I think," Donovan said, feeling sorry for himself, "a skin irritation is the least of my problems."

A few minutes later, Shafter completed his bandaging and stood. "Your ribs are bruised but not broken, so that's some good news." He looked down at his patient, his face thoughtful. "That must have been a vicious horse that kicked you, Mister Donovan. Horses like that are dangerous. I'd stay away from the brute in future." He hesitated, choosing his words. "I wouldn't want something considerably worse to happen to you."

"I plan to stay away, Doc," Donovan said, refusing to meet Nancy's eyes. "Believe me, I plan to."

"Right," Shafter said, snapping his bag shut. "That will be three dollars for today."

"We'll have to pay you later, doctor," Nancy said. "I mean, later today or tomorrow."

The doctor took it in stride, as though he'd heard this many times before. "Just stop by my surgery. I'm usually there unless I'm called out to a difficult birthing or a mine accident or something."

Shafter smiled. "The bandages can come off in a couple of weeks, Mister Donovan. In the meantime, just remember what I said about staying away from dangerous animals."

After the doctor left, Nancy said, "Donovan, do you think he knew?"

"Knew what?"

"About you and Ike Vance."

"Of course he knew. I bet the whole town knows by this time that Ike plans to kill me." Then, as an afterthought, "And you."

Donovan swung his legs over the side of the bed and rose painfully to his feet. He shuffled over to the dresser and what he saw in the mirror shocked him.

The taped bandage across his swollen nose covered most of his face, leaving only his mouth and eyes clear. Both eyes were swollen and black, mottled with angry yellow, and his lips were puffed and cracked.

"God," he whispered, "I look like the mill ends of hell."

Standing behind him, looking over his shoulder into the mirror, Nancy said, "It could be worse, Donovan. You could be dead. You came awful close to drawing on Ike back there at the livery barn."

"Well, there's one thing," Donovan said, pulling his eyes away from the terrible sight in the mirror, "If I had, it would be all over by now and I'd have nothing to worry about."

"You mean, you would have killed Ike and the other three?"

Donovan turned to face Nancy, irritation riding him hard. "Now, do you really think that's what would have happened?"

The girl dropped her eyes to the floor. "No, I guess not." Without looking up, she asked, "What are we going to do, Donovan?"

"Well, Ike told us to be in the street at seven tonight as the miners come in from the diggings. Only thing is, we won't be there."

"Where will we be, Donovan?"

"The one place Ike won't think of looking for us."

"Where's that, Donovan?"

"That fancy new Mount Moriah Cemetery where Charlie Utter wants to plant Wild Bill. Charlie says it's real nice up there, so we can hide out in the cemetery until it's time to go meet him."

The girl's eyes were frightened. "Ooh, I don't like cemeteries, Donovan."

The gambler shook his head. "Don't worry about it. The dead can't do you any harm. Only the living can do that."

"After that what are we going to do, Donovan?"

"Just before midnight we go see Charlie and then help him dig up Wild Bill."

"Donovan, when we get the money from Charlie, can we head for Tombstone? Can me and you—"

"Of course we can, both of us, sure as shootin'," Donovan said, cutting in quick.

Nancy raised Donovan's hand to her mouth and gently brushed it with her lips. "I trust you, Donovan. And you know why I trust you? Because you're the only person in all the world, in my whole life, that ever cared about me."

For a moment, Donovan was glad of the bandage that covered his face. The girl couldn't see the scarlet color that suddenly stained his cheeks—a vivid, shameful mark of Cain.

Mount Moriah Cemetery was carved out of a steep slope on the northern edge of Deadwood. The graveyard had only been in operation for a year but was already well occupied and prime grave sites were going for a premium price.

The rain showed no signs of ending, driven by a gusting wind that rattled the branches of the pines growing here and there throughout the cemetery, gleaming wetly on the new granite and marble headstones.

As Nancy and Donovan walked through the iron gates, the cold breeze sighed around them, tugging at their clothes, teasing them unmercifully as they made their way, heads bent, through the gathering gloom of the fading day.

"Where can we shelter, Donovan?" Nancy asked. "I don't see a place to shelter."

"We'll find a place," Donovan said, pretending a confidence he didn't feel. "There's got to be a place."

He was still weak from the beating he'd taken and he swayed wearily on his feet as he looked around at a bleak landscape of gravestones and wind-tossed pines.

"Over there," he said finally. "See where the tree overhangs that big tombstone with the angel on top? We can shelter there out of the wind."

"It isn't much, Donovan," Nancy said, her voice small and doubting.

"Well, it's all there is, so let's make the best of it."

They sat on the wet grass and huddled behind the tombstone, the final abode of the late Jeremiah T. Pearce, Warehouseman and Beloved Father, Sadly Missed, 1823–1877.

There was little shelter from the rain but the huge tombstone acted as a windbreak and they sat close together, backs to the cold marble, silent in their own world of rain-soaked misery.

"What time is it, Donovan?" Nancy asked after a while.

Donovan consulted the watch, the notes of "Beautiful Dreamer" oddly appropriate in a place where so many slumbered.

"It's almost five," he said, snapping the watch shut.

"I'm so cold, Donovan."

"Come closer," Donovan said. He unbuttoned his sheepskin coat and held the right side of it open and Nancy snuggled next to him, Donovan holding what little of the coat he could spare around her thin shoulders.

"Better?" he asked.

The girl nodded. "A little better." She looked up at him with eyes that revealed a growing adoration. "You're so good to me, Donovan."

The young gambler smiled. "Damn right I am."

They sat in silence for a few minutes, then Nancy

shivered and said, "Will this rain ever stop, Donovan?"

"Sometime. Maybe soon."

"It's a long time until midnight, Donovan."

"Not so long."

What Donovan knew and didn't say was that the long hours would pass very slowly, each building on the other, increasing their hardship. And the rain would keep falling, the wind would keep blowing and soon they might just melt away into the damp earth and join Jeremiah T. Pearce, Warehouseman and Beloved Father, in his narrow, clammy lodging.

But if by some miracle they survived, they had yet another hurdle to face. Ike Vance and his gunmen would be out, prowling Deadwood's Main Street, hunting them like animals.

The odds were slim and in his heart of hearts Donovan realized there might be no bucking them.

Slowly the light of day died around them, melting into thick darkness, and with the gloom of night the rain lessened to a determined drizzle that gusted in the wind and spattered Donovan and Nancy with huge, cold drops.

Beside him, Donovan felt the girl shiver uncontrollably and he did what he could to cover her with his coat.

Above them a bone white moon played hide-and-seek behind scudding black clouds rimmed with silver, and lower down the slope the oil lamps of Deadwood were being lit, glittering like fireflies in the darkness.

"Donovan," Nancy asked through chattering teeth, "what time is it?"

Donovan thumbed open the watch and tilted the face toward the thin moonlight. He squinted at the hands for a few moments and said, "Almost ten. We'll move out soon."

"I'm so cold," Nancy said, shivering. "And I'm so hungry."

"Maybe when we meet Charlie he'll have something to eat," Donovan said, offering a slender hope. "At least he might have hot coffee."

The girl was silent for a few moments and then said, "You know, Donovan, a couple of weeks from now, when we're in Tombstone, we'll look back on tonight and we'll laugh." Her eyes sought his in the darkness. "Won't we, Donovan?"

Donovan smiled. "Sure we'll laugh. We'll be sitting real pretty and by and by we'll get to recollecting and say, 'Hey, wasn't that funny, being up there in the cemetery in the rain?'" He nodded. "Yup, that's what we'll say, all right."

"Will you buy me another pretty new dress when we get to Tombstone, Donovan?"

"Hell, yes. I'll buy you three or four and maybe even five."

Nancy snuggled her head against his chest. "I can't wait to get to Tombstone. We'll be happy there, you and me, won't we, Donovan?"

"As cows in a field of belly-high clover."

Then, because he couldn't bear to lie to her any more: "Nancy, you sit there quiet as a mouse now. I've got some thinking to do. I have to study on things."

"About you and me in Tombstone, Donovan?"

"Yeah, that's right. About you and me in Tombstone."

Time passed and Nancy dozed on Donovan's shoulder, a slight smile on her lips.

Dream, little girl, Donovan thought, looking down at

her. *Dream on while you can and build all those shining, fairytale castles in the air.*

He felt hollow inside, empty of emotion. He wanted this thing over. He wanted Charlie's five double eagles in his pocket and the long road opening up in front of him, taking him back to what he once had been and could yet be again.

At eleven-thirty Nancy wakened to the chimes of the Berthoud of Paris watch and Donovan said, "It's time to go."

They rose, stiff from cold, and Donovan stamped his feet to get the circulation moving again.

Despite the rain, Deadwood was ablaze with light, bursting at the seams. A dozen pianos in a dozen saloons, each playing a different tune, competed for the ears of thousands of roaring miners and from the Gem Theater an entertainer billed only as Ol' Rubber Face did his city slicker meets country rube routine and had them rolling in the aisles.

The smell of frying meat and onions wafted up from a restaurant and Donovan's stomach growled as he took Nancy's arm and led her toward the gates of the cemetery.

Under the bandage, Donovan's broken nose throbbed and his ribs ached where Ike Vance had kicked him.

"We have to step light and keep our eyes open," he told the girl. "By now, Ike Vance and his boys will be looking all over for us."

"How will we avoid him, Donovan?" Nancy asked. "I'm really, really scared, Donovan."

"Just stick close to me and do as I do. There will be all kinds of people on the street and maybe we can pass unnoticed in the crowd."

Nancy hesitated a moment, then said, "It's real hard

not to notice that bandage on your nose, Donovan."
She looked up at the young gambler, studying him intently, frowning. "It really sticks out, if you know what I mean."

"There's always broken noses in Deadwood. Nobody's going to notice or even care."

"I hope so, Donovan."

"So do I, for both our sakes."

As Donovan had predicted, the boardwalks on both sides of Main Street were crowded. Bearded miners, thin Chinese laborers in pigtails and round hats, well-fed businessmen with their wives and here and there lanky punchers from the surrounding ranches, their spurs chiming as they walked, all competing for space.

Of Ike Vance and his gunmen there was no sign.

"So far, so good," Donovan whispered as he took Nancy's arm and pushed her along the boardwalk toward the edge of town.

The rain had finally stopped, but a steady wind blew through the Deadwood gorge, setting the flames of the oil lamps along the boardwalks to dancing, banging saloon doors that had been left open by careless patrons.

It was a drying wind and Donovan appreciated it, soaked as he was. But he had no way of knowing, at least then, that within the stiffening breeze lurked the seeds of future disaster.

Donovan saw Frenchie the Bottle Fiend, a clanking sack on his back, walk along the boardwalk on the opposite side of the street. The man stopped every now and then, his eyes searching the alleys, and occasionally he'd pounce on a bottle like a demented, scrawny chicken hawk.

The boardwalk ended at the general store and ahead lay the open ground of the tent city.

Donovan and Nancy stepped off the walk and squelched through mud toward the scattered rows of tents. A few were aglow with lamps, but most were dark, their owners in the saloons or theaters.

Charlie Utter's tent was one of the lighted ones, the canvas blushing yellow and then orange as an oil lamp flickered inside. A spring wagon stood outside the tent, hitched to a team of four oxen, the animals standing head-down, waiting with dull, bovine indifference for whatever was to happen next.

Two men stood near the wagon and Donovan recognized them as the husky youngsters who had served as unlikely high priests for Charlie's ritual bath.

As Donovan and Nancy drew nearer, the tent flap opened and Charlie, wearing a fringed buckskin coat, his Colts buckled around his waist, watched them suspiciously as they stepped closer.

"That's far enough," he said finally. "I don't allow a man to get closer than that in the dark unless he speaks his name."

"It's me, Zeke Donovan." Then as an afterthought: "And my dove."

"Step closer," Charlie said. "Let me get a look at you. And I'm pretty good with these here guns, mind."

Donovan and Nancy walked to the tent and Charlie took one startled look and yelled, "What the hell happened to you?"

"Horse kicked me," Donovan said, not wanting to go into it and maybe scare Charlie off.

"How did a horse kick you?"

"It's a long story."

"You must tell me about it sometime."

"Sometime, Charlie, but not tonight."

The little gambler studied Donovan and Nancy

closely, then said, "If you don't mind me saying so, you two look like hell."

"We got caught in the rain," Donovan said. He nodded toward the wagon, quickly changing the subject. "Is that for Bill?"

"Sure is. I decided to rent oxen because they'll keep on going through the mud long after a mule would give up." Charlie paused, thinking it through, then added, "Maybe that's on account of how mules are a sight smarter than oxen." After a few moments he waved a hand toward the animals. "Anyhow, an ox is a more solemn animal than a mule and this here is a mighty solemn occasion."

The cold wind gusted Nancy's coat against her legs and Charlie saw her shiver.

"Come inside," he said. "I don't want you two coming down with pneumonia before we even get Bill dug up."

Charlie turned to the two young men. "You boys head up to Mount Moriah and get that grave dug. I showed you where."

The younger of the two, a towhead with dull blue eyes, said, "Supposing we run into the sheriff?"

"What the hell would the sheriff be doing in a graveyard in the dead of night?" Charlie asked, hitching his gunbelt into place around his slim waist. "Right now ol' Seth's getting laid at Dirty Em's or he's lying drunk somewheres. Now, haul ass up there, Zebulon, and do like I told you."

"Well, we'll go, Mister Utter," the towhead said, his head hanging. "But if we run into somebody, we sure got some explainin' to do."

Charlie held the tent flap open for Nancy and called out to the two young men as they left, shovels in hand.

"Dig that grave deep, now. I want Bill lying full six feet under. He wouldn't have it no other way."

Charlie followed Donovan and Nancy into the tent, which was heated by a stove and felt warm and cozy, and he said, "With all the young men trying to strike it rich in the hills, good help is hard to find around here. Take Zebulon. Now, most times he's willing enough, but he isn't the sharpest knife in the drawer and neither is his brother Obadiah." Charlie shrugged. "But I guess we have to make the best of what we have."

He frowned as an unsettling thought struck him. "I sure hope they dig that hole deep enough. I don't want folks to say I skimped on Bill."

The little gambler turned his attention to Nancy, standing damp, cold and forlorn, her parasol in her hands, hair tumbling wetly over her face.

"Young lady," he said, "if you take off that muddy coat, I'll make an exception and allow you to sit on my bed."

Gratefully, the girl did as she was told and perched, somewhat uneasily, on the very edge of Charlie's immaculate cot.

Charlie studied her for a few moments, lost in thought, then said, "What I told you earlier about paying for a poke doesn't go no more. See, I'm always horny when I come out of my bath and this morning I got that particular itch scratched at Dirty Em's."

He smiled, trying taking the sting out of what he was about to say. "Now, when I look at you, I can see you just ain't my type. I mean, I like my women big up top and mighty broad in the beam and, hell, you're so skinny you could walk through a harp and not strike a note."

"As you wish, Mister Utter," Nancy said simply, her eyes downcast, the expression on her face unchanged.

It came to Donovan then as he looked at her that this girl had been used and abused by men for years and nothing they said or did could upset her any longer. In times like this her professionalism kicked in and she wore it like a suit of tarnished armor against all hurt.

Donovan felt a pang of sympathy, regretting it instantly. This was not a time for weakness he could ill afford. "Well," he said, sighing his impatience, "now we got all that settled, should we be about our business?"

"Not yet," Charlie said. "We have to haul Wild Bill clear through Deadwood so it's best we wait until Main Street has cleared out some."

"When will that be?" Donovan asked, his restlessness growing.

Charlie shrugged. "Oh, in a couple of hours from now. The miners have to rise early to get to the diggings so most don't linger much after two in the morning. Well, except them as is too drunk to walk and they won't notice."

A perceptive and essentially kindhearted man despite his brusque ways, Charlie looked at Nancy closely as he said, "Little lady, you look hungry enough to eat the stuffing out of a rag doll."

Nancy nodded, saying nothing.

"Thought so," Charlie said. "You?" he asked Donovan. Then, doubt clouding his face, "Hey, can you eat with that busted nose?"

"I don't eat through my nose, Charlie," Donovan replied, peeved.

Charlie shrugged. "Just wondered, with the breathing and all."

The little gambler unbuckled his guns and laid them carefully on the nightstand. He grabbed a coffeepot from the top of the stove and shoved it toward Donovan. "Take this down to the creek and fill 'er up."

"We don't need coffee," Donovan said, annoyed at being treated like a servant.

"I do," Charlie said.

"And so do I, Donovan," Nancy said, looking at him with brown, puppy dog eyes.

Donovan shook his head and took the pot. "It's dark out there. Suppose I fall into the damned creek?"

"Hell, we'll come and fish you out." Charlie shrugged, smiling without much humor. A couple of heartbeats of hesitation, then, "Maybe."

What he left out, but what was implied in that humorless smile and careless shrug, was the unspoken observation, "What's one broke, down-on-his-luck gambler, more or less?"

Donovan understood the implication perfectly and it stung.

21

As it happened, Donovan returned from the creek without incident and Charlie boiled coffee and made thick sandwiches of sourdough bread and bacon, frying the bacon perfectly and with great concentration as he did most things.

The sides of the tent flapped like a ship's sail as the wind blew harder and Charlie sat on the cot beside Nancy as he ate, Donovan standing head bent under the V of the canvas.

After they ate, Charlie wiped his mouth with the back of his hand and asked, "What time is it?"

Donovan consulted his watch. "It's almost one."

Charlie nodded. "We have time for a game."

A moment's hesitation, then Donovan said, "What stakes?"

Charlie shrugged. "What have you got?"

"Nothing."

"Then we'll play for fun. Draw set all right with you?"

Donovan nodded and Charlie dealt the cards on the

cot. Donovan picked up his hand. He kept his single ace of hearts and discarded the rest. Charlie kept three cards and then dealt Donovan four, adding two to his own hand.

"Right about now is the time to bet," Charlie said. "But on account of how you don't have any money"— he gave Donovan a puzzled, sidelong look—"despite the hundred dollars I gave you earlier, I guess I'll just have to see you."

"Ace high, over ten," Donovan said, throwing his cards on the cot.

"Three ladies." Charlie smiled, showing Donovan his hand. "My deal."

Donovan lost the next ten hands in a row, his only decent cards a pair of nines that Charlie blew away with an ace-high straight.

Finally Charlie brushed the cards together and expertly squared the deck, laying it on the table beside the cot. "This is too easy," he said. "I don't want to play another hand. You just ain't much of a challenge no more, Donovan."

"If we'd been playing for money things would have been different," Donovan said, his professional pride hurt. "Money makes all the difference."

"Maybe," Charlie acknowledged, his face serious, "but I doubt it. I always said you were a poor poker player, Donovan, but now your luck has deserted you, seemingly for good, well, maybe you should be looking into another line of work."

Anger flaring in him, Donovan snapped, "Luke Short doesn't think so. He always reckoned I could play poker with the best of them."

Charlie waved a dismissive hand. "Luke is always full of crap. He told me one time Doc Holliday was a great player but when it came right down to it between him and me in Dodge, all Doc would bet was nickels and dimes. Besides, he was drunk as a pig and a man shouldn't play poker when he's drunk as a pig."

"Doc is sick," Donovan said, not to defend Holliday but to disagree with Charlie.

"Yeah, I know," Charlie said. "A man who coughs up bits of his lungs into a handkerchief shouldn't be playing poker either." He looked at Donovan, trying to make himself appear wise. "Gambling is an unhealthy life and that's a natural fact. Too much whiskey, too many late hours, they can take their toll on a man."

"It hasn't done you much harm, Charlie," Donovan said grudgingly.

"That's because I watch my health. I have a bath every day, I don't smoke and I never drink when I'm at the gaming table. I tried to teach Wild Bill these things, but no matter how hard I tried, I never got through to him."

"And look what happened to Wild Bill," Nancy said, nodding, as if agreeing with herself that she'd said something profound.

"Exactly," Charlie said. "But when you come right down to it, there's nothing worse for a man's health than a bullet in the brain." He made a helpless gesture with his hands. "Not much he can do about that."

"Not much," Nancy said, still nodding.

This melancholy reference to the assassination of Wild Bill plunged Charlie into gloomy silence, but after a few moments he brightened and said, "It's time we was going. Let's get Bill buried proper where he'd want to be."

Charlie buckled on his guns and led Donovan and Nancy outside.

The wind had strengthened, blowing cold from the north, and Donovan had to go running for his hat after it blew off his head and went tumbling among the tents.

Charlie stood by the oxen, a bullwhacker's whip in his hand, as Donovan finally retrieved the hat and jammed it on his head.

His impatience betrayed by the way he tapped the coiled whip against his boot, Charlie greeted Donovan's return with a curt "Now the foot races are over, maybe we can get started?"

Donovan bit off his sharp reply and said only, "Ready when you are."

"Right. Let's go."

The working ox is a quiet, gentle, patient and sensible animal who readily bows his head to the yoke, itself no light or comfortable burden. The animals hitched to Charlie's wagon were in the prime of their working life, each being about seven years old and close to three thousand pounds in weight. In another year or so, they'd be fattened up even more and sold to a butcher.

Lately, in addition to stints as a trapper, hunter and prospector, Charlie had owned his own transportation business and had applied himself to learning the bullwhacker's trade. He showed considerable expertise as he uncoiled his whip, cracked it over the team and yelled, "Yahawoot!" the traditional old English command for "Go thither!" that was still occasionally heard in parts of the West in preference to the more familiar "Get up!"

But Charlie used the American bullwhacker's "Haw!" to turn left and "Gee!" to turn right, the orders reinforced with his constantly snaking bullwhip.

"See what I mean?" Charlie asked Donovan as he and Nancy walked beside the plodding oxen. "When

an even, steady movement is required, without jerks,
the ox is far superior to the mule or horse."

"Whatever you say, Charlie," Donovan replied,
tired and wishing fervently that he was anywhere but
here, about to roll along Deadwood's Main Street and
then into a cemetery to dig up a dead man.

Harsh gusts of wind rattled the panes in the windows of the buildings as they passed and Donovan
buttoned his sheepskin coat against its cold, exploring
fingers.

A drunk reeled out of Sammy McGuire's saloon and
stood on the boardwalk, blinking like an owl as the
wagon rolled past. "Hey, you!" he yelled to Charlie.

Charlie turned his head. "What do you want?"

The drunk waved a hand. "Aw, nothing."

The man spun on his heel, fingers probing in the
pocket of his dirty pants for coins, and stepped back
inside the saloon.

Donovan looked around him. Charlie had been
right about one thing. The street was pretty quiet, most
of the miners having sought their blankets against the
early morning rise of the coming workday. The saloons were still lit and smoking oil lamps smoldered
behind their steamed up windows, but the pianos had
fallen silent and about now the worn-out soiled doves
would be thinking about packing up and going home.

The wind had cleared the rain clouds and the moon
rode high, giving the night sky a dull silver sheen, and
just above the walls of the gorge Donovan saw a few
scattered stars glitter like holes in a tin roof.

The ox team plowed steadily through the mud of
the street and Donovan's pants were covered in black,
clinging ooze to the knees. Mud splashed Nancy's coat
as high as her waist and only Charlie, small and elegant in fringed coat and pants, a white shirt and a red

bandana at his throat, seemed unaffected by it. Mud thrown up by the churning wagon wheels hit him all right, it just didn't stick to him, a source of wonder to Donovan.

"Not far," Charlie said, sticking his whip under his arm as he hitched his gunbelt into place. "We're almost at Ingleside."

Donovan's head acted like it was on a swivel as he turned this way and that, his straining eyes searching for Ike Vance and his gunmen. But they were nowhere in sight and the wind mocked his fear, picking up a page from an old newspaper and blowing it, fluttering, along the empty boardwalk.

Beside him, one of the oxen snorted through its nose and shook its huge head, as a dim and random thought penetrated its dull brain. Or perhaps, speculated Donovan, the beast was sound asleep as it walked and had just woken up from a bad dream.

The stone gates of the cemetery emerged from the gloom and Charlie halted the team, the tired oxen shambling to a stop.

Charlie brushed a hand across his eyes and whispered, "I'm coming, Bill. Charlie's a-coming to take you home." He turned to Donovan and Nancy. "This is such a solemn and holy occasion I swear I'm already all used up."

Donovan, his impatience to be away from this place growing, said, "Charlie, let's get it done. Do you have the shovels?"

"In the wagon."

"Then what are we waiting for?"

Charlie nodded. "Yes, yes, no time to be wasted. Let's go get Bill."

He opened his mouth to yell the team into motion, then stopped as a thought suddenly struck him.

"Nancy," he said, "this ain't woman's work and I don't want you to get to hollering and calling out for your mama once we get to digging up ol' Bill and opening the coffin."

Nancy gave him a wan smile. "I've buried a man before."

Charlie nodded. "Just so you know and pay heed to what I just told you."

The girl nodded. "I will, Mister Utter. Have no fear on that score."

For his part, Charlie's reference to opening Bill's coffin took Donovan by surprise, but he let it go, figuring the little gambler had misspoken himself. Or had he? Donovan gave Charlie a hard look, but the man had already stepped beside the lead ox, his face revealing nothing.

"Yahawoot!" Charlie yelled and the team lurched into motion, plodding through the cemetery gates and into dark, windblown Ingleside.

Charlie led the team to the southern edge of the graveyard and stopped the oxen at a simple wooden marker. He got the lantern from the wagon and after a couple of tries succeeded in lighting it.

Moving closer to the marker, Charlie held up the lantern, yellow light splashing on the weathered, cracked timber.

Donovan peered over Charlie's shoulder and read the words, crude block capitals dabbed on with black paint.

A BRAVE MAN. THE VICTIM OF AN ASSASSIN
J.B. HICKOK (WILD BILL), AGED 39 YEARS
MURDERED BY JACK MCCALL
AUG. 2ND 1876

"I wrote them words my ownself three years ago," Charlie said, sniffing. "And I still reckon they're right pretty."

"Real nice," Donovan said. He glanced around at the pines tossing in the wind and the looming bulk of the huge boulders scattered throughout the cemetery. The moon looked down on them with cool indifference and an owl hooted from the branches of a spruce near the cemetery gate, questioning the wind about the identity of the intruders, asking over and over again, "Who? Who?"

Donovan shivered and he felt Nancy step closer to him, her cold hand sliding under the back of his coat. "Charlie," he said, "how deep is ol' Bill? Do you recollect?"

"Deep," Charlie replied. "Maybe all of six feet. Could be more."

"Hell," Donovan said bitterly, "that's a lot of digging."

"Can't be helped," Charlie said. "I wanted Bill planted deep so the coyotes couldn't get at him."

"Pity it never crossed your mind that you might dig him up again."

If Charlie took offense, he didn't show it. "I'd no way of knowing that they was going to build a whole new cemetery," he said, shrugging. "Things change. Nothing stays the same."

He stepped to the wagon and returned with a couple of shovels, handing one to Donovan. The lantern Charlie gave to Nancy, telling her to hold it close. Charlie spat on his hands, rubbed them together and nodded at Donovan. "Let's get to digging."

He raised his shovel and speared it into the soft dirt, then pushed the blade deeper with his right foot. He threw his spadeful of soil aside and delved into the ground again.

Donovan hadn't moved and Charlie leaned on the handle of his shovel and said, "My plan was the both of us would do the work."

"Sorry," Donovan said. "I was thinking."

"Thinking what?"

Donovan shrugged. "That this is no task for a gambling man."

"Well, if you want to make that other hundred dollars you best get started. Otherwise I'll dig up Bill my ownself and the deal is off. And Donovan, then there will be the matter of paying back the hundred I gave you this morning." Charlie's face hardened, the light from the lantern making shadows of his eyes. "That could become a shooting matter."

Donovan sighed and bit into the wet, dark ground with his shovel. It was going to be a long night.

22

After an hour of steady digging, Donovan's hands began to blister and blood stained the handle of his shovel. He straightened, getting the crick out of his back, and noted that the top of Bill's grave was almost level with the brim of his hat.

"Hell, Charlie, we must have gone six feet by this time and there's no sign of him," he said. "You sure Bill's here?"

"Sure I'm sure. Didn't I plant him my ownself? Maybe he's sunk some." Charlie wiped sweat from his forehead with the back of his hand. "Just dig a little deeper."

Donovan dug his shovel into the dirt again, his aching back and bleeding hands a constant reminder of just how heavy was the wet, reddish clay. He and Charlie, working awkwardly in the narrow confines of the grave, were constantly getting in each other's way.

Above them, on the edge of the pit, Nancy held the lantern aloft, its light staining the head and shoulders of the digging men with yellow while the muddy dirt under their feet remained in darkness. The spinning wind tossed the lantern this way and that, casting grotesque shadows over the grass around Nancy's feet and on the growing mound of dirt at the side of the grave.

Charlie bit his shovel into the soil and both he and Donovan heard the thud of metal hitting wood.

"We've reached it," Charlie said, making a strange little hop of delight. "We've reached ol' Bill at last."

"Donovan!" Nancy whispered, urgency edging her voice. "There's somebody coming!"

"Where the hell?" Charlie asked. He cocked his head to one side, looking up at the girl. "Where is he?"

"Listen," Nancy said, putting a finger to her lips.

All three of them heard it then, a man's voice carried by the wind, singing loudly, sounding a whole lot drunker than he should be at this time of the morning.

"He's coming this way," Nancy said. She bent and put the lantern at her feet. "Oh, he's sure to see us."

The voice came closer, the song louder.

> Goodbye, Old Paint, I'm a-leavin' Cheyenne.
> Goodbye, Old Paint, I'm a-leavin' Cheyenne.
> I'm leavin' Cheyenne. I'm off to Montan'.
> Goodbye, Old Paint, I'm leaving Cheyenne.

"Hell," Charlie said, scrambling out of the grave with amazing speed and agility, "it's a drover. He's got to be a puncher from one of the ranches around here. Ain't nobody else would sing that dumb song."

"What's a drunk doing in a cemetery?" Donovan asked, looking up at Charlie from the grave.

The gambler shook his head. "Who knows what a drunk does and why he does it."

"What are we going to do, Mister Utter?" Nancy

asked, her eyes wide and scared. "We could all get hung for being resurrectionists. That's what they call people who steal bodies from cemeteries and sell them to doctors. I was told about that one time by a traveling man who was in the profession and he said if a resurrectionist was caught, he always got hung."

"Well, first off," Charlie said, "we're not resurrectionists. We're what you might call relocaters of the dearly departed. And secondly, I'm going to get rid of that drunk before he sees too much."

"Oh," Nancy said, her voice shrill with agitation, "please don't shoot him, Mister Utter."

"We'll see," Charlie replied, and in the moonlight his face was grim and determined.

Donovan peered over the rim of the grave and saw a rider walk his horse toward them. The man swayed in the saddle, a bottle in his hand, singing about Old Paint at the top of his lungs.

The puncher, easily distinguishable as such in a wide-brimmed hat and Texas wing chaps, reined up his horse and looked in the direction of the grave, blinking like a lizard as he tried to get his eyes in focus.

"Wha . . . what's going on there?" the man asked, quavering and uncertain, the natural superstitious nature of the cowhand making him wary.

Charlie acted quickly.

He stooped, picked up the lantern and rushed toward the rider. Charlie waved the lantern above his head as he ran and hollered in a disembodied whoop, "Whoooo . . . whoooop . . ."

The cowhand reeled back in the saddle and even at a distance Donovan saw the man's face pale under his tan, his eyes wide and scared.

Now, had the rider been one of the town drunks or even a miner, Charlie's scheme might have worked perfectly. But this was a tough ranch hand who didn't wear a gun for show and there wasn't much back up in him—even in the face of a howling specter rising from the grave.

The puncher made up his mind real fast, went for his Colt and cut loose, slamming five quick shots in Charlie's direction.

Charlie yelped and dived for the ground, bullets kicking up fountains of dirt close around him.

The puncher let out a wild whoop of his own, waved his hat over his head and spurred his horse, riding hard toward the cemetery gate, chaps flapping.

Charlie rose to his feet, yelled, "Goddamned drunk!" and drew his own guns, thumbing round after round at the fleeing cowhand.

But the man reached the gates, galloped through them and was soon lost in the darkness, a last, derisive whoop reaching Charlie in the wind.

"Goddamned drunk drover," Charlie said again, holstering his Colts. "God, I hate drunk drovers."

He stepped to the edge of the grave and looked down at Donovan. "Did you see those chaps? He was a Texan. What the hell is a Texan doing all the way up here in the Dakota Territory annoying folks?"

Donovan shrugged, suddenly tired of the whole business. "I don't know." He leaned on his shovel. "We got maybe two hours left till daylight, Charlie. Let's do what we came here to do and get out of here before that Texan comes back with his friends."

Charlie jumped into the grave, scrambled for balance, didn't make it and ended up on all fours, his head between Donovan's knees. When he got to his feet again, his face was livid. "That damn puncher has completely spoiled it for me," he said. "He done destroyed the solemnity of the occasion."

Wordlessly, Donovan handed Charlie his shovel.

"I wonder what Bill is thinking right now?" Charlie asked, speaking to no one but himself. He tapped his shovel on the lid of the coffin. "Don't let that Texan get to you, Bill. Them Texans never corralled William in life and they sure as hell ain't going to do it to you in death."

"Dig," Donovan said, his voice weary. Above him Nancy held the lantern high and the wind rustled restlessly among the pines, as if urging them to be gone from this place.

It took Donovan and Charlie the best part of half an hour to clear the coffin of dirt and manhandle it to the edge of the grave.

Charlie stood in silence, gazing down at the rough pine casket. "I'm all choked up," he said. "Now Bill is so close, I just don't have the words."

"Let's get him in the wagon," Donovan said, more than ever determined to get it over with. Sweat had trickled under the bandage covering his throbbing nose and now an irritating itch added to his misery.

"Not yet," Charlie said. "I want to behold the brave and noble countenance one last time." He turned to Nancy. "Girl, bring that lantern closer and we'll gaze upon the face of Bill."

"Hold up a minute, Charlie," Donovan said, horrified. "He's been lying there for nigh on three years. He isn't going to be as sweet as a grandmother's kiss."

"Bring the lantern closer," Charlie ordered and Nancy did as she was told, holding it high above the coffin.

"Don't do this, Charlie," Donovan said, the hair on the back of his neck prickling.

But the little gambler ignored him and worked on the coffin lid with the edge of his shovel. The nails, badly rusted, squeaked out of the wet, porous wood and Charlie lifted the lid free.

"It's Bill," he said, his breath coming in short, excited gasps as he looked into the coffin. "It's Wild Bill as ever was."

Warily, Donovan peered over Charlie's shoulder. He started at the body for a few moments and was forced to admit that, despite his long interment, Wild Bill Hickok was in mint condition.

"He's crackerjack," Donovan said. "Like he was buried yesterday."

"Sleeping like a little, bitty baby," Charlie said, dashing tears from his eyes. "An' fresh as a daisy."

The black, broadcloth suit and frilled gambler's shirt Bill wore had begun to decompose, falling away in shreds from the body, but the salts and minerals in the soil had caused some form of petrifaction, hardening the skin to the consistency and color of marble. His thick hair fell over his shoulders in perfect blond ringlets and his mustache was trimmed and neat, the work of a fastidious undertaker. His eyes were closed, his long lashes lying over his cheekbones like fans.

Charlie stroked Bill's face with his forefinger, ruffling the edge of the drooping mustache. "He's turned all to stone," he whispered. "Bill has become a statue."

"Maybe we should just haul him to his feet and set him up in Main Street." Donovan smiled. "It would save us the trouble of planting him again."

Nancy, completely missing the irony, said, "You could put a nice plaque under him, Mister Utter, like they do with all those old Civil War generals."

Charlie rounded on both of them. "That's not funny," he snapped. "It seems everybody's determined to ruin this for me."

He turned to the coffin and again stroked Bill's petrified cheek. Soft and low he said, " 'Goodnight, sweet prince.' "

Charlie replaced the coffin lid and hammered in a few nails with the back of his shovel. "I will never gaze upon his sweet countenance again," he said. He turned to Donovan and Nancy, as though seeking confirmation. "That is so terribly sad."

"Sure it is," Donovan said. "Now he's all boxed up, let's get him loaded into the wagon and haul him up to Mount Moriah before daybreak."

The two men carried the coffin, which was heavy and slick with damp mud, to the wagon and after a struggle managed to get it loaded.

Charlie urged the ox team forward while Nancy led the way, holding the lantern aloft in one hand.

Donovan, like a mourner at a funeral, took up the rear, head bent as though in prayer and Charlie gave him a pleased nod of approval.

The things I have to do for a miserable hundred dollars, Donovan thought, hating Charlie, hating Wild Bill and above all hating himself. He was a man who had once bet five thousand dollars on the turn of a card, but those days seemed so distant it was as though they'd never been.

And, he suspected, bitterness rising in his throat like vomit, they may never be again.

The oxen trudged through the mud of Main Street, now almost deserted, except for a few late revelers who glanced at the wagon without interest, but for one man who stood on the edge of the boardwalk and watched them intently until Charlie swung the team toward Mount Moriah.

Ox wagons were a common sight in Deadwood and there was nothing about this one to suggest that the famed gunfighter Wild Bill Hickok lay stone-faced and slumbering under a tarp in the bed, though the drunk's interest made Donovan more than a little uneasy.

The wind was whipping up hard as Charlie urged the team through the gates of Mount Moriah. The pines tossed their heads in the harsh breeze and Nancy kept the lantern close to her, sheltering the flame.

Charlie led the team directly to the fresh grave his men had dug for Bill. The two youngsters, apparently uneasy about the legality of their task, had fled as soon as the hole was dug, leaving their shovels sticking in the pile of dirt beside the yawning opening.

Charlie brought two ropes from the wagon and handed one of them to Donovan.

"Now we'll lower that sweet soul into the grave and cover him up," he said. "After this night's work is done, Bill will rest content."

It was no easy task getting the coffin into the grave. For some reason, mostly because Donovan was stronger than Charlie, it kept descending at a steep angle, Bill's head lower than his feet. But after a struggle the two men succeeded in getting the coffin level and dropped it to the bottom of the narrow hole.

Charlie removed his hat and Donovan, wanting to please Charlie again now that the payment of his hundred dollars was close, did the same, both of them looking down at the coffin. "You want to say anything?" Charlie asked, the wind whipping strands of his long hair across his face.

Donovan shook his head. "I got nothing to say."

"Damn it, you should say something. Bill's lying down there all quiet and still, expecting a few kind words."

Rankled, Donovan said, "I told you I have nothing to say, Charlie. Hell, I didn't even know the man."

"That's mighty low," Charlie said, his eyes hard, hands close to his guns. "I might just decide to take exception to that."

Nancy, alarmed, stepped into the rapidly widening breach between the two men. She quickly reached into the pocket of Donovan's coat, took out the watch and thumbed open the case.

The notes of "Beautiful Dreamer" chimed above the sighing of the wind and Nancy raised her husky voice, singing along with the tune.

Charlie listened in silence, head bent, and when the song was over he wiped tears from his eyes and said, "That was right pretty, little lady. I know Bill appreciated that and no mistake."

"Let's get the beautiful dreamer covered up," Donovan said, abruptly taking the watch from Nancy.

"You still didn't say anything," Charlie said, steadfastly refusing to let it go.

Donovan had his Colt under his arm and he briefly entertained the notion of putting a bullet into Charlie Utter, a course of action he felt was maybe long overdue.

But Charlie was no bargain. He had killed his man in the past and there were some who said he was as fast as Hickok, if maybe just a tad more humble about his abilities.

Donovan quickly thought it through, weighing his chances, and decided against a shooting scrape. Besides, he had enough problems with Ike Vance and he didn't care to add Charlie to his list of gunfighting enemies.

Removing his plug hat, Donovan sighed, knowing there was no way out. He bowed his head and said in a loud, solemn voice, "Dear God, receive unto you the noble soul of Wild Bill Hickok, paladin of the plains, peerless prince of pistoleers. Ol' Bill was always kind to women, little kids and orphans and he hardly ever kicked a dog. He never shot anybody in the back either, unless they was asking for it. You're right, God, maybe he was too fond of whiskey and whores, but he never meant no harm, so don't hold it against him. He was shot by a coward when his back was turned but he bled out real quick and didn't feel no pain."

Donovan paused, mustering his thoughts, then continued, "These words are in memory of Wild Bill Hickok, loving father, sadly missed by all his true friends, including Colorado Charlie Utter." Donovan gave Charlie a sidelong glance. "Nuisance."

Charlie stood in silence for a few moments, looking down at the coffin, then he dashed away his tears and ran to Donovan, throwing his arms around his neck. "That was beautiful," he sobbed. "The most beautiful words I ever heard in all my born days."

He took a step backward, holding Donovan at arm's length. "You was just funning, wasn't you?" he asked, his eyes searching Donovan's bandaged face for an answer. "I mean, about not having any words to say about Bill?"

Donovan nodded, settling his hat back on his head. "Just funning, Charlie. That's all there was to it." He nodded toward the grave. "Now let's cover up that meek, modest and generous soul and let him rest."

Charlie Utter patted flat the last shovel full of dirt on Bill's grave, took a step back and nodded his approval.

"Donovan," he said, his face shining, "I plan to erect a marble monument for ol' Bill and put an iron fence around his grave so the wild sheep don't crap on top of him."

Donovan shook his head. "Charlie, there are no sheep in Deadwood, wild or otherwise."

The little gambler was irritated and it showed. "Well, wild cows then." He waved his hands. "Whatever." Charlie glared at Donovan, angry that he'd destroyed his moment. "You're sure a picky ranny. I always said that about you."

Nancy had missed this exchange. Her head was turned toward the gates of Mount Moriah, intently watching something.

"What's that?" she asked finally, in a voice so small it was almost a whisper.

Donovan followed the girl's eyes. A tiny point of red light bobbed toward them, flaring brighter every now and then as the wind gusted.

"It's a firefly," Charlie said. "It's got to be a firefly."

The breeze brought a scent of cigar smoke, an elusive whiff that lasted for a second and then was gone.

The red dot came closer and the three of them saw a man slowly emerge from the gloom, walking toward them with a long-legged, purposeful stride. A glowing stogie was clamped between the man's teeth and his long hair streamed wild.

"My God," Charlie gasped. "It's Wild Bill. He's come back to haunt us at last."

But as the man walked closer, Donovan made out the white bandage that covered his nose and most of his face.

"That's not Wild Bill," he said, his words rising alarmed and shrill. "That's Hack Miller. I think the drunk who was watching us must have given him the word we were here."

23

Donovan turned wildly. "Charlie, he's—"

The little gambler was gone. He'd faded into the darkness of the cemetery so completely it seemed like he'd fallen into a grave and pulled the opening in after him.

"He's skedaddled, Donovan," Nancy said. She stepped closer to Donovan, her face very white in the gloom. "I told you when the chips were down, we could only depend on each other."

Miller was much closer now, and Donovan yelled, "Let's talk, Hack." He spread his hands wide. "Hell, man, we can talk this thing through."

The gunman kept walking with no break in his stride, displaying not a moment's hesitation, the cigar smoking between his teeth.

"Real nice to see you again, Hack," Donovan tried, his desperation growing. He reached slowly for his Colt in the shoulder holster.

Miller made no reply. He was an experienced, professional revolver fighter and such men knew the difference between a time for talking and a time for doing.

Hack Miller knew this was a time for doing.

He stopped, took a moment to measure the distance between him and Donovan and using a practiced, lightning movement drew his gun and fired.

Donovan felt a sledgehammer blow to his side and he took a single step backward, triggering his Colt in Miller's direction. He missed.

Miller fired again, and this time Donovan fell, a bullet in his right leg. The gunman, tall and terrible in the darkness, kept coming, the cigar in his mouth glowing like a fearsome red eye.

Donovan, raised his Colt, holding it at arm's length and fired. Miller, grinning now around the stub of his cigar, stepped closer, then stopped again. Less than ten yards separated the gunman from Donovan, and Miller's mouth twisted into a sneer. "Your mama should have taught you how to shoot, boy."

His head swimming, wildly trying to focus, Donovan raised his short-barreled Colt. Hurt, supporting himself on his left elbow, he yelled his outraged anger, a series of loud, primitive shrieks without words. He fired, fired again and then again, the racketing roar of his shots echoing loud in the graveyard quiet.

He missed each time.

Miller raised his gun, smiling, the unwavering muzzle pointed at Donovan's head. He thumbed back the hammer, the oiled triple click a small, metallic voice of doom. "This is for the broken nose," he said. "And other things."

He didn't see it coming.

Nancy threw the lantern. It tumbled through the air and crashed into Miller's face. Charlie had filled the lamp to the brim and the coal oil splashed through the wick opening and over the bandage across the gun-man's nose.

Either Miller's cigar or the lantern flame, Nancy and Donovan would never determine which, set the bandage over his nose afire. Oil had also splashed over the man's chest and it too began to smolder.

Miller screamed and ripped the flaming bandage from his nose. But now the front of his bearskin coat was ablaze and he screamed again and again, beating at the flames.

Horrified, Donovan watched the shrieking gunman fast become a pillar of yellow and scarlet fire, the skin on his face already beginning to melt, bared teeth gleaming in a screeching, wide-open mouth. This was no way for a man to die, even a man like Hack Miller.

"No!" Donovan yelled. "Oh, God, no!"

The young gambler, determined to put the man out of his unspeakable agony, raised his Colt, sighting carefully with two hands on Miller's burning chest. He squeezed the trigger.

Click!

The gun was empty.

Miller, demented now as the ravenous fire de-voured him, turned and stumbled down the slope, arms cartwheeling, toward sleeping, unaware Dead-wood.

Despite the recent rain, the timbers that framed the buildings, especially the heavier beams under the roofs, had baked through three years of relentless sum-mer suns and were tinder dry. The strong wind that now swept through the gorge was also rapidly drying out the warped planks of the shacks, saloons, hotels and storefronts and on the slopes hundreds of dead, fallen trees stood ready to sacrifice themselves in any conflagration.

Fire was a constant hazard in the huddled, wooden towns of the West and Deadwood, its buildings jammed close together, shouldering each other for breathing space, was no exception.

Into this vulnerable and volatile tinderbox ran the screaming, blazing Hack Miller, the rounds in his shell belt exploding, sparking like firecrackers.

Miller staggered to a small frame and tarpaper shack at the bottom of the slope, tried to reach the door but fell at the base of the rear wall. Immediately the shack burst into flames and in the harsh glare of the fire Donovan saw Frenchie the Bottle Fiend run outside, hairy, skinny legs pumping under a nightshirt as he frantically dashed this way and that.

The fire spread quickly. Sparks from the burning shack jumped to the roof of the Montana and then the rod and gun store next to it. Soon both buildings were blazing and in the guttering light Donovan saw Frenchie scurrying here and there like a scared, frantic chicken.

Cartridges went off in the gun store with a sharp *Pop! Pop! Pop!*, flying lead whining off the board walls. Then the fire found the stacked barrels of gunpowder. With a tremendous roar, the roof of the store was lifted clean off, the blast leveling the walls, sending scorched and splintered timbers flying across the street.

Suddenly more buildings were alight. And then more and more. Deadwood was doomed, embraced by fire as destructive as an overly ardent lover, flickering tongues of flame licking at the dry timbers, crackling, smoking, destroying, blistering the paint on the store and saloon signs. The sky above the gorge shaded from dark gray to cherry red, barred by dozens of tall, slender columns of sooty black.

Nancy tore her eyes away from the nightmare

below, kneeled beside Donovan and asked, "How bad are you hurt?"

Donovan winced and opened his coat. Blood fanned upward from above his belt on the left side, soaking his shirt and the top of his pants. When he glanced at his right leg, he saw the thigh was also splashed with blood.

"I'm hurt bad, Nancy," he said. "I'm shot through and through."

The girl shook her head. "The bullet just grazed your side and your leg doesn't look too bad either. Lucky for you Hack Miller was shooting in the dark."

Donovan grabbed Nancy's wrist. "Nancy, tell me the truth. Am I going to die?"

"I told you, both bullets just grazed you, Donovan," Nancy said. "Quit being such a crybaby."

"You're not the one lying here all shot to pieces," Donovan said, annoyed that the girl was taking his wounds so lightly.

Nancy turned away from him and looked down the slope where flames were jumping from building to building, the wind surging down the gorge creating a roaring, crackling firestorm that was cartwheeling in a scarlet ball through the city.

There were thirty thousand people in Deadwood that morning and it seemed most of them were already fleeing their burning town. Wagons, buggies, horses and men and women on foot, many of them carrying what few possessions they could salvage on their backs, jammed Main Street, a jostling, frightened tide of humanity, their faces carved from black soot and smoke, only their terrified eyes showing white.

Here and there a man fell, to be trampled underfoot into the bottomless mud, never to rise again. A miner, his entire back on fire, ran from a blazing saloon and dived headlong into the black ooze. Nancy did not see him get up.

Like a huge, undulating serpent, the refugees of Deadwood fled their doomed city and poured across the open ground of tent town. Gray and black ash and glowing sparks rained on them like a hailstorm in hell and from somewhere, loud above the roar of the fire, a woman screamed, screamed again and then fell silent.

Horrified, the glare of the flames touching her forehead and cheeks with red, Nancy turned back to Donovan and asked, "What are we going to do?"

Donovan glanced down the slope to where Bearden's livery stable still stood untouched by the fire.

"We're going down there and get us a horse," he said. "Then we're getting out of here."

"Can you make it, Donovan?" Nancy asked. She was frightened and it showed in the way she tightly clutched her tattered parasol to her breast.

"Like I told you, I'm all shot to pieces," Donovan gritted between his teeth. "But I guess I have to make it. If we stay up here we'll die." He held out a hand to Nancy. "Help me to my feet."

With the girl's assistance, Donovan rose and was surprised that neither of his wounds hurt real bad. But he felt weak and light-headed and his broken nose throbbed.

"I just can't believe it," he said.

"Believe what, Donovan?"

"That Charlie Utter ran away when Hack Miller appeared."

Nancy put her arm around his waist, supporting him. "Donovan, the only person you can depend on is me, and the only person I can depend on is you. Nobody else gives a damn about either of us, including Charlie Utter." She gently took his cheek and turned his head so he was looking at her. "People want to be happy, Donovan. They don't want you to keep serving them your pain, or mine."

She held up her hand with its bandaged stump of finger. "Even with this, I'm so small, most times they don't even see me."

Donovan nodded. "There's something in what you say, Nancy. Words a man should think about, I guess."

Helped by Nancy, Donovan unhitched the oxen from the wagon. Now they'd have to fend for themselves, like everything and everyone else in Deadwood.

Donovan and his dove made their way to the cemetery gate and then slowly down the hill to the livery stable. And around them Deadwood blazed, columns of smoke rising into the scarlet sky like the sooty souls of the damned.

Of Bearden there was no sign. The man had presumably fled, leaving behind his horses in their stalls. Perhaps he'd meant to return but the fire had caught and trapped him somewhere.

Between them, Nancy and Donovan led the six horses in the barn outside and turned them loose, all except a tall, rangy palouse gelding with black spots on his rump and the look of the racer about him.

Donovan, wincing now and then against the pain in his side and the throbbing in his nose, saddled the animal and led him outside.

People streamed past the livery stable not sparing them a glance, but one burly miner noticed the saddled horse, stepped out of the crowd and stomped toward Donovan.

"That's what I need, "the man said in a strong Irish brogue. He waved a hand at Donovan. "Now, if you'll kindly step aside I'll be taking that horse."

Donovan shook his head. "I need this animal. There are others around."

The miner was huge. He had wide muscular shoulders, and strong hairy hands, the knuckles scarred, hung loose and ready from the dirty sleeves of his vest. His forearms bulged, massive from heavy manual labor with pick and shovel, and his determined eyes revealed that there was no give in him. The man scowled and waved his hand a second time. "Stand aside, I say, or it's myself will be breaking your jaw as a match to your nose."

Donovan shrugged. He handed the miner the reins of the palouse and stepped aside. The man gave Donovan a triumphant little grin, then turned away from him, placing a hand on the saddle horn and a booted foot in the stirrup as he prepared to mount.

Quickly, Donovan stepped close, drew his Colt and slammed the barrel down hard on the back of the miner's head. The man collapsed without a sound, ending up between the legs of the scared, prancing horse.

"It's myself will be breaking your head," Donovan said, mimicking the miner's accent. He turned to Nancy. "Let's go before he wakes up."

"That's about what I'd expect from a low-down, no-good skunk like you. Buffalo a ranny while his back is turned."

The voice, low, flat and hard came from the corner of the stable. A man walked toward Donovan, grim and terrible, framed by the flaming city behind him. It was Ike Vance and he was primed for a killing.

He'd tried it with Hack Miller and failed, now Donovan tried it one more time on Vance.

"Ike," he said, backing up as the gunman walked toward him, "we can talk about this." Then, keenly

aware that his Colt was empty, added without much
real hope, "I'm sure you'll agree that we don't need
gunplay here. Let's settle it between gentlemen."

"Too late," Vance said, "and damn ye for a scoundrel
and no gentleman. I told you not to wear that watch."
The man's handsome face broke into a brutal grin. "We
end the thing right now."

Vance went for his gun. And several things happened very quickly.

The gunman fired and Donovan felt a bullet slam
into his chest, low on the right side. He staggered back
a few steps and fell, his back slamming against the
wall of the barn. Donovan rose quickly and lurched
behind a low pile of stacked lumber, grateful for its
cover.

He raised his head and saw Vance steady himself
for another shot, his Colt extended at arm's length. He
fired again. But the dazed miner, who had struggled to
his feet, stumbled into Vance's line of fire. The bullet
crashed into the man's belly and he yelled once and
went down.

Cursing, Vance thumbed back the hammer of his
Colt. From somewhere close, Donovan heard a rifle
roar and he saw a fountain of mud kick up at Vance's
feet. The rifle fired again and this time Vance winced
and spun around, bending over as the bullet burned
across the heavy meat of his left bicep.

Vance straightened, steadied himself, and fired at
the hidden rifleman, missed and fired again. Nancy
was standing close by and Vance stepped toward her
very fast. He grabbed the girl, holding her in front of
him. Using Nancy as a human shield, Vance caught up
the reins of the palouse and led the horse toward the
street where hundreds of people were still streaming
past, oblivious to the gunfight, heedless of everything

but their own all-consuming fear and the desire to get as far away from Deadwood as possible.

There were no more shots from the side of the barn. Donovan surmised that the rifleman, unsure of his aim in the flickering glare of the fire, did not want to shoot and miss and hit Nancy or the innocent people behind her.

On the other hand, it seemed Vance wanted out of there. He was caught in the open, being shot at by a well-concealed rifleman, and he knew the odds were against him.

Vance grabbed Nancy by the arm and roughly shoved her into the saddle. He mounted behind her, throwing one last glance of demonic hatred at Donovan as he savagely raked his spurs across the horse's belly. The big animal reared, fighting the bit, then galloped forward and crashed into the crowd, scattering cursing men and screaming women right and left.

An enraged miner reached up, trying to pull Vance from the saddle. The gunman lowered his Colt and shot into the man's face and the miner fell, his features a sudden, scarlet mask.

A moment later Vance was through the crowd and gone, firing his gun into the air, a demonstration of futile anger and a warning, as he galloped away.

Footsteps sounded, coming closer, and Donovan wearily turned his head and saw Charlie Utter walking toward him, leading a horse, a Winchester rifle hanging from his right hand.

Charlie grinned and said: "Boy, Donovan, you cut it close. I thought ol' Ike had you for sure that time. Lucky I was around."

"He could have run over here and finished me off," Donovan said, his face puzzled. "Why didn't he finish it?"

Charlie kneeled beside Donovan. "Because Ike is a gambler. He knew I was ready with the rifle and he didn't like the hand he was being dealt. He folded, knowing he'd play another day when he held all the aces."

"He took Nancy," Donovan said, his mouth dry.

"Uh-huh. Figures you'll go after him to get her back. Then he'll finish it for sure." Charlie grinned. "'Course what he doesn't know is that you won't. You ain't gonna risk your life for no nine-fingered, brown-eyed whore, and a right homely one at that."

Donovan shook his head. "You got that right. I've had enough of whores to last me a lifetime." He looked hard at Charlie. "How bad am I hit?"

Moving Donovan's sheepskin aside with the muzzle of his rifle, Charlie glanced at the bullet wound in his chest. "It's bad. But maybe I can save you." He shrugged. "Or maybe not. It kinda depends on my doctoring."

Charlie looked up at the blazing city, the flames reflecting in his blue eyes. "We got to ride, me and you. The fire will reach this far pretty soon."

"Why are you helping me?" Donovan asked, his voice thin and weak. "Figure you owe me something?"

"I figure I don't owe you a damn thing except maybe a hundred dollars. But since I'm leaving for a cabin I own on the Two-Bit, I reckon I might as well take you along."

Donovan caught Charlie's arm. "Why did you run away up there at the cemetery when Hack Miller showed up? That was low down."

Charlie grinned, cheerful and unrepentant. "Hell, like Vance just a minute ago, I didn't like the odds. I wasn't about to stand toe-to-toe with Hack Miller in a standup gunfight. Besides, I didn't have the drop on

Hack like I had with ol' Ike." Charlie laughed and slapped his thigh. "Hell, did you see his face? Ike didn't know his ass from his elbow, on account of how he couldn't figure where the shots were coming from."

Rising to his feet, Charlie looked at the blazing city. "Deadwood's done for," he said, shaking his head, "and it ain't never coming back."

"I wonder what happened to Frenchie the Bottle Fiend?" Donovan asked, fighting to retain his consciousness.

From a long distance away he heard Charlie say, "Who the hell knows?" Then he heard nothing more.

24

Zeke Donovan woke to sunlight.

The angling yellow rays streaming through the window of the cabin were surrounded by a bright opalescence that stained the rough pine log walls and sod roof with a pearl white light.

Donovan closed his eyes, opened them again. All was still the same. Realization slowly dawned on him that the light was caused by snow outside. How long had he been out?

He tried to sit up but was stopped cold by the sudden pain in his chest. He pulled back the blanket and looked at himself. He was naked except for a white bandage that covered most of his upper body. His thigh where it had been plowed by Miller's bullet looked angry and red, but it showed no sign of infection. Donovan gritted his teeth against the pain and struggled to a sitting position.

He lay in a bunk in a narrow cabin that felt snug and warm. There was a stove against the other wall and it glowed a dull red and smelled of burning pine.

A table and a couple of benches made up the rest of the furniture, except for some blankets and a pillow on the floor. The blankets were clean and carefully folded and the pillow had been fluffed and placed neatly on top of them.

The cabin had been swept clean of dust and cobwebs and the rough wood floor had been polished with wax.

An open cupboard beside the stove held neatly arranged cans of beans, peaches, vegetables and coffee, and the coffeepot itself stood on top of the stove where it would keep warm.

Donovan's Colt, in its shoulder holster, hung on a chair beside him with his washed and folded underwear, socks, shirt and jeans. His sheepskin coat hung on a nail behind the door with his hat, and his boots, cleaned of mud and buffed with a cloth, stood in a corner.

Donovan pulled the Colt and spun the cylinder. Charlie had loaded five chambers, leaving the one under the hammer empty as was the custom in the West, that being the safest way to carry a single-action revolver.

The door swung open and Donovan swung the Colt in its direction. Charlie, the wool collar of his canvas mackinaw turned up, stepped inside carrying an armful of firewood.

"That's a hell of a way to greet a man," he said, motioning with his head toward the gun. "Especially a man who saved your life."

"Sorry," Donovan said, reholstering the Colt. "I'm a mite jumpy."

Charlie laid the wood beside the stove, straightened and said, "Hungry?"

"Some."

"I bet you're more than some."

"Okay, more than some." Donovan studied Charlie's face for a few moments, then asked: "How long have I been out?"

"Out of your head or just plain out?"

Donovan sighed. "Both."

"Four days. You stopped raving two nights ago. And that's just as well, because I was getting so little sleep I seriously considered putting a bullet into you."

"I'm glad you didn't study on it too deep." Donovan paused, then said, "So I was raving. What was I raving about?"

"Well," Charlie said, pulling a frying pan closer to him across the stove, "you was took with fever, mind."

"But what was I raving about? I must have been raving about something."

"Ike Vance. Some about him. Luke Short, too, and something about Denver and poker. But mostly it was about Nancy."

"Nancy? You mean my dove, Nancy?"

Charlie looked exasperated. "Now, who the hell else do you know called Nancy?"

"Strange," Donovan said, shaking his head in wonder. He looked at Charlie, who was slicing bacon into the pan. "What did I say?"

"What does a man say when he's out of his head?" Charlie shrugged. "I don't know. It was all nonsense. Something about saddling up and going after her." He smiled. "That kinda shows just how far gone you was."

"Maybe. Maybe not. I think maybe I will go after her."

The bacon was sizzling and smoking and Charlie shook the pan to allow the slices to brown evenly. He waved a negligent hand, dismissing the girl entirely. "Ah, forget it. She's only a whore."

Donovan took some time to absorb that, then he said, "Nancy says her and me, we only have each other and that nobody else gives a damn about us. Maybe she's right."

"Hell, man, I cut that bullet out of you and saved your life," Charlie said. He shook his head. "People give a damn."

"I guess I should thank you," Donovan said. "And you're right. You didn't have to do that."

"Damn right, I'm right." He turned to Donovan, grinning. "But you're lucky Deadwood is mostly gone and I'd nothing else to do, especially since Dirty Em's place burned down. I guess you could say I took you on as a project." He shook the pan again. "They're rebuilding it, by the way. The merchants and the saloon owners are already hauling in timber all the way from Cheyenne and they say Deadwood is going to be bigger and better than before."

Satisfied that the bacon was done, Charlie cracked eggs into the pan and then dropped in two thick slices of sourdough bread.

"When can I ride, Charlie?" Donovan asked.

"Never," Charlie replied, getting two blue plates from the cupboard. "On account of how you ain't got no horse."

"I can borrow yours."

"No, you can't." Charlie handed Donovan a filled plate and a fork. "Me, I got to head back to Deadwood and stand guard at Mount Moriah. Folks are in a peculiar frame of mind right now, a might testy, and I don't want them digging up Bill again in a fit of spite."

Talking around a mouthful of bacon, Donovan said, "Then I'll head out on foot."

"Head out where?"

"After Nancy."

"Hell, Donovan, she's only a whore."

"I know. But"—Donovan hesitated—"I think maybe I love her. At least some."

Charlie shook his head, his eyes puzzled. "You don't just fall in love with a whore right quick. It doesn't happen that way."

"It wasn't right quick. I didn't fall in love with her fast. I think it was in me all along and I just realized it that night up at the cemetery. And maybe before. I don't know."

"Does she love you?"

"Don't know that either."

Charlie chewed his eggs, casting around for a comment, found none, then compromised by throwing an obstacle in Donovan's path. "It snowed last night. The rain turned to sleet and then to snow. Must be four, five inches on the ground."

Donovan nodded. "Figured that. By the light."

"Man can't go far in the snow on foot, especially if his nose is broke."

"No, he can't," Donovan agreed, letting it go at that.

"You ain't got no horse."

"You already done told me that, Charlie."

Charlie nodded. "Just so you know." He took Donovan's empty plate and sighed long and loud, a man who realizes nothing he can say or do will change the course of history. "Ike's bullet went right through your chest and lodged in the skin of your back. I cut it free and as far as I can tell, it didn't hit any of your vitals." He stood and looked down at Donovan, a smile in his eyes that didn't engage his mouth. "You're young and healthy. I'd say now your fever's broke, you can head out tomorrow or maybe the day after. But all you'll be fit to do is ride a stage, nothing more."

Donovan nodded. "Maybe so, but I'm going after her."

"Then you're a fool."

"I know that."

"Hell, you don't even know where ol' Ike is holed up. And he still might have Clint and Les Fairchild with him. I hear tell they was going around saying they planned to kill you on account of what you did to their brother." Charlie shook his head as though baffled by Donovan's foolishness. "Clint and Les are both top gun hands and they're no bargain."

"I'm going after Nancy," Donovan said. "Charlie, she's got nobody else in the world besides me."

"She's got Ike. She could go back to whoring."

"After Ike kills me, he'll kill Nancy. He doesn't want witnesses left."

"Ha!" Charlie exclaimed. "There, you just said it. You said, 'After Ike kills me,' and that means you don't give a hill of beans for your chances."

Donovan smiled. "I don't. But I'm sure as hell going to try."

Charlie Utter shook his head. "It's your funeral." He hesitated, then said, "Zeke, listen to me. Don't take to believing your own legend. That man folks talk about, the one who rescued the princess from the Chinee pirates, well, he ain't you. He's a braver, better man than you'll ever be, so don't even try to become him. You'll fall way short."

Charlie reached into the pocket of his pants, brought out a handful of coins and thumbed five double eagles onto the top of Donovan's blanket. "Be true to yourself. Use that money. Get on a stage, go to Cheyenne and forget the dove." He smiled, trying to take the barb out of it. "Hell, boy, you just don't shape up to be the heroic type."

Later that morning Donovan rose and dressed. He was weak from loss of blood and unsteady on his feet and the wound in his chest pained him when he breathed.

A small, steel mirror hung on the wall by the stove and Donovan stepped up to it. He looked like hell.

Charlie had changed the bandage over his nose, but lacking surgical tape, he'd tied it around the back of Donovan's head. Above the bandage, both the young gambler's eyes were black and swollen, yellowing at the edges, and his uncombed hair was wild.

Carefully, Donovan untied the bandage and eased it away from his broken nose. The nose itself was twice its normal size and dried blood crusted both nostrils. Beard stubble lay heavy on his cheeks and his mustache was ragged and untrimmed.

Donovan looked around and saw what he was looking for. Charlie's razor, hairbrush and comb lay on a small shelf near the cot. The brush was immaculate, free of even the tiniest strand of hair, and Donovan figured that if he used it, Charlie might consider it sacrilege and a shooting matter.

He compromised and used the comb to get his hair back in place, then stepped outside, the razor in his hand. A barrel of water stood near the wall of the cabin and there was a mirror, a bar of lye soap and a roller towel.

Donovan shaved with ice cold water, carefully washed his battered face, then brushed his teeth with his finger. He glanced in the mirror and considered he looked at least vaguely human.

"You look almost human again," Charlie said, echoing his own thoughts as he stepped beside him.

It was very cold, and to the east the entire rugged peak of Dome Mountain was covered in snow. The cabin was surrounded by low, undulating hills, yellow and scarlet aspen on the lower slopes, spruce and lodgepole pine growing higher.

The morning sun glittered on the snow and jays quarreled noisily among the branches of a pine near the cabin, sending down a shower of green, brown-tipped needles.

His breath smoking in the frigid air, Donovan nodded toward the cabin. "How come you own this?" he asked.

Charlie shrugged. "I took to liking cabins quite a spell back. I have them all over the place. Got one in Colorado, Montana and Texas and I'm looking to buy another down to the Arizona Territory."

Then, in a calm, conversational tone, he added, "Rider coming."

Donovan followed Charlie's eyes and saw a man on a mule loping toward them. The man led a horse and when he got closer, Donovan recognized the big palouse Ike Vance had taken from him.

"Is it Ike?" Donovan asked, feeling naked without his gun.

Charlie shook his head. "I don't think so. Ike would never ride a mule and besides, that man is way too small." He rubbed his chin, thinking, then said, "Still, I'm going to get my rifle."

Charlie stepped out of the cabin again, Winchester in hand, just as the man reined up outside the door.

It was Frenchie the Bottle Fiend. He looked like a scorched rabbit but his face was creased in a smile.

"Howdy, Frenchie," Charlie said. "How's the bottle business?"

Frenchie shrugged and spread his hands. "Alas, all was lost in the great fire." The palouse tossed his head, bit jangling, and Frenchie jerked on the rope. "He is wild, this one," he said. "Hard to ride."

The little Frenchman sat his mule, looking at the two men, and Charlie didn't question him further, figuring he'd soon get to what he'd come to say.

"Deadwood is being rebuilt," Frenchie said, picking up on the story of his personal tragedy, "and soon the miners will start drinking again." He smiled, tapping the side of his head with his forefinger. "Frenchie, he ees smart, he knows there will be even more bottles than before."

"Well," Charlie said, "I'm right glad to hear that. You're the best bottle man in the territory and no mistake."

Frenchie gave a little bow from the saddle. "I know that. But it's always nice to hear it from someone else."

Charlie was content to let the man talk himself out, but Donovan was feeling the cold out here in the open and he wanted Frenchie to come to the point. "What brings you all the way out here, Frenchie?" he asked. "And where did you get that spotted horse?"

"Ah," the little man said, "I am here because I have a message for you, Mister Donovan."

Donovan turned to Charlie. "It can only be from Ike Vance."

"Precisely!" Frenchie said. "You are, 'ow you say, very perceptive."

"Frenchie, I saw Ike Vance ride away from Deadwood on that horse," Donovan said. "It didn't take much figuring."

"What's Ike's message?" Charlie asked, suddenly all business now that Donovan had led the way.

"Right, now to the point. Mister Donovan, Mister Vance told me to give you this horse. He said you are to ride him to the . . . ah, let me remember . . . oh yes, ride him to the southern slope of Bear Den Mountain where it meets the bend of Strawberry Creek. He says he will meet you there tomorrow at noon." Frenchie's face screwed up in thought. "Oh yes, there was one thing more. He said to make sure you bring a gun and that you should wear your watch."

The Frenchman shrugged. "A strange message, but he gave me five dollars to deliver it."

"Where's Ike now?" Charlie asked.

Frenchie shrugged again. "I met him in the fair city of Lead, but that was early this morning. Who knows where Mister Vance goes."

"Did he have Nancy with him?" Donovan asked.

"The not very pretty girl you brought to my cabin? Yes, she was with heem."

"How was she?"

"Laughing."

"Laughing?"

Frenchie spread his hands. "Mister Vance said something and she laughed." He shrugged. "That's all I know."

Charlie fished in his pocket, came up with a silver dollar and spun it to Frenchie. The little man caught the coin expertly and Charlie said, "You best be going now, Frenchie. We got things to do around here."

"As you wish," Frenchie said. He extended the rope toward Donovan. "Your horse."

Donovan took the rope and Frenchie said, snapping his fingers. "Oh, there was one more thing. Mister Vance, he said he'll be alone and that you should be alone too, Mister Donovan. He said if he sees more than one rider coming toward the creek at Bear Den he'll cut the girl's throat."

Charlie shook his head. "Frenchie, you sure have a happy knack of leaving the most important stuff to the last."

25

That night after supper Charlie lit his pipe and studied Donovan across the table. He sat for a few minutes, then broke his silence.

"You still plan on going through with this?"

"That's what I have in mind."

Charlie nodded. "Thought so." He took the pipe from his mouth and thoughtfully studied the glowing coal in the bowl. "You're no match for Ike Vance, you know. He's good, real good and he'll kill you for sure."

"I'll have to take my chances," Donovan said, trying to sound defiant even as he felt his confidence slip. "He tried back at Deadwood and didn't kill me." Donovan smiled, a grimace that added no light to his eyes. "I'm right hard to kill, Charlie."

"Ike's shooting was off because I was taking potshots at him," Charlie said, his face wreathed in smoke. "If I hadn't been there you'd be dead."

He shook his head. "Hell, you're in no condition to ride. You've been shot through and through and your damn nose is broke."

"I'm going after Nancy and I'm wearing Ike's watch," Donovan said, banging his fist on the table. "I want this thing over. I can't go on living like this, always looking over my shoulder, wondering if this time Ike Vance will be standing there." He paused, his eyes searching Charlie's face. "You have to understand. I feel I owe Nancy this much. She's got nobody else but me. And besides, like I told you this morning, I think I love her."

"You pay a whore for a poke. You don't fall in love with a whore."

"I did. I didn't even see it coming, but suddenly I realized I did."

Charlie sighed, sensing the futility of further argument. "I'm playing solitaire with a deck of fifty-one, ain't I? I keep talking and talking but you don't hear a word I'm saying."

"You're right, Charlie, so save your breath. Like you said, you're just hollering down a rain barrel."

Charlie's pipe had gone out and he laid it on the table in front of him.

"What will I tell your friend Luke Short when I see him?"

"About what?"

"About you being gunned down by Ike Vance."

Donovan shrugged. "Tell him I died game. That's something Luke will understand."

Donovan saddled the palouse just after sunup the next morning. His breath smoked in the air and flurries of snow tossed around in a wind blowing long and cold across the Black Hills from Canada. Around him the aspen trembled and the dark green arrowheads of spruce showed a frosting of white on their lower branches.

A jackrabbit bounded across the snow toward Donovan, then stopped, kicking up little spurts of snow. He sat for a few moments, nose quivering, head turned, watching the man, then ran back the way he'd come. Looking up, taking pleasure in each passing moment, Donovan watched a hawk slide across the pale, rose-tinted sky and vanish behind the crest of a hill.

Charlie came toward him, leading his horse. He stopped and nodded, drinking from the steaming cup of coffee in his hand.

"One last time, Donovan," he said. "Ride with me into Deadwood and help me mount guard over Bill's grave. After that, maybe we can both head for Cheyenne."

Donovan shook his head. "No deal, Charlie. I can't step away from this. I've got it to do."

Charlie stood in silence for a few moments, thinking this through. He took his .44. 40 Winchester from his saddle boot and handed it to Donovan. "This might help even the odds. If you live, return the rifle back here to the cabin. I'll find it."

"I appreciate it, Charlie," Donovan said. "I owe you."

Ignoring that remark, Charlie threw away his cup, brown coffee spilling into the snow, and stuck out his hand. Donovan took it.

"Maybe after all is said and done it's better this way," Charlie said. "Sometimes it's preferable that the man die and the legend live on." He smiled. "At least, that's how folks seem to favor it."

He swung easily into the saddle, looked down at Donovan and touched his hat brim. "*Hasta luego*, Zeke."

Then Colorado Charlie Utter touched spurs to his

horse, cantered across the snow and was soon lost to sight among the tall hills and sweet-scented pines.

Watching Charlie go, Donovan wanted to call out after him, telling him he'd changed his mind and would join him in Deadwood after all.

He couldn't.

The words stuck in his throat, clogging his windpipe so that he suddenly found it hard to breathe. His heart hammered against his ribs, hurting his chest, and he laid his head on the saddle, feeling the world spin around him.

It came to Zeke Donovan then that he had moved beyond fear of Ike Vance and was now stepping along the ragged edge of stark terror. But somehow forcing himself to come face to face with that realization brought him a strange sense of peace.

He was scared beyond scared, and all he could do now was swallow his fear whole, feel it churn like a yellow serpent in his belly, and keep on going.

As he'd told Charlie, he had it to do.

There could be no turning aside.

The palouse was a tall horse, and Donovan, weak and hurt as he was, had trouble getting up on him. But after several tries he finally succeeded, caught up the reins and swung the horse toward Two-Bit Creek.

The creek was still running free, bubbling over rocks scattered along its bottom, but lacy, fragile shelves of ice were forming along both banks, a warning of the big winter freeze to come.

Donovan rode the horse into the creek and the gelding splashed through the icy water and climbed the opposite bank.

Ahead lay open grassland and steep-sided hills, most of them covered thickly in pine and aspen with gray outcroppings of rock showing here and there, and around him the snow lay everywhere, white and quiet, muffling the stillness into an even deeper silence.

The only sound Donovan heard was the steady *crump, crump* of the palouse's hooves in the snow and the jangle of the bit as the horse tossed his head, nostrils smoking, in the crisp air.

A pack of wolves moved like ghosts through the aspen covering a hill to Donovan's right and the palouse lifted his head high, ears pricked as he tested the wind and caught their scent.

But the wolves ignored horse and rider and faded among the trees like woodsmoke only to reappear a few moments later higher up the hillside, trotting among inverted Vs of rock that jutted like the prows of ancient galleys from the slope.

Donovan caught his first sight of the full sun as it climbed over Bear Den Mountain to his east. It was still a long ways from noon but he decided he would not be bound by Ike Vance's timetable.

He swung off the flat into a stand of mixed spruce and aspen at the base of a hill and fished in the pocket of his shirt for the cigar Charlie had given him that morning after breakfast.

The palouse, eager to keep going, tossed his head impatiently as Donovan bit the end off the cigar, spat it out and found a match in his pocket. He flared the match into flame with his thumbnail and lit the cigar, puffing it rapidly into life.

On all sides of him lay the rugged, magnificent land, an enormous vista of breathtaking beauty, timbered hills cut through by deep-shadowed canyons rising high above wide plains and the only sound the sound of the wind sighing through the pines, teasing the trembling aspen. The great arch of the sky where the hawk and the eagle soared opened up above the land and from horizon to horizon clutched hills, plains and rivers in its grasp. The Sioux and the Cheyenne, who held the Black Hills sacred, knew this place and sometimes when the moon rode high and the wind was just right the air still smelled of the smoke of a hundred thousand campfires, though the land itself bore no mark of their ever having been here.

Yet lovely as it was, this was a harsh and unforgiving wilderness and the weak or the hurt or the sick found little solace in its bosom and knew well not to cry out for mercy, because there would be none. Nature is cruel and entirely without sentiment.

All this Donovan saw and all this he knew not by prior knowledge but by instinct, as powerful and primal a force in the human, if heeded, as it is in the wolf.

Donovan smoked his cigar down to a stub and pitched it away into the snow.

He stood in the stirrups, easing the pain in his back and chest, then kneed his horse out of the trees and back onto the flat.

Bear Den Mountain lay a few miles ahead and he swung south toward Strawberry Creek where it skirted the southern slope of the peak. Donovan rode head up and alert, the Winchester ready across the horn of his saddle.

Vance said he'd be alone, but where were Clint and Les Fairchild? The two men were dangerous and they held the death of their brother against him. It would be no easy thing to go against three skilled gunmen—as though Ike Vance himself wasn't a handful all on his own.

The sun rose higher and it felt warm on Donovan's face. The air smelled of pine and snow and it was a day that made a man feel glad he was alive. It was not a day for dying, if any can be said to be such.

Now the bend of Strawberry Creek lay directly to Donovan's south. He swung wide toward Butcher Gulch, then crossed the creek well to the west. He then headed northeast, keeping the south slope of the mountain to his left. If Vance expected him to ride directly into his camp, he was going to be sorely disappointed.

Donovan recrossed the creek about a quarter of a mile east of the mountain's south slope and picketed his horse on a patch of grass that was relatively free of snow among a sparse stand of a few spruce and aspen trees. He took his rifle and headed toward the spot Vance had said he'd be, his head turning this way and that, his every instinct clamoring, alarmed because he couldn't account for Clint and Les and they could be here, very close by.

Donovan was very weak and he had to stop often to catch his breath. The bullet wound in his chest hammered at him as he crouched low, running from tree to tree, sometimes finding welcome cover behind an outcropping of rock.

The great bulk of the mountain loomed above his head as he stopped in a shallow depression and listened. He heard nothing but the rustle of the wind in the trees and the rapid thump of his own heart in his ears. His breath steamed in the air and it was very cold.

He moved again, and this time came up on a fallen pine, its branches still carrying dry, brown needles. He kneeled behind the trunk, blew on his numb hands and readied his rifle. Again he listened. Still nothing.

Then he caught it, the slight scent of wood smoke, as elusive as a will o' the wisp, drifting in the breeze.

Donovan glanced upward at the tops of the trees ahead but saw no telltale misty column. Vance, an experienced woodsman, had sited his fire so that the branches of the pines would disperse any smoke.

Since he'd taken care to conceal his camp, it dawned on Donovan that Vance didn't want him to walk right up to his fire and say howdy. He was hidden somewhere, waiting with his rifle for a sure kill as soon as he showed up.

But why? Vance was a skilled revolver fighter and he knew Donovan was no match for him. Thinking the thing through, Donovan recalled seeing men slow on the draw take their hits and still stand on their feet, shooting back. And as long as a man was shooting, even the most deadly gunfighter, all stings, horns and rattles, was in danger of taking a wild bullet.

It seemed Ike Vance, knowing this well, did not want to take the chance. Out here in the wilderness, with no crowd of gaping miners to witness his triumph, the fact of Donovan's death and the return of his watch would be satisfaction enough for him.

Besides, there was always the possibility that Donovan would be down and wounded and unable to fight back and then Vance could have his fun, a thing he could not do in Deadwood.

Donovan shuddered.

The night before, as they lay in their blankets, Charlie, who'd still been trying to talk him out of going after Nancy, told him Vance had once skinned a man alive. It had taken three days for the wretch to die and by that time the screams coming out of the man's mouth were no longer human.

"Ike lived with Apaches for a spell and he's worse than any of them," Charlie said. "He can track like an Apache and he can fight like one too, remember that."

Donovan swallowed hard. Where was Ike? And where was Nancy? And where were Clint and Les?

He had plenty of questions, all worrisome, and no answers.

His wounds were telling on him and Donovan felt weakness hang on him heavy as an anvil, dragging him down. He badly needed to rest, but he knew he could not. Vance was too dangerous an adversary and to shut his eyes, even for just a moment, could mean death.

He had to move.

Vance's fire was straight ahead and if the fire was there, then the gunman could be close by.

Donovan rose painfully to his feet and crouching low, made his way forward. Slowly, trying to make as little sound as possible, he moved from tree to tree. The sun had risen higher in the sky and the tops of the pines were touched with gold. Sunlight bathed the slope of Bear Den, washing out the last of the night shadows from the shallow ravines and crevasses, and the air Donovan breathed was cold and brittle, filling his lungs like sharp shards of shattered crystal.

The smell of smoke was stronger now and Donovan knew he must be close to Vance's camp. He paused, listening.

Not a sound.

Carefully he edged forward, his finger ready on the trigger of his Winchester.

CRACK! A twig snapped to his right, higher up the slope.

Donovan caught a glimpse of gray cloth moving quickly among the trees and he fired, cranked a round into the chamber and fired again.

Despite the pain of his wounds, he threw himself to

his right, came up on one knee and triggered another shot into the trees.

There was no return fire.

Donovan rose to his feet and let out a wild whoop of triumph.

He'd killed him.

He'd killed Ike Vance!

26

Warily, Donovan moved higher up the slope. He was sure he'd hit Vance, but the man was tough. He could be down but not out—and even now waiting. Donovan reached an outcropping of gray, gnarled rock, a stunted spruce growing on a narrow ledge jutting out from its side. He kneeled behind the rock, his Winchester close to his shoulder.

"Ike," he whispered. His voice was unsteady and his breath came in short, nervous gasps. "Ike, are you there?"

Silence. Above him the wind stirred the pines and a flurry of snow fell from a branch, scattering fat flakes over his plug hat and the shoulders of his sheepskin coat.

Donovan tried again, talking louder this time. "Begging your pardon, Ike, but did I kill you for sure?"

"No, Donovan, you idiot, but you damn near killed me!"

It was Nancy's voice!

Donovan left the shelter of the rock and headed

higher. He found Nancy sitting at the base of a pine, her parasol in her hands and an annoyed, exasperated frown on her face.

"I . . . I saw something gray," Donovan said, knowing well how lame that sounded.

"You saw my coat," Nancy shot back. "Didn't anyone ever tell you to make sure of your target before you pull the trigger?"

"Hell," Donovan said, disappointment heavy on him. "I thought you were Ike Vance. I figured I'd killed him for sure."

"You put three bullets right close to me, Donovan," Nancy said, her brown eyes accusing. "And if you don't get down pretty quick, Ike will put one into you."

Alarmed, Donovan dropped to a knee, his eyes frantically scanning the trees around him.

"Where is Ike?" he asked.

Nancy shrugged. "He's around. He left me alone at the camp and I decided that was the time to make a break for it. I was climbing the slope when you started shooting at me." The girl's face was a study in many conflicting emotions, the predominant one disillusionment. "You tried to kill me, Donovan."

"Hell, I didn't know it was you."

"How can I be sure of that, Donovan?"

The young gambler shook his head. "I came back for you, didn't I? I'm all shot to pieces, yet I came to find you. If I did all that, why would I try to kill you?"

Nancy sat in silence for a few moments, absorbing this information. Then, with the aggrieved woman's unwillingness to concede that a man had made an honest mistake, said, "You shouldn't go shooting at people, Donovan."

Donovan hung his head. "Sorry," he said. He

wanted to tell her he'd come back because he loved her. But he couldn't bring himself to say it. He didn't know if it was true.

"Sorry doesn't cut it, Donovan," the girl said, breaking into his thoughts.

Realizing further apologies were useless until Nancy's present mood had passed, Donovan reached down, took her hand and pulled her to her feet.

"Where are Clint and Les?" he asked. "Are they around?"

"They're not with Ike. He told me he thinks maybe they died in the fire."

"We got to get off this damn mountain," Donovan said. "If Ike's close he can shoot us like fish in a barrel."

"He doesn't want to shoot you, Donovan," Nancy said. "At least not clean."

"Huh?"

"He's crazy, Donovan. I think his hatred for you has driven him out of his mind. He's gone way over the edge. He told me he wants you to scream and beg for mercy so he can laugh and spit on you. He says he wants to gut you like a hog. He says—"

"Enough already," Donovan snapped, fear raking him savagely like roweled spurs. "I don't want to hear any more."

Nancy looked at him then, her eyes shadowed, revealing only a desperate pity and something else, something that bordered real close on contempt. "Donovan, we don't have a hope in hell of making it out of here alive if you won't reach deep down inside yourself to find your manhood and dry it off."

"Dry it off? What do you mean, dry it off?"

"I mean that, since I've known you, all you've ever done is piss on it."

Donovan was stung into silence. He opened his mouth to speak but failed to find the words. Finally, he could only manage "Let's go. My horse is nearby."

The two of them came down the slope of the mountain, what had been spoken and left unspoken hanging heavy between them.

The palouse was gone.

In its place, a scrawled note torn from a tally book sat atop a rock. Donovan picked up the scrap of paper. The words were written in a fair hand and their meaning was inescapable:

I'M KUMMING TO GET YOU SOON. I PLAN TO BURY
YOU WITH MY WATCH BUT YOU WON'T BE
WEARING IT BECAUSE IT WILL BE INSIDE YOU.

Wordlessly, Donovan passed the note to Nancy and her eyes grew wide with horror as she read.

"What are we going to do, Donovan?" she asked. "I'm real afraid."

Something brittle snapped in Donovan then. He looked wildly around at the surrounding trees and yelled at the top of his lungs, "Vance! You bastard! You dirty, no-good bastard!"

He ran to the base of the hill and fired into the trees, cranked another round and fired again. "You bastard!" he screamed. He fired again and again, shooting from the hip, his bullets smashing into the pines, sending the roosting jays scattering into the air, splintered branches and pine cones tumbling to the ground.

"No!" Nancy yelled, running toward him. "Donovan, stop!"

Donovan was beyond hearing, venting all his pent-up frustration, seized by a fear he recognized he was increasingly unable to handle.

He fired again and again, sending bullets into the trees around him and when the rifle ran dry, he kept on cranking and pulling the trigger, the hammer falling each time with a forlorn *click, click, click*. . . .

Finally Nancy took the Winchester from him and Donovan fell to his hands and knees, head hanging, sobs racking his entire body.

The girl kneeled close to him, her arm across his back. Her mouth close to his ear, she whispered, "Reach deep, Donovan. You must reach deep."

He turned wild eyes to hers. "I can't do this, Nancy. I'm hurt real bad and I can't do this."

"You can do it, Donovan. You came back to rescue me, just like in the story they tell about you. You're making it all come true, Donovan, can't you see that? You don't have to be ashamed no more when they tell that story."

Donovan shook his head. "I can't rescue you, Nancy. I'm scared, my nose is broke, I'm shot through and through and I can't rescue nobody."

"You have to reach, Donovan."

"I can't reach any further. I'm not brave, Nancy. You know me, damn it, I'm scared all the time."

"It's not so hard to be brave. All you have to do is keep right on going even though you are scared."

"Have you done that?"

"Every single day of my life."

Donovan stayed where he was for a few moments, breathing deep, working through in his mind what Nancy had just said. Then slowly he rose to his feet, his face stiff and expressionless. He picked up the Winchester and worked the lever. "I guess I used up them all," he said.

Nancy nodded. Then, apparently trying to keep any

hint of accusation from her voice, she said in a neutral tone, "You still have your revolver."

"I can't hit anything with a revolver," Donovan said. "Unless I get lucky or I'm real close like I was with those Louper boys."

"It will have to do," Nancy said.

Donovan nodded. "Yes, I guess it will." He looked around at the surrounding trees, then the slope of the mountain. "Where is he?"

"I think," Nancy said, "that we'll see him soon enough."

Donovan and Nancy found Ike Vance's camp at the base of the mountain. The fire was out and the gunman had left nothing of value.

In the distance the sun had turned ice crystals in the snow to diamonds and the pines and aspen stirred in a gentle breeze. It was very cold and Nancy's breath smoked in the air as she talked.

"What are we going to do, Donovan?"

Donovan looked around him. There was no sign of Vance but he sensed the man was close by, maybe even now watching them.

"We can't stay here," he said, trying to draw on whatever small reserve of strength he had left. "If we stay here we'll starve to death, or freeze. We'll head back toward Two-Bit Creek. Charlie Utter has a cabin on the creek and there's food and maybe shells for the Winchester."

"We'll be out in the open, Donovan," Nancy said, doubt clouding her face.

"Don't you think I know that?" Donovan asked, annoyed. "Unless you have another idea?"

The girl shook her head. "I don't know what to do."

"Then we'll head for Charlie's cabin like I said."

"Will we make it, Donovan?"

Donovan reached deep. "Sure we'll make it. I still have this here Colt and it will make Ike Vance stay his distance and no mistake."

"Can you walk that far, Donovan?" Nancy asked.

Donovan reached deeper still, wondering how far he could go before he finally hit rock bottom. It must be real close by now. "I can walk that far. Just pick me up when I fall."

"That's what I've always tried to do, Donovan."

Together, walking close, they left the slope of the mountain and headed out onto the flat.

Strawberry Creek lay just ahead of them. Nancy took off her shoes and stockings and splashed through the icy water barefoot and Donovan helped her dry her feet before she put them back on again.

Butcher Gulch lay to their left and they walked parallel to its tumbled rock walls, making slow going in snow that was deeper here than it had been back at Charlie's cabin.

Donovan was very weak, his mouth hanging open as he fought for breath. The wound in his chest hurt dreadfully and when he unbuttoned his coat, the front of his shirt was stained with blood.

"How much further do you think, Donovan?" Nancy asked.

They'd been walking for an hour and Donovan knew it was him that was slowing them down.

"Not far. We'll see the Two-Bit soon. Maybe another hour, maybe less."

"My eyes are burning," Nancy said. "I can hardly keep them open."

"It's the glare of the sun on the snow." He held out his hand. "Just keep your eyes shut as much as you can and hold on to me. I'll guide you."

The girl did as she was told, took Donovan's hand and closed her eyes. They walked on.

Once Donovan stumbled and fell and pulled Nancy after him. They both rose, brushing snow off their clothes and Donovan apologized profusely.

"It's all right, Donovan," Nancy said. "It could have been me that fell. I can't feel my feet anymore."

"You can soon warm them at the stove," Donovan said, smiling. "I'll get you some hot coffee and maybe a blanket for your shoulders. Would you like that?"

The girl nodded. "I'd like that just fine."

As they trudged through the snow, Donovan kept turning this way and that, trying to catch any sign of Ike Vance. Once something startled a small herd of antelope in the distance, near the aspen line at the base of a hill, sending them running. But of the gunman there was not a trace. Donovan was carrying the rifle and he figured maybe that's what was keeping Vance at a distance. Perhaps he hadn't figured out that it was empty.

"We're getting close," he said to Nancy. "Damn it all, girl, I think maybe we're going to make it."

The bullet smashed into him just above his left knee, followed a split second later by the angry roar of a rifle.

Donovan fell, taking Nancy with him, the Winchester spinning out of his hands.

The girl rolled off him and sat up. "Donovan, are you hit?"

"My leg. He blew my damn leg right out from under me."

Donovan looked around wildly. About thirty yards away a clump of aspen grew around a tall, broad-based spire of rock at the base of a shallow, humpback hill.

"Over there," he said. "We can get cover."

Donovan rose to his feet, hobbling toward the hill. He turned and yelled to Nancy, "Get the rifle."

The girl dived toward the Winchester, but another bullet slammed into the stock, splintering the wood, skidding the rifle across the top of the snow.

"Forget the rifle!" Donovan yelled.

Nancy ran to him and put her arm around his waist. "Here, Donovan," she said, handing him her parasol. "Use this like a cane."

Supporting some of his weight on the parasol, Donovan stumbled toward the rock. Gritting his teeth against the pain in his leg.

Ike Vance let them go.

They reached the aspen and Donovan sat down heavily, his back against the rock spire. He drew his Colt and looked around. They were surrounded by aspen and a few spruce and the steep slope of the hill loomed behind them. Where the hell was Vance?

A bullet chipped pieces of rock inches above Donovan's head, then whined away among the aspen, scattering yellow and scarlet leaves. Donovan saw a puff of smoke to his right, about twenty yards further down the tree line, and he fired, thumbed back the hammer and fired again.

Another of Vance's bullets whined off the rock and then another. This time the smoke of Vance's rifle was closer, almost lost among the slender, silver trunks of the aspen. Donovan fired, aimed a yard to the left of his first shot where a branch moved, and fired again.

There was no answering bullet.

"Did you get him, Donovan?" Nancy asked, her face pale with fright.

"I don't know. Maybe I did."

A bullet pounded into the ground near his right leg,

kicking up dirt and rotten leaves. Then a second and a third.

"You didn't get him, Donovan," Nancy said, her voice a low, soft whisper in the stillness after the racketing boom of the shots had echoed and rung away among the hollows and heights of the hills.

Then Vance's laughter, mocking and crazed, sounded among the trees. "Soon, Donovan," the man yelled. "I'm coming to get you right soon."

Because of the surrounding trees, Donovan's view was restricted and he couldn't peg where the voice was coming from. He had one round left in his Colt and he didn't want to use it needlessly. He might need it for Nancy.

That horrifying thought was confirmed for Donovan when Vance called out again.

"Hey, Donovan?"

"Yeah?" Donovan hollered back, desperately trying to pin down the direction of Vance's voice.

"Know what I'm going to do to that whore of yours?"

Donovan didn't answer, but Vance was undeterred.

"I'm gonna cut her tits off and stuff them into your mouth!"

The man's insane laughter ran through the aspen and he yelled again, "Know what else I'm gonna do, before I even get started on you? I'm gonna cut her—"

Nancy shook her head and covered her ears with trembling hands, and Donovan roared, "Vance, you no-good son of a bitch, shuck your iron and come on down here and face me like a man!"

Vance laughed again. "Too easy, Donovan, way too easy. But don't you worry none, I'll be there soon, real soon now."

Donovan wiped sweat off his forehead with the

back of his gun hand. Then he reached out and gently moved the girl's hands away from her ears.

"How are you doing?" he asked.

Nancy's face was stricken. "Donovan, don't let him to do those terrible things to me."

Donovan forced a smile. "I won't. You can depend on that."

She studied him closely. "Donovan, you're reaching deep aren't you?"

"Reaching deep, drying it off." His smile grew wider. "It's not so hard when you really try."

"Hey, Donovan!" Vance's voice.

"Go to hell!"

"I'm getting closer."

"Good, you son of a bitch, then I can't miss."

Vance's laughter, the insane cackle of a madman, rang through the aspen.

"How's your leg, Donovan?" Nancy asked. "Does it hurt much?"

"It's bad."

"How bad?"

"I think the bullet's still in there."

"What are we going to do, Donovan?"

"Wait right here for Vance to come at us, I guess. If we try to move, he'll nail us for sure."

"How many bullets do you have left, Donovan?"

"Enough."

"How many?"

"One."

"Donovan, will you—"

"Don't even think that way," Donovan said. "We're walking out of here. Together."

"I'm not brave, Donovan," Nancy said. "I'm not brave at all."

"Hell, girl, neither am I. But we got it to do."

The day wore on, the sun sliding lower in the sky. The aspen cast blue shadows on the snow, and the bottoms of the canyons and ravines among the surrounding hills and mesas were shading into wedges of darkness.

Vance must come soon.

Donovan laid his head against the hard rock. He desperately wanted to close his eyes and sleep. Now he thought about it, he figured he couldn't place a postage stamp on any part of his body that didn't hurt and when he looked at his leg, it was swelling, straining against the stretched canvas of his pants.

He closed his eyes, Nancy laying against him, her head on his shoulder. All he needed was a few minutes sleep. Just a few minutes . . .

A fine shower of gravel rattled on the top of Donovan's hat and he woke with a start.

Where was Vance?

More gravel fell and Donovan looked up. Vance was standing on the rock above him, rifle in hand.

A huge, blurred figure jumped, boots first toward him. Donovan rolled away from the rock and his gun blasted. A moment later Vance's feet crashed into his chest and Donovan felt the wind knocked out of him.

He tried to rise, but Vance swung a fist that crashed into his chin. He was falling, but Vance grabbed him by the front of his coat, holding him upright. The big gunman viciously backhanded him, then slapped him hard with his palm and Donovan's head jerked back and forth under the stunning impact.

Suddenly Vance let him go and Donovan fell heavily against the rock. He dug his heel of his right boot into the dirt and pushed himself into a sitting position, his back again against the cold stone.

"Stay there," Vance growled, his eyes wild, "or by God I'll cut you right now."

Donovan's heel dug deeper as he tried to push himself to his feet. Vance stepped in close and backhanded him across the face again. Donovan's broken nose spurted a sudden, scarlet fountain of blood and he slammed against the rock, not moving.

From somewhere he heard Nancy scream, "You leave him alone!"

Donovan was vaguely aware of Nancy springing at Vance like a wildcat, but the huge gunman easily brushed her aside and swung a powerful punch to the side of the girl's head. Nancy fell beside him, unconscious.

Donovan closed his eyes, opened them again and saw the huge, blurred form of Vance looking down at him.

The gunman carefully took off his coat and laid it on the ground, placing his brass-framed Henry rifle on top of it. He settled his gunbelt on his hips, then reached behind him. When his hand reappeared it was holding a wicked-looking Green River knife.

"Donovan," Vance said, his voice real quiet and low, "are you awake?"

Through cracked, puffed lips, Donovan whispered, "Go to hell, you crazy bastard."

Vance smiled. "Good, I'm glad you're still with me." He tested the edge of the knife with his thumb. "Me, I got me some cuttin' to do."

27

Ike Vance stepped closer to Donovan, looming over him, an insane, evil grin playing on the man's wide mouth.

"First I'm gonna cut you up some, Donovan, then I'll work on the girl for a while so you can watch, then back to you . . . and so on and so on until it's over." Vance held the knife low and ready. "Though that will take some time. Maybe tomorrow, or if I'm lucky and you're not, the day after."

"Vance," Donovan pleaded, desperation edging his voice, "let the girl go. She can't do you any harm."

"No deal," Vance said, shaking his head. "Me, I like cutting women. I enjoy hearing them scream, all high and girly like."

Vance came closer. His eyes were odd, strangely luminous and more green than blue, like those of a rabid cat.

"The watch," he said. "Give me the watch."

"Hell, Ike," Donovan said, even now, at the eleventh hour, trying to smooth things over, "you could have had it back in Deadwood. Glad to give it to you."

Donovan reached into his pocket and handed the watch to Vance.

The gunman fondled the smooth gold and enamel case, like he was seeing it for the first time. With excruciating slowness, he wound the Berthoud, forefinger and thumb moving forward and back, his eyes never leaving Donovan. When the watch would wind no further, Vance put it to his ear. He nodded, satisfied that it was ticking.

He thumbed open the case and the butterfly notes of "Beautiful Dreamer" fluttered around the trees. Vance laid the watch carefully on a small ledge in the rock and said, "Now I'll have music while I work."

He hefted the knife. "Ahh," he whispered, his eyes busily scanning Donovan's prostrate frame, "the question is, where to begin?"

Donovan braced himself as Vance brought the point of the knife close to his belly. He reached out a hand to steady himself and his fingertips touched Nancy's parasol, a seemingly harmless object Vance had ignored.

Donovan's hand closed on the handle of the parasol as Vance started tugging at his jeans, trying to rip the fly open.

"First I'll geld you," the gunman said. "Ah, yes, that first."

Donovan picked up the parasol, a movement missed by Vance as he savagely tore at Donovan's pants. Donovan drew back his arm then shoved the sharply-pointed tip hard into the side of Vance's belly. Four inches of steel plunged into the gunman and Donovan rammed the point in further as Vance screamed.

Vance staggered back, the now bloody parasol sticking out of him. His face had a shocked, disbelieving expression, his bottom lip suddenly stained scarlet. Vance dropped the knife and grabbed the parasol with both hands and pulled it free. Donovan, summoning what remained of his feeble strength, rolled, grabbed the knife and rose to his feet. As Vance staggered toward him, he stepped close to the man and shoved the long blade straight into the gunman's throat and then sprang away from him and his reaching hands.

Vance took a step or two to his right, the brass guard of the knife jammed against his prominent Adam's apple, and dropped to his knees. He opened his mouth and made a gagging sound, raised his right arm and pointed at Donovan, his eyes bulging and wild.

"Gaaa . . . gaaa . . ." Vance gasped, blood spilling over his mouth.

Vance's hand dropped to his gun but he never made it. His eyes rolling upward in his head, he stumbled forward, still trying to draw a gun that now seemed heavy as an anvil. He lurched a few more steps, then fell and crashed onto his back.

Donovan stumbled to the gunman's side, picked up the parasol and raised it high again, ready to strike. There was no need, Vance lay unmoving. Donovan turned Vance's face toward him with the toe of his boot. The man's eyes were wide open, but he was staring into nothing but eternal darkness. He was dead.

Donovan shook his head. "Ike Vance," he said, "you were one crazy son of a bitch."

Then his own darkness took him and he fell on top of Vance's body.

Donovan woke to see Nancy's pale face hovering over him. The girl had a bruise on her cheek where Vance had hit her and there were huge dark circles under her eyes.

"Oh, thank God you're alive, Donovan," Nancy said.

"You were lying there so quiet and still I thought you were a goner."

"Vance?"

"He's still dead, Donovan."

"Help me sit up."

Nancy helped Donovan into a sitting position. He glanced over at Vance's body, the huge, muscular frame lying in a widening pool of blood.

"He died hard," Donovan said. "In the end he died a dog's death."

"Better him than you, Donovan," Nancy said with a woman's practicality. "As it is, your leg looks real bad." She studied the young gambler for a few moments, her face grave. "Donovan, you can't keep on getting shot up this way. Pretty soon there will be nothing of you left."

Despite his pain and the weakness that drained him, Donovan tilted back his head and laughed.

"It's not a laughing matter, Donovan," Nancy said, annoyed. "What are we going to do about your leg?"

Donovan's laugh faded to a smile, then to a pained grimace and he said. "You're right, it's no laughing matter. Nancy, Ike's bullet is still in there. You'll have to dig it out."

The girl was shocked. "I can't do it. What would I get the bullet out with?"

Donovan nodded to the Green River knife, its five inches of steel sticking in Vance's throat. "With that," he said.

"No!" Nancy screamed. "It's all bloody and horrible. I can't do it, Donovan!"

"You have to do it," Donovan said, not raising his voice. "There's only me and you and nobody else. So reach deep, Nancy."

The girl sat in silence for a few moments, fighting

down her revulsion. Finally she said, "Donovan, can you get it? The knife I mean."

Donovan lay very close to Vance's body. He leaned over, grabbed the bone handle of the knife and tugged it free.

"Take this and wash it in the snow," he said, extending the knife toward Nancy. The girl swallowed hard and with her forefinger and thumb grasped the very end of the pommel. She rose and walked to the edge of the aspen line and dropped the knife into the snow.

Carefully, using handfuls of snow, Nancy washed the knife free of blood, then she walked back and dropped to her knees beside Donovan.

Nancy looked down at her coat and shook her head. "My English coat has blood on it, Donovan. All the nice new clothes you bought me are ruined."

"I'll buy you others," Donovan said. He touched the back of the girl's hand with his fingertips. "Hell, we'll visit England and buy you another coat there."

"Will we cross the ocean by steamship, Donovan?"

"Uh-huh. I wouldn't have it any other way."

The light of day was fading around them and high above the trees the night birds were pecking at the first faint stars. The air had grown colder and the aspen leaves stirred in a chilling breeze from the north.

"Nancy," Donovan said, "do you know how to build a fire?"

The girl nodded. "I think so. You use twigs and dry leaves and stuff."

"That's right." Donovan said. "That's how it's done." He glanced at Vance. "We're moving away from here. I don't want to spend the night next to a dead man. Then you're going to dig that bullet out of me before it gets much darker. After that, build a fire to keep us warm. You'll find matches in my pocket."

Nancy was puzzled. "Why are you telling me all this, Donovan? Where will you be?"

Donovan smiled. "I'm not going to be around to help you. I think I'll be unconscious." He gave the girl his arm. "Help me get up."

With Nancy's help, Donovan struggled to his feet. He stood, swaying with weakness for a few moments, then, when the spinning world around him had steadied itself, he took the watch from the rock.

As Vance had done, he wound it, looking down at the dead gunman. "Donovan, are you giving it back to him, now he's . . . he's . . ."

"Dead, you mean?"

The girl nodded, her eyes wide.

Donovan slipped the watch into his pocket. "Hell, no," he said, "I don't owe that no-good son of a bitch a damn thing."

He shucked the empty brass from the cylinder of his Colt and then reloaded it from Vance's gunbelt. He strapped the belt and its holstered revolver around his waist and picked up the Henry.

Leaning heavily on Nancy, using the rifle as a crutch, Donovan stumbled with the girl through the aspen. After five minutes he found what he was looking for, a narrow, V-shaped depression in the ground. It was a dry creek bed, overgrown with grass, and its banks were high enough to shield them from the worst of the wind.

It was maybe an hour to full dark when he and Nancy stepped down into the depression. Donovan looked around him and said, "I think you'll find enough wood around here to keep a fire going. Just remember, start with small twigs and dry leaves if you can find them, and then slowly add the bigger stuff."

His eyes searched the girl's face. "Can you remember all that?"

Nancy nodded, saying nothing.

"Good." He handed her the knife. "Now do what you have to do."

"I can't." The girl shook her head, her mouth clamping into a straight, determined line.

"Nancy," Donovan said, "it will be soon too dark to see. If that bullet stays inside me much longer my leg will rot." He reached out and touched her pale cheek. "The chips are down, and there's nobody else here but you."

"Donovan," Nancy said, tears springing into her eyes, "there's veins and arteries and stuff in your leg. I could cut into one and you'll bleed to death."

"That's a chance we'll have to take. If the bullet doesn't come out, I'll die anyway."

"We can make it to Deadwood," Nancy said desperately. "There's a doctor there, Donovan."

"Deadwood is gone and maybe the doctor with it," Donovan said. "Besides, I'd never make it that far on this leg." He unbuttoned his pants, rolled on his belly and turned his face to the girl. "Now, do it."

Nancy was silent for a long time, then she said, "It looks horrible, Donovan. All bloody and red, like a piece of raw meat."

"Damn it, Nancy! Do it."

Donovan felt the girl's finger probe in the wound and he bit his lip against the sudden stab of pain.

"I feel it, Donovan," Nancy said. "I think the tip of the bullet is right up against your thigh bone."

"Get it," Donovan said, his voice so weak it was only a whisper. "Cut the damn thing out of there. Use the point of the knife."

"It's very deep, Donovan. It's way too deep."

"Nancy . . . please . . ."

The point of the knife levered into the wound as Nancy probed for the bone and white hot pain hammered at Donovan. He pushed the fleece collar of his sheepskin into his mouth and bit down hard.

The knife probed deeper and with it came more pain and this time Donovan screamed, a wild, agonized shriek that sent the roosting birds scattering out of the aspen branches, showering him and Nancy with leaves and snow.

"I can't do this!" the girl wailed, a despairing cry almost as loud as Donovan's scream. "The bullet is too deep. It's right into the bone."

Donovan was in blinding, searing pain. "Cut!" He roared. "Get it over with."

Again the knife plunged deep and again Donovan screamed. He screamed over and over again, shattering the quiet of the surrounding night like the sudden fall of plate glass.

"I can't get the bullet out of there, Donovan!" Nancy howled. "It's stuck fast in the bone and it's all slippery with blood. I can't get the knife to work."

Donovan was beyond speech. He was beyond anything but the awareness of his own bright scarlet universe of torment, the clustered stars spinning within his head exploding one by one into white hot, searing fragments. He gathered his strength and managed just two words, both of them coming hard as he battled to hold onto consciousness. "Do it!"

The knife dug. Pried. Skidded. Dug again. Scraped bone. Scraped again.

"I got it!" Nancy yelled. "I got the bullet!"

Donovan didn't hear. He had already fallen headlong, shrieking, into a darkness where there were no longer stars.

28

When Donovan woke, Nancy was sitting beside a large fire, her knees drawn up to her chin. She was watching him intently, the reflection of the flames moving across her still face, changing the color of her eyes to glowing amber.

Donovan still lay on his belly, his pants down around his ankles. He rolled onto his back and looked at his leg. Nancy had bandaged it with a piece of cloth torn from her shift.

"Did you get it out?" he asked.

The girl nodded, saying nothing.

"Where's the bullet?"

"I threw it away. It was a horrible thing."

Nancy watched Donovan struggle to pull his pants up and she said, "I tried to move you but I couldn't. You were too heavy for me."

Donovan slowly pulled up his pants, gingerly coaxing the waistband past his bandaged thigh. "Feels all right," he said. "My leg doesn't hurt near as bad as I thought it would. I mean, don't get me wrong, it hurts like hell, but not as bad . . ." Seeing Nancy watching him and realizing how lame he sounded, he finished quietly, ". . . as I thought it would."

A horse stomped and blew through its nose. Donovan turned and saw the palouse and Ike Vance's bay standing in the darkness, just outside the circle of firelight.

"They came in about an hour ago," Nancy said. "They just walked up and stood there."

"Horses will do that," Donovan said. "They get used to human companionship and on a dark night like this with wolves around, they'll seek people out."

"They just came in the night and stood there," Nancy said, her voice flat, like it was no remarkable thing.

"We can ride to Charlie's cabin," Donovan said, aware of the weakness in his voice. "Just as well, I don't think I can walk."

Nancy sat in silence for a while, looking at him, the firelight playing over her face.

"You did real good with the fire," Donovan said, the girl's amber stare, as unwavering as a cat's, making him uneasy.

Nancy smiled slightly. "You only had one match, Donovan. I had to make it count."

"You did real good. Damn right you did."

Somewhere in the hills a coyote howled its haunting call, stopped as though listening, then howled again. The breeze that whispered among the aspen smelled of falling snow and distant places where icebergs floated on cold white seas.

"I heated the knife red hot, Donovan," Nancy said. "I couldn't get the bleeding to stop so I laid the red-hot knife blade on the wound and burned it shut. Your leg smelled real bad, Donovan. It smelled like burning meat."

"You did good," Donovan said again, his eyes haunted as he tried to imagine what Nancy had gone through and the courage it had taken. "That was the right thing to do."

Nancy looked at him for a few moments, then she said, "We've come a long way, me and you, haven't we Donovan?" Then, without waiting for reply, "We've had to grow up real fast."

Donovan nodded, feeling somehow inadequate. "You've grown up, Nancy. I'm not so sure about me."

The girl turned her head and laid her cheek on her knees. "You've grown up, Donovan. I think you have."

"Listen, Nancy, I want to tell you something," Donovan began, "I . . . I . . ." he couldn't bring himself to say it. "I . . . like you a lot."

The girl nodded without lifting her head. "I like you too, Donovan."

The night was cold and Donovan inched closer to the fire, an effort that made his head spin and the pain in his leg flare.

"It hurts, doesn't it?" Nancy asked.

Donovan nodded. "It do."

"The bullet was right into the bone. It's going to take a while before you can walk real good."

"We'll rest up in Charlie's cabin for a spell, then we'll head for Tombstone," Donovan said. "There's nothing to hold us here."

Nancy's eyes glittered in the darkness. She threw a few more sticks on the fire, sending up a crackling shower of red sparks.

"I think I saw Ike Vance," Nancy said. "An hour ago, while you were sleeping."

Donovan looked around uneasily. "That's not possible. He's dead."

"I know he's dead, but I think I saw him." She pointed into the snow-laced gloom among the silent trees. "He was standing right over there. He just stood and looked at me."

"You're tired, Nancy. You imagined it."

"Maybe. But I think he'll haunt this place forever," Nancy said. "I think his ghost will never move from here." She looked over at Donovan. "He died a terrible death."

"It was a sight better than the one he planned for us," Donovan said. "Get that son of a bitch out of your mind."

"Maybe that's it. Maybe his soul is so evil it can't move on," Nancy said as though she hadn't heard. "Too much hatred and all the killing he done is weighing down his spirit with invisible chains."

Donovan sighed, drew his Colt and placed it on the ground beside him.

"What's that for?" Nancy asked.

"Ghost or not, if Ike Vance shows up again, I'm going to put a bullet into him," Donovan said.

They rode to the cabin on Two-Bit Creek just after sunup.

Charlie had left the place well provisioned and over the next couple of weeks Donovan was able to rest up and let his badly-mangled leg start to heal. But the leg would never be the same again and Donovan knew his limp, caused by badly damaged tendons, would become a permanent thing.

The stump of Nancy's finger had scarred over, but the hand would never be pretty. She didn't consciously try to hide the mutilation, but she had a way of moving the hand so it was never in sight long enough for him, or anyone else, to notice.

Occasionally a bullwhacker or muleskinner on his way to or from the diggings stopped by for a cup of coffee, and Donovan and Nancy learned that Charlie Utter, assured that Wild Bill's body could remain where it was, had left Deadwood and was rumored to be heading for Colorado.

The city itself was being rebuilt and some of the saloons, hastily thrown up using green timber, were already back in business and thriving.

That was a fact that Donovan noted and stored away.

He saddled the palouse and rode every day, sometimes exploring as far as Rubicon Gulch to the east and Deadman Mountain to the west.

He shot a deer that had come to the creek for water and later another big buck, the animals providing meat that was a welcome change from their steady diet of bacon and beans.

Donovan and Nancy had been living in the cabin for almost a month, she sleeping on the cot while he spread his blankets on the floor, but being this close to a young woman was beginning to wear on him.

It was in Donovan's mind that it was time cozier sleeping arrangements were considered.

The heavy snows of December were falling and Nancy had just cleared the plates from the table. She stopped on her way back and stood on tiptoe to look out the cabin window.

"Snow's getting thicker, Donovan," she said.

Donovan looked at her then, the way her worn dress molded against her slim body and how the lamplight played on her dark hair and he felt something stir inside him.

"Did you hear what I said, Donovan?" Nancy asked. She turned—and saw the way he was looking at her, a look she'd seen on the faces of men many times before.

Donovan had the decency to turn away. "It's going to be a cold night," he said, looking into his coffee cup. "Maybe too cold to sleep alone."

It was unsubtle and awkward and Donovan knew it and he felt his cheeks burn.

Nancy, experienced in such things, sat opposite him at the table. She lifted her coffee cup to her lips and then, speaking real soft, said over the rim, "You want to sleep with me, don't you, Donovan?"

"Something like that," Donovan said. He forced himself to look into Nancy's eyes. "Don't you think it's about time?"

"It might be," Nancy said. She sat in silence for a few moments, then very carefully laid her coffee cup on the table. "Do you love me?"

That took Donovan by surprise. "I . . . I don't know. Maybe I do."

Again: "Do you love me?"

"Maybe," Donovan said. "I just told you. I said maybe I do."

"I'm a whore," Nancy said. "I'm your soiled dove. You own me, remember. Tell me to take off my clothes and lie on the cot, and I'll do as I'm told."

"Not like that," Donovan said, his misery growing. "I don't want it to be like that."

"I won't charge you two dollars, you know."

"Forget it, Nancy. Forget everything I said."

Nancy rose and stepped to the stove. She brought the coffeepot and filled Donovan's cup and then her own. She returned the pot to the stove and then took her seat again.

"Donovan," she said, "I've been poked by a lot of men and none of them loved me. They didn't care about me. Most didn't even ask me my name. After it was over they just threw the money on the dresser and walked out of my life. They didn't even look at me, like they were afraid of what they might see. Maybe they regretted it afterward, I don't know. I never want to feel used like that again. When you can look me in the eye and honestly say, 'Nancy, I love you,' then we can sleep together and I'll give you all I have to give."

"Do you love me?" Donovan asked, frustrated and annoyed.

"Yes, Donovan, I love you very much."

"Odd way to show it."

"I've grown up."

She looked at him long and hard. "Donovan," she said, "what's my name?"

"Nancy, your name is Nancy. Hell, I know that."

"What's my last name?"

"Huh?"

"Everybody has a last name. Yours is Donovan. What's mine?"

Sensing a crushing defeat coming, Donovan shook his head and said weakly, "I don't know."

"It's Brown."

"Brown?"

"That's it. Nancy Brown. My name is every bit as plain as I am, don't you think?"

Gathering what was left of his dignity around him like a tattered cloak, Donovan snapped, "Well, maybe I will tell you to get nekkid and lie on the cot. I think I'll just do that. Hell, you know what they say, a hard pecker has no conscience."

"As you wish, Mr. Donovan," Nancy said. She

stood and began to undo the buttons at the back of her dress.

Donovan watched her for a few moments, then stood and barged through the door and into the snow. He stood with his back against the cabin wall and drew in deep breaths of cold, icy air.

He stood there for several minutes, then walked around the cabin through the falling snow to the lean-to barn in the back and checked on the horses. When he came back inside, numb with cold, Nancy had turned down the lamps and was asleep in the cot.

He stretched out on his blankets on the floor, put his hands behind his head and looked up at the dark roof. "Women," he muttered. "There's no understanding them."

Donovan had no way of knowing it, but Nancy was still awake. And she was smiling.

29

Donovan rose early next morning and saddled Vance's bay, tying him next to the palouse at the hitching rail outside the cabin.

He had washed, shaved and dressed with care, and stood drinking coffee near the stove in his gambler's finery. The Berthoud watch was in the pocket of his vest, the chain draped just so across his lean belly. The cut of his frock coat concealed his holstered Colt and when he examined himself in the small square of mirror he considered that he looked both prosperous and confident.

He felt stronger this morning as his wounds began to heal. Even his swollen nose was beginning to look human again, and the yellow disc of the sun rising over the pine-covered hills added to his sense of bright optimism.

Ike Vance was dead and his luck had surely turned for the better. It was high time he got back to practicing his profession.

Nancy poured more coffee into Donovan's cup and

asked, her eyes wary as she took in his fine, newly brushed clothes, "You're all dressed up. What do you have in mind, Donovan?"

"I have a horse and a hundred dollars," he said. "It isn't near enough to get us to Tombstone."

"You have two horses, Donovan," Nancy said.

Donovan shook his head. "The palouse belongs to Bearden. I'm taking it back to him, if he's still there. One thing I don't need is to get hung for a horse thief."

"Then what are you going to do, Donovan?"

"Play poker. I'm going to turn this hundred dollars into five hundred or a thousand. Then me and you can travel to Tombstone in fine style."

"Suppose you lose?" Nancy asked, doubt clouding her eyes.

"I won't lose," Donovan said, smiling. "Hell, Nancy, I'm a professional gambler and I'll be playing cards with miners and rubes. How can I possibly lose?" He put his crooked forefinger under the girl's chin and lifted her eyes to his. "Besides, Ike Vance is dead and I'm certain my luck has come back."

"You didn't get lucky last night, Donovan," Nancy said, totally without guile.

"That was different. I'm talking about poker here. And unlike women, I know a little about poker."

"Donovan, I wish you wouldn't," Nancy said. "We can get to Tombstone on a big bay horse and a hundred dollars."

"No, we can't. At least, not in style. When that Wyatt Earp feller sees us for the first time I want him to turn to his brothers and say, 'Cut off my legs and call me shorty, but I say those two pilgrims have style.'"

"Donovan, leave forty dollars here," Nancy said. "We can still travel far on forty dollars."

Donovan laughed. "Trust me, Nancy. My luck is

back. I can feel it. It's something a gambler can sense, like how some folks can tell when it's going to rain." He kissed her lightly on the cheek and said, "We can leave for the Arizona Territory tomorrow or maybe the day after and with a pocket full of money. Trust me."

Donovan stepped outside and swung into the bay's saddle, catching up the lead rope of the palouse, loudly singing "Brennan on the Moor" as he remembered his mother singing it.

> *It's of a fearless highwayman*
> *A story I will tell,*
> *His name was William Brennan*
> *And in Ireland he did dwell.*

Nancy came outside and Donovan, cheerful and smiling, said, "I'll be back before sundown and we'll sit together over a cup of coffee and count our money."

He touched the brim of his plug hat, then rode away in the direction of Deadwood, singing again, and when he looked back Nancy was standing there, watching him.

He waved, but she didn't wave back.

It was still two hours short of noon as Donovan splashed across Deadwood Creek and rode into the devastated city.

Two-thirds of Deadwood had been destroyed, the charred framework of ruined buildings a long series of black triangles and crazily leaning spars rising out of a gray sea of ash.

As far as the eye could see, the walls of the gorge were a fire-blasted wasteland, and there was no way to distinguish where the slopes ended and the burned out town began.

To Donovan, it looked like the avenging hand of

God had smote this mining Gomorrah and leveled it for its sins, which were endlessly creative and many.

But like a phoenix, the city was fast returning to life, spreading its wings as it grew again out of its own ashes.

Mule and ox teams, hauling heavily laden wagons, competed for space with riders in the muddy street, now changed by fire, ash and smoke from black to a dull ochre brown, and crowds of miners and even a few stalwart women picked their way carefully along the scorched boardwalks.

The Montana had been rebuilt, though the entire structure tilted a few degrees to one side as green timbers bent under the weight of the roof. Several other saloons were up and running, and in the absence of the destroyed pianos, fiddles and banjos were valiantly attempting to take up the slack.

The smell of stale smoke still hung in the air, but Donovan saw no sign of defeat in the faces of the men and women around him, just determination and a grim sense of purpose.

Deadwood had burned to the ground and they would rebuild it again. It was a simple proposition, one that would brook no argument and only the bare minimum of discussion. Such was the nature of Western men and women. Accustomed to danger and hardship, they had long learned to endure. They would, after hard times, straighten their backs, pick up and start all over again. It had been that way in the past and would be so in the future.

To Donovan's surprise, Bearden's livery stable still stood, seemingly untouched by the fire. Bearden himself, looking even more sour if that were possible, stepped out of his office as Donovan rode up.

"Brought you your horse back," Donovan said before the man could speak. "Found him wandering in the hills."

Bearden searched the young gambler's face, looking for the lie, couldn't find it and said, his voice a low growl, "Damn looters. Took everything that wasn't burned away or nailed down."

"Looters?"

"Yeah, no-accounts and hangers-on, dance hall loungers, razor grinders and ferrymen and sich. Sheriff Bullock is out scouring the hills for them right now, got a fair-sized posse with him an' all."

"Well," Donovan said, "you got your horse back." He looked beyond Bearden to the stable. "I want to put this bay up for a few hours. Maybe you could throw him some oats."

Bearden thought this over and, slow and grudging, said, "I guess I owe you that much since you brung back the palouse." Then, to make up for his moment of weakness, "Be back for him afore sundown, mind. Otherwise I'll be charging you two bits."

Donovan left the livery and stepped along what was left of the boardwalk. In some places the boards had burned away and only the charred support timbers were left and he had to tiptoe along these like a high-wire artist.

Even at this early hour the Montana was busy and smoke belched from the chimney of its Franklin stove, a cast iron monster made by the Stafford Foundry in New England that had survived both the blaze and the exploding gun store next door.

Donovan stepped inside and looked around. Men lined the bar and poker was being played at several tables, considerable amounts of coin, paper money and gold dust changing hands or lying in the middle of the green baize.

To Donovan's great satisfaction, all the players seemed to be miners or rubes and he saw no professionals, it being too early in the morning for those nocturnal gents who seemed to survive on less sleep than nightingales.

A sooty coffeepot hung from an iron hook next to the stove, a selection of tin cups close by and Donovan poured himself a cup. The coffee was Arbuckle, strong and bitter, the way he liked it, and he sipped as he strolled among the tables.

One table in particular attracted his attention, as the five men around it seemed to be high rollers. One of the men rose as Donovan stepped closer, disgustedly throwing his hand on the table. "I'm out," he said. "You boys is too rich for my blood."

That left four—three rough-looking, bearded miners and a young, slack-jawed, dull-eyed rube, Adam's apple bobbing in a scrawny turkey neck that stuck out of his high celluloid collar.

Donovan tipped his hat at a jaunty, devil-may-care angle. Three miners and a plowboy right off the farm. This was going to be too easy.

"Mind if I sit in?" he asked, smiling.

The rube looked up at him, slowly taking in his frilled shirt, flowered vest and frock coat.

"I fear, sir," he said, "you have the stamp of the skilled, professional gambler about you and might seek to take unfair advantage of us."

Donovan shook his head. "Just passing time. The big spenders don't come in until tonight. I've got some hours to kill is all."

One of the miners, a huge man with a scar down his right cheek, said, "Hey, ain't you Zeke Donovan, the man who saved the German princess from the heathen Chinee?"

Donovan gave a little bow. "You've heard that story, huh?"

"Sure did." The miner waved a hand to the empty chair. "It will be a right honor to play poker with you, sir."

"Alas," the rube said, half rising out of his chair, "I think I'm about to be badly outclassed. This is one of those situations my sainted mother warned me about."

"Don't worry," Donovan said, smiling, pushing the reluctant pumpkin roller back into his seat. "I'll take it real easy on you."

Thirty minutes later, badly burned, he walked out of the Montana owning only the clothes he stood up in and the Berthoud watch that he couldn't bear to part with.

Who would have guessed a gambler would disguise himself as a dumb farm boy to lure and then trap the unwary?

There should be a law against it, Donovan thought to himself, his face drawn and bitter. A self-respecting, professional gambler should look like a self-respecting professional gambler. Like himself, come to that.

God, the pretend rube was good. Better even than Luke Short and that was saying something. And he played straight poker. He won because he was a lot more skilled than Donovan, and that rankled.

Or was it just that his luck was still forsaking him?

As Donovan picked up his horse and cantered out of Deadwood, he thought that over. And it was true.

He was on a losing streak that showed no sign of ever ending. It seemed that some dark fate had ordained that it must go on and on forever.

"And now," he said aloud to his uncaring bay, "I have to face Nancy."

*   *   *

"You what?" Nancy asked, her eyes blazing.

"Lost it all. Every last penny."

"How could you do that, Donovan?"

The young gambler shrugged, his face bleak. "How was I to know the rube imposter would draw a fourth queen? I was holding a full house, aces over deuces and I figured he had three of a kind. Then he draws the fourth queen. Nobody draws the fourth queen, for God sakes. What are the odds? You don't know, but let me tell you, they're pretty damn high."

Nancy let this pass without comment, then said, "So we're broke?"

"Flat. Busted. I don't have a tail feather left."

"What are we going to do, Donovan?"

Donovan shook his head, his misery apparent. "I don't know. Maybe"—he shuddered—"I could get a riding job. There are plenty of ranches around here. They might be hiring."

"When did you last nursemaid a cow, Donovan?"

"A long time ago. Look, Nancy, cowboying is something you do when you can't do anything else, but once you've done it, it's a thing you never forget." He paused, trying to read the girl's reaction. "I can still fork a bronc with the best of them."

"Forget it, Donovan," Nancy said. "Better you buy yourself a pick and a shovel and go digging for gold."

"A lot of men are doing that and most of them are as broke as I am."

"What are we going to do, Donovan?"

"Eat," Donovan said. "I'm hungry."

Nancy fried venison steaks and they ate them with beans and in silence. Afterward, Donovan shoved back his chair and stood. He crossed to the window and stared moodily outside at the snow-covered landscape around him.

"How much wood do we have?" he asked. "I mean, for the stove."

"Enough to last for another day or two," Nancy said. Then, anticipating his next question, "We'll run out of coffee tomorrow, salt, meat and beans the day after. There are still a few cans of peaches left."

Donovan nodded, as though he'd made up his mind about something. "We're leaving for Tombstone tomorrow morning at first light. Whatever food is left, we'll take with us."

"With no money?"

"That's right. With no money. I'll earn it as we go along or steal it if I have to. But we're getting out of here." Donovan took the watch from his vest pocket and glanced at it. He wasn't interested in the time, it was a wholly symbolic gesture. "We've been here too long already," he said. "Winter is closing in on us fast."

Nancy was silent for a long time, then she crossed the floor and sat on the edge of the cot.

"Go without me, Donovan," she said.

"What?"

"You'll have a better chance of making it if you go alone. I'd only slow you down and one mouth is cheaper to feed than two."

"I'm not leaving without you," Donovan said. He hesitated. "Hell, woman, I love you! There, I've said it."

Nancy's head snapped around and she look at him with startled eyes.

"You mean that?"

Donovan nodded. "Yeah, I do. Every word. Well, all three of them."

The girl stood and ran into his arms, her mouth hungrily searching for his. They kissed, then clung to each other while the cabin seemed to spin crazily around them.

Finally, Nancy whispered, "We'll make it, Donovan. As long as we're together, we'll make it. When it comes right down to it, we only have each other."

Donovan smiled. "We're a pair, aren't we? A no-good, down-on-his-luck gambler who isn't too brave or too bright and a ragged little brown-eyed dove with nine fingers." He shook his head. "Seems to me, there ain't nobody going to be looking out for us."

"But us," Nancy said.

Gently, Donovan pushed Nancy away from him. "Hey, before this gets serious, I better fork some hay for the horse, and we're running out of that too."

"I'll be waiting for you, Donovan," Nancy said, her eyes bright with promise.

Donovan swallowed hard and stepped outside . . .

. . . where Les and Clint Fairchild sat their horses, glaring at him, the fire in their bellies and the urge to kill writ large on their hard, bearded and unforgiving faces.

30

Acutely aware of the danger he was in but trying to make the best of it, Donovan smiled and said, "Hi, boys, long time no see."

Les, the older of the two, leaned forward over the saddle horn and said, his voice low and thin and heavy with menace, "You killed our brother, Donovan. He was but twenty years old and Ma's favorite. It wouldn't set right with Ma if'n we didn't gun you and make sure you have the knowing of your own dying."

"That," Clint said, taking it up from where his brother had left off, "is why we're gonna shoot you in the belly."

The brothers sat easy and loose in the saddle, but Donovan knew they'd shuck their revolvers with blinding speed and hit where they aimed.

His Colt was in the shoulder holster but it was an awkward draw and mighty slow. And he seldom hit where he aimed.

"Boys," Donovan said, his voice edged with desperation, "we can talk this over. We don't need gunplay to settle this, especially now that Ike Vance is dead."

That took them aback. "Ike is dead?" Clint asked.

Donovan nodded, deciding it would be safer not to tell the truth. "His horse fell on top of him and his neck broke." He spread his hands. "Let's talk about this."

Clint shook his head, never taking his eyes from Donovan. "We didn't come here to talk, we came here to kill a man." He smiled, real thin and mean. "That man is you, Donovan."

The gunman inclined his head slightly toward his brother. "Want to get it done, Les?"

"Yeah, let's do it," Les shrugged. And he drew.

Donovan's hand was moving toward his gun when Les's bullet crashed into his chest. He gasped and stumbled backward, slamming hard against the wall of the cabin.

Somehow he was still alive and moving and he jerked his Colt as Les's second bullet thudded into the wall an inch from his head. Les now steadied his gun with both hands, aiming carefully.

Donovan fired.

Then someone fired from the cabin.

Les, hit hard, threw up his arms, his Colt spinning away from him, and fell backward over his horse.

The gun from the cabin slammed again, missed. Clint fired at the cabin window and Donovan heard glass shatter. Donovan thumbed back the hammer of his Colt and fired. The gunman jerked in the saddle as the bullet slammed into his shoulder.

The gun in the cabin roared again and Clint's horse reared as a bullet burned across its neck. The gunman went down, thudded hard into the snow on his back but came up fast on one knee, his gun ready.

Donovan fired, the boom of his gun echoed an in-

stant later by the one in the cabin. Hit twice, Clint
stumbled to his feet, staggered a step or two and
yelled, "Damn ye for a scoundrel!" Then his eyes
turned up in his head and he pitched forward, stretching his length on the snow.

The cabin door opened and Nancy stepped outside,
Ike Vance's smoking Henry in her hands. She hurried to
Donovan as he slumped to the ground and asked, her
face chalk white, "Are you badly wounded, Donovan?"

Donovan tried to smile. "I'm killed, Nancy. I took a
bullet in the chest."

Nancy dropped the rifle and opened up Donovan's
frock coat, frantically searching for the wound. She
sat back on her heels and said, "There's no blood,
Donovan."

Donovan looked down at his vest. "There's got to
be blood. Les hit me square."

Nancy reached inside Donovan's pocket and took
out the Berthoud of Paris watch, holding it by the
chain. Clint's bullet had hit the watch. It had smashed
through the gold and enamel cover but had been
stopped by the sturdy steel mechanism, the flattened
lead bullet embedded in a tangle of wheels and
springs.

Free of Donovan's pocket, the buckled cover
flopped open and a few forlorn notes of "Beautiful
Dreamer" chimed into the smoke-streaked air, then
faltered to a stop, never to chime again.

"He saved your life, Donovan." Nancy whispered.
"In the end, Ike Vance saved your life."

Donovan took the ruined watch from Nancy's
trembling hand and threw it away as far as he could.
"Ike Vance didn't save my life, Nancy," he said. "You
did." He leaned over and kissed her gently. "If you
hadn't opened up from the cabin, those two lowlifers

would have done for me for sure. I'd be a dead man by now and you'd be putting silver dollars on my eyes."

"We don't have any silver dollars, Donovan," Nancy said, her face serious. The girl looked over at the bodies of Les and Clint Fairchild. "It's a terrible, lonely thing to kill a man."

Donovan nodded. "It is all that. Let's hope we never have to kill another."

Hooves sounded in the distance, muffled by the snow, and Donovan and Nancy stood as a dozen riders came over the crest of a low hill and thundered up to the cabin, reining up their wild-eyed horses in a flurry of kicked-up snow.

The big man in the lead, a star pinned to his mackinaw, rose in the stirrups and hollered, mustache bristling, "I'm an officer of the law on the hunt for looters and low persons. What's going on here?"

Donovan nodded to the two dead men. "Those two low persons rode up here aiming to kill us, Sheriff. We fought back and done for them both."

"Oh, you did, did you?" Seth Bullock said, swinging out of the saddle. "We'll just have to see about that for our ownselves."

A couple of vigilantes dismounted and joined Bullock as he inspected the bodies.

"Here, Clem, don't these two look familiar to you?" Bullock asked one of the men at his side. "I saw them around town a spell back, but I recollect something more recent."

The man called Clem rubbed his chin and studied the dead gunmen for a few moments, then snapped his fingers. "Well, I'll be damned! Seth, I swear that's them two we just got a dodger on, the pair that robbed the Cheyenne mail coach last week and killed the guard."

"It's them, all right," Bullock said, his huge mustache lifting, "I knowed I'd seen them recent. That's the Fairchild boys as ever was an' about as dead as they're ever gonna be."

The lawman turned to Donovan, recognition suddenly sharp in his eyes. "Here, ain't you Zeke Donovan? And ain't that your dove, the Spanish princess?"

Donovan nodded. "You gave us the keys to Deadwood, Sheriff. You and the mayor."

Bullock nodded. "I recollect that real well." He smiled, his teeth showing white under his mustache. "Well, boy, you struck the mother lode this time. The stage company has put up a five hunnerd dollar reward for them two, dead or alive. I guess you can ride into town at any time you care to and pick up your money."

"I'm obliged, Sheriff," Donovan said, feeling Nancy's eyes on him. "Maybe I'll ride on into Deadwood with you. Strike the iron while it's hot, you might say."

"Don't make no difference to me," Bullock said. He turned to his deputies. "Throw them boys on the backs of their horses. We'll take 'em in with us as proof." He turned to Nancy, giving her a slight bow. "Sometimes dead men do tell tales. That's a little American lawman humor there, your majesty."

Nancy inclined her head and smiled. "Your sense of humor does you credit, sir."

Pleased at Nancy's reception of his joke, Bullock grinned, swung into the saddle and waved a hand. "Let's move out."

Donovan followed close behind on the bay. "I'll be back," he told Nancy. The girl looked up at him, a worried frown on her face. "Donovan, no gambling, remember."

Donovan smiled and touched fingers to his hat brim. "I'll remember."

He rode after Bullock, his horse's hooves kicking up little spurts of snow as he urged the bay into a canter.

Nancy watched him until he was out of sight, and then a little longer. Finally she went back inside.

It was full dark, the moon riding high in the sky, when Donovan returned. He put his horse up in the barn and walked to the cabin, his boots crunching in the crisp snow. Nancy was waiting for him at the door, one eyebrow raised in a question.

"I got the money," Donovan said. "I got it right from the hands of a director of the stage line and he seemed right happy them Fairchild boys was brought in across their saddles."

"Do you still have the money?" Nancy asked, her eyes wary.

Donovan smiled. "Of course I still have it. Me, I'm steering well clear of the saloons until my luck changes."

He followed Nancy inside and she poured him coffee. Donovan pulled off his coat and his elastic-sided boots and stretched his feet to the stove, wiggling his toes.

After a few moments he fished in the pocket of his frock-coat and brought out a canvas bag tied at the neck with a drawstring. "Here it is, five hundred dollars in gold." He looked at Nancy and smiled. "Our passport to the Arizona territory."

The girl hefted the bag in her hand, hearing the coins chink.

She laid them on the table and stepped to the window. Outside, the moon was plating the snow and the branches of the surrounding pines with silver and the sky was a dark, cobalt blue. There was no breeze and the intense cold had frozen the land into immobility.

"Creek's freezing up, Donovan," Nancy said.

Donovan turned his head, the cherry-red glow of the stove reflecting on his cheek. "Just as well we're getting out of here tomorrow. Another few weeks and we'd be snowed in until April for sure."

"It's a cold night, Donovan," Nancy said.

Donovan nodded. "I reckon it's aiming to get colder."

The girl stepped closer to him. "It's too cold to sleep alone," she said.

Donovan looked up at her, the breath catching in his throat. He stretched his arms and yawned. "God, I'm tired," he said. "Time to turn in, I guess."

Later, lying on his back in the cot, Nancy snuggled close beside him, Donovan put his arms behind his head and studied the reflected glow of the stove staining the ceiling red.

"Nancy, you awake?" he asked.

The girl shook her head and said, her voice drowsy, "No, I'm asleep."

"I've been thinking," Donovan said. "I've been thinking about us."

"What have you been thinking, Donovan?"

"Well,"—he moved his shoulders into a more comfortable position—"I was studying on the idea that maybe we could stay in the Dakota Territory instead of traipsing all over the country." He leaned on one elbow, looking down at Nancy. "We could buy a farm and settle down and raise a bunch of young 'uns. I think, in fact I know, we'd make a real good team."

"You think so?" Nancy was fully awake now and interested.

"Sure I do. I wouldn't have said it if I didn't."

The girl nodded. "Mmm, Zeke Donovan as a farmer. That would be a sight to see. In fact, I can see it all now, you walking behind a plow, gazing at a mule's ass. 'C'mon, Rosie ol' gal,' you'd say, 'we got to be a-plowin' a whole acre today and then get to plantin' them 'taters an' a-cleanin' out the hog pen.'"

Donovan laughed. "Is that how it would be?"

"Bet your life," Nancy said.

"And how about you?" Donovan asked. "You'd be in the kitchen sure enough baking a soda cracker pie with a couple of wailing younkers hanging onto your skirts. Then I can see you come to the door of the cabin, yelling, 'C'mon inside, Zeke dear, and leave off that plowing for a spell. Your soda cracker pie is a-cooling.'"

They both laughed, bouncing up and down on the cot until the springs squealed.

"And we'd drive to church every Sunday, all dressed up in our go-to-prayer-meeting duds, and when we came home, you'd sit by the fire, Donovan, a-reading of the Good Book to the younkers," Nancy said. "Telling them the error of their ways and the perils of drinkin', whorin' and gamblin'."

"And you'd be busy in the kitchen, a-baking of another one of them soda cracker pies," Donovan said.

They laughed until tears started in their eyes, bouncing harder, making the cot springs squeal even louder.

And they were still laughing the next day as they saddled the bay and rode south.

Lighting a shuck for Tombstone.

31

Zeke Donovan, in a brand-new broadcloth suit, a diamond stickpin in his cravat and a gold ring on the little finger of his left hand, sat at a gaming table in the Oriental Saloon in Tombstone, idly shuffling a greasy, well-thumbed pack of cards.

Opposite him, Wyatt Earp, looking just as prosperous, watched with a benign, almost fatherly interest. Earp smiled, the usual thin grimace that never quite reached his eyes, his long piano-key teeth showing yellow under a sweeping dragoon mustache.

"Damn it, Zeke, I like you," Earp said. "You play straight-up, honest poker, yet you bring in more money for the house than any other dealer I have."

Donovan nodded. "Luke Short taught me that. About playing honest poker, I mean." He moved his legs under the table, wincing slightly as his wounded thigh, still only partially healed, pained him.

Doc Holliday coughed into his handkerchief, studied how much lung he'd brought up, shrugged his unconcern and poured himself another drink from the bottle on the table.

"You're true blue, Donovan," Doc said. "You're the kind of man we need around here."

Earp, who seldom drank, sipped delicately from his coffee cup, then ran a forefinger across his mustache, smoothing a few wayward hairs back into place.

"How's Nancy?" he asked.

"She's fine, real good," Donovan replied, smiling fondly, as though seeing an image in his head. "She and I are thinking about getting hitched. Maybe in the spring."

"Marriage is a good thing for a young man," Doc said, his mustache lifting. "Though I never did take to it myself."

Donovan shuffled the deck, then squared it off and laid it on the table in front of him.

"Wyatt, I've been meaning to tell you this before now, but I really appreciate all you've done for Nancy and me in the past few weeks."

Earp waved a dismissive hand. "Glad to do it. Any friend of Charlie Utter is a friend of mine."

"Still, for the first time in a long time I've got new clothes on my back and money in my pocket and I owe it all to you," Donovan said. "And Morg and Virgil, come to that." He smiled across the table at Holliday. "And you too, Doc."

The little dentist nodded, the blue veins very prominent in the slender white hand that lifted the whiskey glass to his lips. "I always like to help an up-and-coming young man, and you'll go far, Zeke. You'll make your mark one day."

"Well, if there's anything I can do to repay you gentlemen, all you have to do is let me know," Donovan said.

He saw Wyatt and Doc exchange a quick look, then Earp said, "No repayment needed." He paused for a long time, long enough to sip his coffee cup dry and for Doc to get over another fit of coughing.

Finally, moving a little in his chair, Earp said, "But now I come to study on it, Zeke, maybe there is something you can do."

"Name it." Donovan's hazel eyes, more green than brown, were eager.

Earp shrugged, like a man reluctant to shape his thoughts into words. "To put it bluntly," he said after a while, "I could do with your help."

"Anything, Wyatt, you know that. Since I've been in Tombstone my luck has really taken a turn for the better, and you're the cause." Donovan leaned closer to Earp, trying to read the man. "Don't be shy. Name it."

Again Earp and Doc exchanged looks, then Wyatt said, "Zeke, will you ride with me?"

"Wherever the trail leads, Wyatt."

Earp was silent for a few moments, seemed to make up his mind about something, then said, "Well, it's like this, Zeke. I've been having a lot of trouble with this no-good, cattle-rustling bunch of outlaws called the Clantons and . . ."

HISTORICAL NOTE

By the time Zeke Donovan rode into Deadwood in August 1879, the era of the frontier gambler was already drawing to a close.

After 1884, many of the wild cow towns and mining towns in the West underwent a metamorphosis as the farmer and the homeowner, the businessman and the churchgoer, took over and changed the West forever.

Here and there, a place like Tombstone would flare up, all sound and fury for a few years, but for the most part the excitement of the six-gun frontier was gone.

Like that of the cowboy, the time of the Western gambler was very short, from about 1870 to 1890, a span of just two decades.

True, as more and more states outlawed games of chance, gambling went undercover and millions were still wagered across the baize cloth. But gamblers like Luke Short and Zeke Donovan knew they were now operating outside the law. As an outlaw, the gambler not only lost status in the community, he felt degraded in his own mind and this eventually led to his demise.

Like Tombstone, Deadwood was truly a town too tough to die.

Following the fire of 1879 that burned it to the ground, the town was rebuilt, only to be swept away by a flood four years later.

Deadwood was rebuilt a third time, and today is a major tourist attraction with its Adams Museum, the site of Wild Bill's last poker game, and the graves of both him and Calamity Jane.

Bill's friend, the elegant gambler Colorado Charlie Utter, is said to have died of yellow fever in 1904 while working as a laborer on the Panama Canal.

Joseph A. West

"I look forward to many years of entertainment from Joseph West."
—**Loren D. Estleman**

"Western fiction will never be the same." —**Richard S. Wheeler**

Silver Arrowhead 0-451-20569-3
When the bones of the world's first Tyrannosaurus Rex are
discovered in Montana cattle country—and the paleontologist
responsible for the find is murdered—it's up to San Francisco
detective Chester Wong to find the killer.

Johnny Blue and the Hanging Judge
0-451-20328-3
In this new adventure, Blue and his sidekick find themselves
on trial in the most infamous court in the West.

Johnny Blue and the Texas Rangers
0-451-20934-6
Infamous shootist Buck Fletcher befriends a female victim of
a range war and finds himself threatened by one side, courted
by the other.

Available wherever books are sold, or
to order call: 1-800-788-6262